THE BITE

THE BEAUTIFUL RIP-OFF

Four guys with shotguns had crashed a very exclusive party, walked out with a quarter of a million dollars worth of jewels, and left two corpses as calling cards. Wylie Lincoln and Russ Turner couldn't have cared less – until one of the party's beautiful people offered them a lot of money to care more.

The blonde had paid off a blackmailer for some very incriminating negatives, and had stashed them in her cigarette case just before the heist. Unfortunately, the cigarette case went along with the rest of the haul, and now the blonde was desperate to get it back.

Lincoln and Turner didn't have much to go on, but that was the least of their problems. The hard part was keeping the Mafia off their necks, the police off their backs – and four cold-blooded killers off their tails . . .

THE BITE

Eric Corder

A STAR BOOK

published by
WYNDHAM PUBLICATIONS

A Star Book
Published in 1976
by Wyndham Publications Ltd.
A division of Howard & Wyndham Ltd.
123 King Street, London W6 9JG

First published in Great Britain by
W. H. Allen & Co. Ltd.

Copyright © 1975 by Eric Corder

Printed in Great Britain by
Richard Clay (The Chaucer Press), Ltd., Bungay, Suffolk

ISBN 0 352 39873 6

CHAPTER ONE

The crowd erupted from Madison Square Garden like some great flock of fantastical birds fleeing an aviary of the exotic. They were riotously plumed in silks and brocades, startling cottons and wools, leather, polyethylene, even flexible aluminum. Ornaments glittered on their fingers, arms, and ears and in their hair. They crowed, they strutted, they preened. They flowed in liquid bubbliness around stony gray-haired men in black tuxedoes whose women wore long gowns and strands of pale gems in silver and platinum settings; furled skin; stiff, elegant coiffures. But mostly the crowd was young, or at least in pursuit of that fountain, many raucous, others studiously languorous, and dazzled by themselves. A CBS camera crew trotted after a band of black-jacketed youths in berets who were managing a fair lockstep against and through the impacted bodies, their clenched fists in the air, booming *'Venceremos!'* and *'Adelante con La Raza!'* Many faces and arms were painted, and one young blonde in a wetsuit, the throat of which plunged to her dimpled navel, had painted the globes of her breasts vermilion. Ranked along the curbs of Seventh Avenue and Thirty-third Street were Mercedeses, a spotting of Rolls-Royces, limousines from Cadillac and Chrysler, two Morgans, a Bentley, a Duesenberg, and other handsome understated excesses, chauffeurs standing at the doors.

It had been a thoroughly satisfying fight – for a New York audience, anyway. Octavio Carreras had battered and bloodied Mississippi's Freddy Lee Scully for eight rounds and then in the ninth had driven him through the ropes and onto a sportscasters' table; Scully had not regained consciousness until Carreras had been proclaimed the new Welterweight Champion of the United States.

Scully, over the preceding weeks, had variously referred to Carreras as 'spic,' 'greaser,' and 'nigger,' demonstrating mastery of the essential vocabulary but ignorance of proper usage. Carreras had responded with 'I go' to beat him. Not jus' win, mon. *Beat* him.'

Heavenly. Quickly co-opted from the mean streets to stylish brownstones, duplexes, and cooperatives on the park. Marcuses with Pulitzer Prizes and Dun & Bradstreets. The greening of the ring.

And tonight the dark knight had slain the white dragon. All was right, and the crowd was delighted with Carreras, with life, and, above all, with itself.

Wylie Lincoln was delighted, too. He rarely involved himself with a cause, *célèbre* or *vulgaire*, but he did like making money, and Carreras had just won him five hundred dollars from a Saluki breeder in Westchester, a man of restrained racist sentiment. Which made it even more enjoyable, although Wylie would also have been pleased to have won the same money from a committed brother.

Wylie and Evadne Jones and Russ Turner were caught in a press on Seventh Avenue between Thirty-fourth and Thirty-fifth. Wylie's feet were stepped on. He was elbowed and jostled and buffeted. Popping flashbulbs – there were as many society as sports reporters – brutally whitened the night and made him blink. But he didn't mind. He liked seeing people have a good time. And there was the five hundred dollars.

A police lieutenant was speaking through a bullhorn in a patient monotone: 'Please keep moving, folks ... We can all get to where we're going a whole lot sooner if we keep a little movement up ... Sir? ... The gentlemen in red velvet by the hood of the silver Rolls? ... Could I ask you, please, to end your interview, or at least have your chauffeur move your car? You're blocking other vehicles ... Please keep moving, folks ... The young lady with the orange blouse, the orange blouse she's waving in her hand? You're causing a jam-up there. Would you mind ... even just draped over the shoulders ... Thank you, miss ... The party by the arch? With the champagne magnums? I salute you too. Could you cork your bottles, sir, until you're out in the open? People are finding it difficult to share your generosity and keep moving ... Folks, if you'd only try...'

Movement was more fluid between Thirty-fifth and Thirty-sixth, but people began to pile up again at a red light on Thirty-seventh. Wylie, Russ, and Evadne slowed. A band of black youths in plum and lime suits with wide velour lapels watched them come. One of these sported a cape and a silver-tipped walking cane. He rested both hands atop his stick, shifted his weight back on his heels, and appraised them.

Wylie stopped when his eyes met the boy's. He lifted his arms a little from his body and made a slow 360-degree turn. His jacket, which he wore over an orange turtleneck, was of wool woven into a tapestry of soft golds and greens and blacks in a faintly Aztec design. His pants were a deep purple, short rise, tight down his legs, and severely flared at the ankles. Wylie unbuttoned the jacket, and spread it to reveal a ferocious paisley lining. He lifted one pants leg to display a glossy London Character boot-shoe. He looked at the boy hopefully.

The youth peered disdainfully down his nose at Wylie, then moved his eyes to Russ. Russ, who was white, stood glumly with his hands in his Levis pockets. He wore a green shortshirt, no jacket. The boy snorted and shifted his gaze to Evadne. Evadne was tall, five ten in flats. She was supple and long-limbed, and her color contrasted with Wylie's in a way that flattered them both – Wylie pitchblende and lustrous, Evadne a soft tan that seemed to absorb and incorporate light in a manner that caused color and texture to merge and become indivisible. Her Afro was a dark halo, her forehead was high and smooth,

9

her large eyes yearned shyly toward an almond shape. On either side of an aquiline nose, her cheeks were sharp flat planes. Her mouth and lips were full. Tonight she wore an ankle-length jersey of gray silk, with a loose collar of pale blue. She was naked beneath it, and the nipples of her high breasts were stiff thumbs against the fabric, the contours of her hips lazy swells, and the junction of her thighs a sweet valley viewed through a morning haze.

'Now you, mama,' the boy said huskily, 'you could steal my sleep away. Oh yes you could.'

Evadne smiled. 'You're sweet.'

'Oh, I could be so, *so* sweet for you, mama! Just float on loose from Chuck an' Tom there and come lay your honey on my sweetness. I buy a whole herd o' cabs t' carry us uptown.'

'Honey, I'm goin' grieve through the night, but the numbers just don't come up for us. That's the truth, it wholly is.'

'Then the world ain't hardly fit t' live in no more.'

'Bye now.'

'Till the numbers turn.'

'Uh huh.'

The light had been green for several moments. The boy and his friends made it across just as the yellow appeared.

'I feel very old,' Wylie said.

'You are,' Evadne said seriously.

Wylie nodded. 'I guess the years did catch us. You turned what, thirty-one, this time?'

'Yes, you prick. But I imagine a boy like that could cut off a few.'

'Wonder if he has a sister?'

'He didn't even like your clothes.'

At Thirty-eighth a silver Rolls swerved to the side and abruptly double-parked to a blare of horns. A man sprang from the back seat before his harried chauffeur could slip from behind the wheel and open the door. Unhappily, the chauffeur closed the door and stood at attention next to it, determined not be be foiled a second time.

'Vadne!' the man called. 'Vadne, wait a moment!'

Wylie, Evadne, and Russ, stepping up to the sidewalk on the north side of the street, stopped, and turned.

The man gained their side. They moved off to get out of the way of the crowd.

'Malcolm tells me you're not coming tonight,' he said. 'Excuse me.' He extended his hand to Wylie. 'I'm Neal Cummings.'

Cummings was a good-looking brown-haired white man in his late thirties. His careful tailoring and grooming were broken, perhaps redeemed, by the teeth exposed when he smiled; they gleamed brightly, but the front uppers overlapped, and one of the eyeteeth was crooked. That he hadn't deemed it important to have them corrected manifested a certain indifference to the values of his class.

'Wylie Lincoln.'

Cummings offered his hand to Russ.

Russ mumbled his name.

'I'm not,' Evadne said.

'I'm sorry. Tell me how I can change your mind.'

'Really, Neal, no. I've been partied nearly to death these last weeks.'

'Malcolm guarantees a boredom factor no higher than two percent.'

Evadne smiled, and shook her head.

'Mr Lincoln,' Cummings said. 'Come, please. Persuade her.'

'Love to,' Wylie said. 'I like parties. But models, you know, very temperamental. And popular ones are the worst. I can't do a thing with her, especially after I wash her hair.'

Cummings smiled in minor confusion. 'Well, what can

11

I say? I'd like to push, but I won't. Can I drop you anywhere?'

'Sure,' Wylie said.

'No thanks,' Evadne said. 'We'd take you a good deal out of your way.'

'I don't mind.'

'You're a love. Good night, Neal.'

'I'll call you soon.'

'Please do.'

'Glad to have met you, Mr Lincoln. Mr Turner.'

Cummings went back to his car. Wylie, Evadne, and Russ headed up Seventh Avenue again.

'It's going to be hell getting a cab,' Wylie said. 'How come we didn't let Cummings take us?'

'I'm trying to discourage him. He wants me.'

'That's sensible.'

'What? His wanting me, or me discouraging him?'

'Both. Who is he?'

'Cummings Enterprises. He was a Beautiful about nine or ten years ago. He got into some kind of merger fight and had his ass whipped. *Really* whipped. Lost every penny. He dropped out of the circuit, then reappeared two years back. Much smoother and nicer than he used to be, but still not my type.'

'Uh huh,' Wylie said, his interest petering out. 'Is that Malcolm Chasteen he was talking about? Didn't we go to a party there about two years ago? A townhouse on East . . .'

'Sixty-third Street. Yes.'

'That was a very good party.'

'This one won't be. Very select – nothing but Beautifuls, local and international. It'll be a night-long scramble for position. No one does that as much as the ones who are already on top. They have to get on top of the top.'

The September night was crisp and pleasant, so they weren't too displeased with having to walk all the way up to Fiftieth before they found a free cab.

Hand on the taxi's door, Wylie said, 'You want to stop in for a drink, Russ?'

'Thanks. Not tonight. I think I'm just going to walk Frank and then catch a late movie on television.'

'Okay. See you tomorrow.'

'Right.' To Evadne, Russ said, 'Good night, lovely.' Russ was not a flatterer. They all understood he was telling Evadne that she was, quite literally, lovely. Evadne kissed him on the mouth, then got into the cab with Wylie.

Wylie gave the driver his address and told him to go through the park.

'The least you could do is ask me, "My place or yours?"' Evadne said. 'Not just usurp my prerogatives as a matter of course.'

'One of my trainers laid an ounce of terrific grass on me yesterday. Ten-plus on a scale of ten.'

'Then you *may* usurp my prerogative as a matter of course. And tomorrow morning you will lay that ounce on me.'

'What for?'

'Because it was our anniversary last week, and you forgot. As of today, we have been divorced exactly six years and five days.'

'Oh. I'm sorry.'

'It's all right. I understand that these things are not as important to men as they are to women.'

Central Park was empty and peaceful along the illuminated roadway. Farther back, in the darkness that lay over the walkways and underpasses, the groves of trees and the ball fields, the miniature valleys and the jutting crags of rock, the thickets of brush, lurked persons hoping to commit one or more of every type of perversion or criminal act known to contemporary urban man. They were checked only by stunted imaginations and lack of victims. Nothing but the fury of bitterest winter could enforce a moratorium upon the nightly arena of the park.

The taxi emerged at Seventy-ninth Street, turned right onto Fifth Avenue, and bore Wylie and Evadne four blocks down. It stopped before a gold awning. A uniformed doorman opened the door. 'Good evening, Mr Lincoln, evening, Miss Jones.'

'Evening, Matt,' Wylie said.

'Hi, Matt,' Evadne said.

Matt assisted her out of the car while Wylie paid the driver.

The lobby was a stubby T, with a single elevator to the right and another to the left. A big cut-glass chandelier hung from the ceiling. There was a short sofa and a grouping of three expensive chairs along one wall, half a dozen live palms in *fin de siècle* pots, and a tall mirror in a brass frame mounted midway between the elevators.

Wylie and Evadne went to the right. A double row of buttons, numbered 1 through 18, protruded from the elevator panel. Above them was a single button marked *PH*. Wylie pushed that one. They whisked up smoothly and quickly. The door opened onto a space not much bigger than a walk-in closet. Directly opposite was a carved, heavy old library door that had been fitted with a knob and lock.

Wylie put his key in the lock. Behind the door, there was a deep snuffling sound.

'My baby smells me,' Evadne said.

Wylie opened the door, and was nearly knocked down by the rush of a massive black-and-rust German shepherd. The dog rose up on his hind legs, head on a level with Evadne's, and danced and pawed the air before her, careful not to touch her, and emitted a frantic series of yips and whines.

'Mommy's *baay*-bee!' Evadne said.

The dog plunged down to all fours, shot up again, shook himself, and panted deliriously.

14

'Would you like to come in?' Wylie said with resignation.

As Evadne entered, the dog shot past her, raced across the wide living room, bounded up on the leather couch and off, barked urgently, leaped over an end table, and came down on a throw rug. The rug skidded across the wood floor, causing the dog to fall. He scrambled to his feet, reached Evadne, and rolled over on his back, whining desperately.

Wylie buried his face in his hands.

Evadne hiked her dress up around her thighs and went down on her knees. She scratched the animal's great head, ministered similarly to his throat, and then began to work his chest with the nails of both hands. 'Big puppy,' she murmured. 'Big baby, lover dog, oh, so good you are, what a beautiful boy, oh yes, you're loved . . .'

The dog groaned. His long tongue lolled from his open mouth, his legs splayed to either side, his tail beat against the floor, and his eyes glazed in ecstasy.

'Your dignity,' Wylie pleaded. 'Ahab, remember your dignity.'

Ahab and Evadne ignored him.

'It's disgusting,' Wylie said. 'That is a noble and a proud and a fearless animal. But when he sees you he turns into Silly Putty.'

'That's because he has excellent taste,' Evadne said, finishing and standing up.

'Maybe I should let him live with you a while.'

'If he hasn't torn *your* throat out yet, then he could live with anyone.'

Wylie took a leash from a wall peg. 'Come on, Hab. Walk time.'

The dog moved behind Evadne.

'Oh, for Christ's sake, she'll be here when you get back. You going to make me be formal? All right. Ahab: Come.'

The dog moved swiftly, stopped, and sat a foot in front

of Wylie and perfectly square with him.

'Good boy.' Wylie patted him on the head. They left, with Ahab glancing over his shoulder at Evadne.

When they returned, ten minutes later, Scarlatti was on the turntable and being driven richly by the powerful amp through four Altec speakers, one in each corner of the room. Evadne had turned the rheostat controlling the ceiling fixtures low, suffusing the room with soft light. She was on the couch with her shoes off and her legs tucked beneath her, a drink in one hand, leafing through a magazine.

Wylie felt a sense of loss. Sometimes he perceived Evadne in an instant's context that stirred mournful longing in him, a hunger to make the moment permanent and never to relinquish her. But he'd tried that once: a marriage of fearsome, incendiary pleasure and rage in which they'd torn at each other like wild, crazed creatures. It was not inconceivable that eventually, if they hadn't fled each other, one might have killed the other.

Fortunately, such wistful sentiments in Wylie quickly metamorphosed into something that was a meld of lust and affectionate camaraderie. As they did now. He went to Evadne and kissed her on the forehead. She laid her arms around his neck and put her tongue in his mouth.

When they parted she said, 'That was nice.'

Ahab insisted on another lavish greeting.

Wylie brought out a cellophane bag with the un-cleaned grass, a flour sifter, and a sheet of typing paper. He laid the paper on the marble-slab table before the couch and emptied the grass into the sifter. He worked the stuff with his hand against the mesh with a steady circular motion. Shredding, the dry leaves dropped through onto the paper, forming a heightening mound of coarse greenish powder, the stalks and hard seeds remaining in the sifter.

Ahab's weighty head rested in Evadne's lap. She scrat-

16

ched him around the ears, asd he gazed up at her in rapture, sighing every few moments.

Wylie finished, put the seeds into a pill bottle, and went for the papers.

Evadne stood, stretched, and drifted toward the damask drapery that covered the opposite wall. The room was twenty feet long, and nearly as wide. The ceiling was high and beamed. The floor was dark parqueted wood. Wainscoting covered the lower portion of the walls. The upper parts, and the ceiling spaces between the beams, were finished in rough plaster. The furniture was mostly wood, massive and simple. Dominating one wall was a fireplace of granite blocks with a stone mantel. A bookcase consumed another. Over the fireplace hung a faded but intact Flemish tapestry depicting a stag harried by sleek dogs, and men with spears in pursuit. There were also a fifteenth-century German mace and a startling oil of one-inch squares of black, red, and white.

Evadne drew the drapes back. The wall was composed entirely of leaded windows. She freed a latch in the center and stepped onto the balcony. The breeze was cool and deferential. To her left were the buildings of Central Park South, farther down the spire of the Empire State Building, and still farther the mountainous jut of the World Trade Center. Directly across, the luxury buildings of Central Park West. And to her right, the lights of Harlem. She hadn't lived there since she was seventeen; only a madman would want to. The night was cloudless, and within the park proper the reservoir shone like glass. Headlights moved like lines of jeweled, regimented insects.

Wylie's arms came around her from behind. He put a burning joint between her lips and drew her in close. She sucked smoke and held it until her lungs hurt. Exhaled and dragged again. Passed the joint back to Wylie. When it was nearly finished, she disengaged from Wylie, went back in, and replaced Scarlatti with B. B. King.

17

Wylie followed, pinched out the roach, and rolled and lit a second joint. Evadne puffed once and began blinking at him.

'I'm ... away,' she said with sudden discovery. She hunched her shoulders and hugged herself. 'Oh. Oh. Oh. Not fair. This dope doesn't warn you. It just ... comes. Like a tidal wave. Oh!' Her mouth opened with surprise. 'There's a herd of tiny rhinoceroses running up and down my back.' She closed her eyes and wriggled with pleasure.

'It's the millennium,' Wylie said, and wondered why he had. He smoked and offered the joint to her.

'No, no. More would annihilate me.'

He took another drag and laid the cigarette on the ashtray.

They returned to the balcony, where they held each other loosely, moving with the music. In a while Evadne stepped away and to the balustrade. She leaned forward and stared. After several minutes she shook her head.

'None of that is real,' she said. 'There's nothing out there. We're ... all alone.' She turned to Wylie. '*I'm* all alone. I can't even find *you*.'

'You can if you try.'

'Can I?' She touched his face. Her fingers trembled. 'Yes.'

Wylie stood the touch, though he was afraid it asked too much. His muscles twitched.

She smiled sadly at him. 'Poor brave Wylie.'

'You'll have me weeping for myself.'

'What I really meant was that nobody can find *me*, didn't I?'

'I can.'

He drew her to him. She stiffened and tried to push away. He locked her tight and placed his lips on her forehead.

'No,' she said. She strained. But then, in moments, she collapsed against him and pulled her arms to her chest, hands touching her chin, and sank into his insistence. She pressed her face to his shoulder. 'Oh God, yes. Do that for me, Wylie. Please. Don't ever let me run that far.'

'Hush,' he whispered into her ear. 'You can never run so far that someone can't find you.'

She floated, buoyed by him, for a long, assuaging time, longer than she needed to. Until she sensed that it had ceased to be difficult for him, too. Gently, she disengaged.

She wiped her moist eyes. 'You have to watch that grass, it can be mean.'

'Some.'

'Despite yourself, Wylie, you're a very good man.'

'There's been talk of giving me a prize.'

She made a face at him.

They returned to the living room, and Wylie locked the door behind them. They listened to music and played lazily with Ahab, who grew near catatonic with pleasure. When they began to sag, they relit the joint, which had gone out, finished it, then stretched out on the floor and toyed with each other's fingers and hair. They talked with intense focus, and their insights were of exceptional profundity, which escaped them only moments later.

In time they went into the bedroom. Wylie's bed was broad and covered with a black leather spread. Batik-patterned leather pillows were scattered about it. The headboard was suede. Above it hung a suprarealistic Perlstein nude. Three tall broad-leafed plants stood in one corner, an English library chair in another. The bureau was constructed of lacquered Japanese travelling chests with brass carrying loops.

'I walk through warm water,' Evadne said. 'I swim through airy clouds.' As an afterthought she added, 'I am also six thousand three hundred thirty-nine feet tall.'

'You'll grow,' Wylie assured her. 'Don't worry.'

'It's so, so good. Why is it against the law?'

'*Because* it's so good.'

They pondered that awhile, and were not sure it made

19

sense. But they agreed it was correct.

Evadne pulled the mushroom curtains away from the casement windows, which also fronted the park. She would the windows open and let the breeze in.

'Mmmm,' she said. 'Like an ice massage, but not really cold, you know what I mean?'

'I think so.'

She pulled her dress over her head and dropped it to the floor, letting the breeze flow over her naked skin. 'Delicious!'

'Somewhere on Central Park West there's a voyeur with a high-power Bausch-and-Lomb scope, and right now you're overloading his nervous system.'

Evadne's breasts were smooth and conical, tipped with big areolas and nipples of a purplish color. She cupped and stroked them with her hands. Her tone was serious: 'If he had anything real, he wouldn't need his scope, would he? So I hope I make him happy. I hope he comes, so he can crawl into bed tonight with a little happiness.'

She turned inward, to herself, and moved her body with fluid effortlessness, a small dance in time to the music of its own motion. 'Poor, poor man,' she whispered.

Wylie watched her. He believed in love so far as it was a thing of the moment. He did not believe that it was something between one man and one woman that endured through the years – that was friendship, and rare enough. And he believed that unhappiness was the greatest stupidity of which man was capable.

So he would never say to himself that he loved Evadne.

She had finished her dance, and stood naked before the window with her head bowed.

Wylie was sitting on the edge of the bed. She went to him.

'I want to fuck you,' he said.

'And I want to fuck *you,* lover.'

He spanned her with his arms and pressed his thumb into her back, drawing it down, feeling the ridge of her spine, until he arrived at the soft fuzz at the lower curve. He caressed this, then ran his fingers down the declivity between her buttocks, took the tense mounds in his hands, pressed his face into her warm belly and kissed the thicket of hair, rolled his tongue in her navel. She teased the hard muscles of his shoulders and back with her nails.

They stripped the bed to the sheets and turned out the lights. Wylie flipped a switch at the base of a cube of cloudy Lucite on the table next to the bed. It encapsulated them in a soft glow.

For a time they simply rubbed their bodies together, sliding and twining as if they aspired to serpenthood. Slowly they added their hands and mouths, the sweet pressures of locked legs and bent arms; they traced patterns on muscles and softness with light fingertips; they grasped and pulled at flesh, licked and sucked each other, nibbled on toes and nipples, thrust tongues into openings and into the soft pockets between lips and teeth and against the backs of knees, strained themselves and each other to trembling doors of pain, tormented and lavished each other, probed sensitive, wet, musk-ridden folds and rigid flesh, stroked and lightly pinched tiny buttons of ecstasy, and then finally she lay back and spread fully open for him and he pierced her just a little and braced against her urgent hands on his buttocks and went only a tiny bit deeper, and it progressed like that for some time until finally he sank the final short distance, hard to his own root, and she groaned as if from deep within a cave, and they moved long together in easy rhythm, and then, in turn, they offered each other hesitations and bucks, claspings and stillness, twitches, and frantic little lunges, and then, after a return to that steady rhythm which neither could endure much longer, they began to drive at each other with grunts and gasps and ratcheting throats and small growls, battering and arching until she lifted from the bed, bent, and froze herself with a moist 'Aaaaaaahhhhh!' and remained thus, trembling ever so smally, while he threw back his head and lashed on until he too was hurled spinning and tumbling over the bright edge and they collapsed together, breathing deeply, little tics and twitches pulling at their flesh; later she rode him, and at the end they lay on their sides facing each other, content, he with one leg lodged between hers and his limp self pressed against her wetness, and even as they drifted near sleep he began to swell and with a slight movement she made it possible for his tumescence to come into her, and when it was complete they rocked each other gently and it was slow this time, but they found it, eventually, half in dreams, and they slept coupled until, sometime much later, one of them rolled over without knowing it.

Morning. And Wylie's body chuckled indulgently at his mind's presumption in ordering it to rise. But Wylie's mind, though sympathetic, remained firm, and at last the body turned to the task, petulant and surly, knowing full well the task was impossible.

Evadne was lying on her stomach. Wylie kissed her shoulder. Sleeping deeply, she did nothing. Wylie slipped a sweatsuit on over a jockstrap and took Ahab down the elevator. The dog, who had been forced to sleep in the hall behind the closed bedroom door, looked at Wylie with reproach, and punished him by being aloof and restrained in his morning greeting. But Ahab was incapable of lasting grudges, and by the time they had crossed Fifth Avenue and entered the park under the bright new sun, he was frisking around Wylie, and his tail was wagging lustily.

They ran their mile around the Sheep Meadow, though it did take somewhat longer than usual. By the time they reentered the lobby, Wylie's body tentatively admitted that it probably could get through the day. But it warned him not to expect anything of quality from it.

He picked up the *Times* from the mat before his door, brought it into the kitchen, and set it on the yellow molded-polythene table. He ran fresh water into Ahab's bowl and cut and squeezed four oranges into a tall glass. He drank the juice, ground coffee beans and put them into a paper cone which he inserted in the top of the Chemex pot, then set water to boil. *Times,* juice, and coffee were necessary before shower.

He sat down and opened the paper.

'Son of a bitch!' he said.

The *Times* had got the story late, and had been able to run only a box on it. Basic facts, little detail. Professional curiosity gripped Wylie several moments. But then he thought of Evadne. He worried some.

He squeezed another glass of juice, poured the boiling water, and let it drip down through the coffee. He took the juice and coffee into the bedroom, sat on the edge of the bed, and began to rub Evadne's back. He didn't hurry her; she woke in time. He gave her the juice and had her sip some coffee. She didn't gain full consciousness until she'd drunk half the coffee. Then she became querulous, and demanded to know why he'd wakened her.

'Listen, babe. Do you know a Julius Hollander, or a Mrs Radfood Greer?'

She frowned. 'Hannah Greer ... yeah, I've met her once or twice. Julius Hollander, I think I know the name. Why?'

Wylie was relieved. 'I was afraid they might have been friends. Someone knocked over Malcolm Chasteen's party last night. Mr Greer and Mrs Hollander were shotgunned to death.'

23

CHAPTER TWO

Wylie picked up the Mercedes's keys from morning-shift doorman. The garage, three blocks away, dropped the gray car at the curb each weekday morning at eight thirty and left the keys. Wylie opened the rear door, and Ahab jumped up onto the plywood platform. The platform extended from the back of the front seat to the vertical cushioning of the rear seat and was hinged on the center and secured with snap catches so it could be removed and stored in the trunk when not in use. It was covered with felt to eliminate the possibility of splinters and to give the dog traction. Large dogs were uncomfortable trying to balance on normal car seats, and the vagaries of traffic could pitch one off – to its distress and anxiety, and possible injury.

The engine turned over instantly and idled with a low, pleasant thrum. Wylie liked the car. He liked fineness in anything.

One of the reasons he didn't like the robbery at Chasteen's was that it had fallen apart. Things that were crude or inferior annoyed him.

He shifted the radio tuner as he drove, picking up different newscasts. The robbery was being played for sensation; little concrete information was offered. Nothing, certainly, that suggested a way into it. He lost interest, changed the selector to FM, and pushed the button for WQXR. Liszt. *Les Preludes*. Very nice on a clear September morning.

He pulled into a garage on Second Avenue between Twenty-seventh and Twenty-eighth streets. Ahab stretched as soon as he got out, a kind of deep bow with forelegs extended straight before him, chest nearly touching the concrete, the line of his back swinging up to his high rump with a curvature that resembled a ski jump. He flexed his toes. Then he stood, shook himself, and ambled to Wylie's side. His tail swung in an unconscious lazy wag. With equal unconsciousness, Wylie scratched the dog's ear as he handed the keys to the garageman.

He said, 'Ahab, heel,' and started down Second Avenue.

The dog matched Wylie's stride, maintaining a position in which his head preceded Wylie by about a foot and his shoulder remained aligned with Wylie's left knee and a foot to the side.

Ahab was linebred from Volker von Zollegren-schutz-Haus, the only German shepherd ever to have twice captured the annual German Sieger award – the equivalent of the breed's world championship. He was a large dog of proud mien, a study in esthetic proportion, a balanced animal that devoured ground with long, floating steps. His head was large and strong-muzzled. He was deep-chested and iron-backed, his ribs well sprung. His tail was full and flowing; his bones were precisely angulated, and their movement was fluid. He was firm-fleshed and muscular, toned like an athlete at peak. His colors, jet black and deep rust, were well demarcated. He was reserved with strangers, but would tolerate their making a fuss over him if they insisted upon it. His spirit was noble and encompassed an element of largesse. He was of subtle and utterly sound character, stable as rock.

By ring standards his muzzle was slightly blunt, and two of his nails were washed, pale gray with hints of pink – faults. Still, he could have been a major champion. But Wylie would not campaign him. The dog-show circuit was a miserable world of hysteria, back-biting, internecine warfare, viciousness, and vulgarity. And it was quite possible – indeed, it occurred with depressing regularity – for a dog with the intelligence of a grasshopper and the personality of an assassin or a slave to become elevated to championship.

Obedience competition was only a bit more pleasant, and American obedience trials were of poor design to test an animal's full intelligence and character. Wylie had entered for Ahab's sake – he thought the dog was entitled to recognition – but had disengaged as soon as Ahab had won his degrees.

Wylie was a good trainer, and not particularly humble, but he knew and readily admitted that the better part of the credit went to Ahab himself: Ahab would have achieved competency even in the hands of a bumbler. Wylie was not a romantic. For example, he considered the sacrifice of one's life on behalf of another person, to say nothing of a dog, a complete and inexcusable absurdity. But were Ahab's existence to hang in the balance, Wylie would have surrendered an arm without hesitation.

Wylie stopped for a traffic light at Twenty-fifth Street. Ahab sat automatically. On the green, Wylie stepped out with his left foot, and Ahab rose and heeled without a word. Had Wylie begun with his right foot, the dog would have held his sit until told to do something else.

They crossed the street, turned right, and walked halfway down the block. The sign over the two long windows read: CERBERUS SCHOOL FOR DOGS. Dog books and training and maintenance equipment were displayed in the bottom halves of the windows. Passers-by could look over them into the panelled room beyond. The room was large enough to accommodate group classes of six owners and their pets, if the animals weren't all of mastiff or Great Dane size. It was one of three training areas in the building, and Cerberus favored it for general instruction and some attack work. Observation by people on the street brought in a surprising amount of business.

At the back of the room, around a cluster of three desks, Russ was talking to Kenroy. Kenroy was a slow-speaking Tennessee boy who frequently reminded Wylie of Will Rogers. He was Cerberus's night manager. Kenroy's eyes were pouchy. He smiled thinly as Wylie entered and lifted a hand. Russ, in chinos and a sweatshirt, strode angrily across the green indoor-outdoor carpet to Wylie. The carpet was washed once a week, and had to be replaced every two years. It was an expense, but tiles and sheet vinyl just didn't offer the footing that dogs in training needed.

'We lost Furcoat Duke last night,' Russ said. There were three Dukes: Furcoat, Duke the Younger, and Oddball Duke. 'Some motherfucker put a crossbow bolt through him.'

'Ah no,' Wylie said. 'Not Furcoat. Oh, *goddamn* it!'

They went to Kenroy.

'Ahab,' Russ said to Wylie.

When Wylie had stopped inside the door, the dog had sat. With Furcoat Duke on his mind, Wylie had moved off on his right foot – Ahab was waiting.

Dogs were Russ's dead center. Bleeding from severed legs, he would have crawled home on stumps to see that his own animal was fed and walked.

Wylie said, 'Okay, Hab.'

Released, Ahab stood and went sauntering toward the corner in which Frank was lying. Frank, a Rottweiler, was Russ's dog. He came to his feet as Ahab approached. The hair on his back rippled. Ahab closed with stiffened legs. Tensed, the animals confronted each other, then slowly swung their hindquarters so that each could sniff a moment. They separated and locked eyes again. The dogs did not like each other, and they performed this ritual each time they met, even if one were simply returning to a room after a few minutes' absence. Having satisfactorily demonstrated to one another that they were as formidable as they had been yesterday, and would take no shit, Frank lay back down, and Ahab walked several neutral feet away before dropping down himself.

27

'Mornin', Wylie,' Kenroy said. 'Awful sorry. He was still alive when I got him to the hospital. But just barely. They asked me did I want 'em to operate, an' I said hell yes, there wasn't nothin' to lose. But when they got him on the table, he gave one last snarl and then he just...' Kenroy raised his hands, palms up.

Wylie was depressed. Furcoat Duke, a monstrosity of a shepherd by breed standards, with a head like a grizzly bear and long, shaggy, yaklike hair that sprang out in a tangle, making him look even larger, had been one of his first rental dogs. Going on eleven years old. Ordinarily, Wylie retired area guards at eight or nine. But three years ago, when he'd sent Furcoat Duke to the school's upstate installation to recuperate from a sprained leg, the dog had grown morose, and had nearly starved himself to death from unhappiness. Furcoat Duke had been one of those very, very few dogs who can truly be called vicious. The animal had lived only to put its teeth into flesh, and Wylie knew that it would have died in misery if kenneled in its old age and denied a reasonable chance to perform the only action it found significant. Wylie had hoped the old berserker would die peacefully in his sleep one morning.

'Where'd they hit him?' Wylie asked.

'The arrow went right through. Collapsed one lung and tore up some other stuff.'

'He get a piece of 'em?'

Russ was squatting down, rubbing a Pembroke Welsh corgi whose leash was tied to a desk leg. He answered before Kenroy. 'Yeah. I just got back from there. They pried off the sheet metal that was covering what used to be a window. It was maybe eight feet up from the ground, and the way it looks – scratch marks on the wall – Furcoat was jumping to get up to them. One of them must have leaned in and let him have it. The shock probably stunned him, and they figured he was dead and they dropped in. But Furcoat put it together for one last play.

Blood all over the wall and the windowsill – out on the sidewalk, too, right to the curb. Good old, tough old dog.'

Wylie nodded. 'You bring him back, Kenroy?'

'Sure. Got him downstairs.'

'Okay. Have Gene take him upstate this afternoon and bury him. Get a little marker for him. Furcoat. I'm going to miss him.'

Kenroy was unable to suppress a yawn.

Wylie said, 'What time did it happen?'

'I got the call about two. A squad car noticed the window job, stopped, and shined a flashlight in. Furcoat tried to take the cop's hand off. They got our number from the sign and called. I phoned Cheryl and asked her to come over and cover here for me, then I went and picked him up, took him to the hospital.'

'Go upstairs and get some sleep,' Wylie said. 'Tell Cheryl she can head home, she's already put in a full day. Thanks, Kenroy. You did everything you could.'

'How's this one doing?' Russ asked. The corgi was nibbling on Russ's fingers.

'Terrible,' Kenroy said.

'He'll learn.'

'I guess,' Kenroy said doubtfully.

'Sure you will, won't you, boy,' Russ said. The dog licked his face, then stepped away and lifted his leg against the desk. 'No!' Russ yelled. *No!* He snatched the dog up, fumbled the leash free and ran for the door. 'That's outside, boy. Outside, old hero. *Outside!*'

The corgi was a housebreaking job.

Wylie had founded Cerberus School for Dogs ten years ago, after his resignation had been forced from the Police Department. It was not the largest in the country – and Wylie wasn't sure he ever wanted it to be – but it was among the three or four finest, and easily the best on the Eastern Coast. Cerberus was a full-service school that trained for general obedience, utility and obstacle work, scent discrimination and tracking, retrieval, attack (both area guards and command-only dogs), theatrical work, and correction of special problems. Excepting guide work for the blind, the school would teach a dog to do anything a dog was capable of doing. One staff member *had* trained for the Seeing Eye in Morristown, but that work was so highly esoteric that it required an organization dedicated to nothing else.

Wylie was a very good man with dogs. There was little he couldn't get them to do, and well and happily. Still, like most trainers, he was somewhat mechanistic in his approach. Russ was not. Russ *understood* dogs. Not theoretically, not through years of experience, but emotionally, with deep natural empathy. He never mis-interpreted an animal's actions, knew precisely what its emotions were, *felt* its emotions, and could tell you what a dog was about to do a moment or two before the dog itself had decided. Russ respected and loved dogs. Rarely did he respect or love human beings. He did not train an animal – he worked *with* it toward a common goal. He had been with Cerberus four years, and was its chief trainer. Last year Wylie had offered him a piece of the school. But Russ didn't want to own anything.

The morning was gloomy with Furcoat Duke's death, but busy. The mail brought eleven letters of appreciation, seven from the older customers. One man's pet had been trained two years ago. He apologized for his dilatoriness, but did want to thank the school for the dog's continued good deportment. Wylie turned them over to Pat, the receptionist-secretary, to write acknowledgment notes. He dictated short answers to several letters requesting information of various kinds. A Cerberus brochure was enclosed with each. With Cheryl gone, another trainer out sick, and the schedule for private lessons thrown off by a few people who arrived late with their dogs, Wylie had to help with the training. He handled a group lesson first. The dogs and their owners were being introduced to the sit-stay, a not very complicated phase of basic on-leash obedience. Two people demonstrated high intelligence and sensitivity with their animals, three were initially flustered and unsure but pulled together toward the end, and one was hopeless. That man had managed to teach his enthusiastic Old English sheepdog nothing over the last two weeks. He blamed Cerberus, and he was surly. The sheepdog was intelligent – it had trained its owner with little difficulty. Wylie was sorry for the animal. The man would not return for the balance of the course. In time, frustrated, he would begin to beat the dog, or he'd give up all hope of control and have on his hands a lunging, barking, totally undisciplined creature that would make an asylum of his house and generate endless need to apologize to neighbors, friends, and strangers on the street, and would probably, therefore, be brought to a shelter where its life would be ended a short time later.

Next Wylie donned a heavy padded sleeve and worked half an hour with a Doberman in for attack training. He was sweating and short of breath by the time he hung the sleeve back up. He got a list from Pat of calls that had backed up, and sat down at one of the desks in the front room.

Four theatrical jobs – a bonanza. He accepted three: an off-Broadway production needing a Great Dane that would be tied to a toilet bowl and would then pull the bowl from its moorings; a swimming-pool commercial in which a cocker spaniel would paddle about sinking plat-forms on which cocktails floated; and a dog-food spot re-quiring thirty-six puppies of different breeds. The last would be a mess. But they had agreed to his price, which was high.

On the fourth, he asked, 'How high is the ledge you want the dog to jump from?'

'Twenty feet,' the assistant director said, 'and it's got to be the real thing, no cut-shots. We can mask about six inches of padding.'

'Padding's no good. A dog doesn't know how to hit it. He can snap a leg or tear a shoulder apart.'

'Well, we might squeeze by at fifteen feet without padding.'

'No good. Ten's the limit.'

'Fifteen's ours.'

'Sorry, then. Not with one of my dogs. Call me back if you think you can make it work with ten.'

There were also three obedience jobs and four dogs for boarding. He called the printer and ordered one hundred fifty signs offering a two-thousand-dollar reward for information leading to the arrest and conviction of Fur-coat Duke's killers, and placed newspaper ads with the same offer.

In the early afternoon he sent out for two bottles of Heineken and a pastrami on rye, and went into the small soundproof office they used for consultation and tele-phone calls when dogs were creating a din in the other areas. The food and respite allowed the previous night to catch up with him, and he began to feel logy. He leaned back in the chair and put his feet up, but guarded against the closing of his eyes. If he dozed, it would be at least an hour before he woke. He lit his first cigarette of the day and watched the smoke rise.

A knock on the door. 'Yes?'

Harold poked his head in. Harold had handled a scout dog in Vietnam. He wore his blond hair short, had kindly blue eyes, was exasperatingly patient and tolerant, and did not smoke, drink, swear, or raise his voice in anger. Harold was always sadly baffled by the amount of pain and anger in the world. At different times, people wanted either to venerate him or beat him to a red pulp.

'There's a young woman to see you, Mr Lincoln. She didn't give me her name, but she said Miss Jones sent her.'

Dogs were barking in the front. Wylie asked Harold to show her in. He dumped the empty bottles of Heineken and the wax paper from the sandwich into the wastebasket.

The girl Harold brought wore silver aviator sunglasses. Her hair was a dark honey color, long and straight. The planes of her face were broad, her nose long but attractive. Large round breasts pouched her thick-ribbed sweater. A short skirt, white knee-high boots. It was difficult not to wonder what she would feel like.

Wylie introduced himself. She waited until Harold had gone, closing the door behind him. Then she removed her sunglasses, in a manner suggesting that the act had significance. The only significance Wylie found was that her eyes were now uncovered. Pleasant but ordinary brown eyes.

'I'm Lesley Marecek,' she said.

Wylie asked her to sit. He went back around the desk. 'Any relation to Pytor Marecek?' he asked irrelevantly.

'He's my father,' she said, surprising him. 'Do you know his compositions?'

'Yes. They're very fine.'

Lesley nodded. 'He is a nice man, too. I don't write to him enough. But he is happy in Czechoslovakia, and I am happy here, and he has nothing to do with us.'

Wylie was disappointed.

'Evadne said I should talk to you, Mr Lincoln.'

'What can we do for you?'

Her tongue flicked across her lower lip. Not in nervousness, Wylie noted, but in appraisal. 'I couldn't think of anyone to call but Evadne. She said I could trust you. I don't know you, and I have no reason to do that. But I trust Evadne.'

Wylie waited.

She took cigarettes from her purse and lit one, exhaling smoke through her nose. 'I am in trouble,' she said.

33

'What kind?'

'There are ... photographs of me.'

'With a man?' He tried for an avuncular tone.

She looked away. 'Yes.'

'And you're engaged in sexual acts in these photographs, and someone is trying to blackmail you.'

She nodded, still not looking at him.

'Did you pose for them?'

'No!'

'I'm sorry. It happens that way sometimes. Do you know how they were taken?'

'No, I can't understand it.'

'Is your face clear in these, Lesley? I mean, would there be no doubt that it was you if someone saw them?'

'There would be no doubt.'

'Are you married?'

'No. But I live with a man.'

'Is it a serious relationship?'

'Yes, to an extent. And it seems to be growing more serious. But it is more than that. He is very jealous and possessive, and a man of temper. It would not be beyond him to disfigure me if he saw them, and possibly do something even worse.'

Wylie lit his second cigarette of the day. 'What do you want from me?'

'To get the photographs. Evadne said you do things like that for people on occasion.'

Wylie did, and more than on occasion. Cerberus was a solidly profitable operation, but it didn't make near the money he needed to support his life-style. Wylie hadn't been a ghetto kid, but he'd been poor enough, and he'd seen his father shuffle and kiss ass most of his life. Wylie's father, a sharecropper in Georgia, had been widely respected as a trainer of coonhounds and rabbit dogs, bear and boar hounds, even by the whites. But up North, where the family moved when Wylie was still young, they wouldn't let the old man touch a leash, wouldn't let him be anything but a shit-shoveler, a cage cleaner and kennel scut man. Wylie had gone to Harvard on a scholarship. He had learned a lot there, including the fact that people with money live incalculably better and more happily than people without it. He missed *Magna* and *Summa,* but did manage a very respectable *Cum Laude,* and turned down offers from IBM, Corning Glass, AT&T, and half a dozen others because that kind of career, in concept, didn't seem much better than slavery, in concept, and he didn't want to be anyone's show nigger. So he messed around in New York a few months, living on the largesse of school friends and their families, and then, being somewhat contrary, and slightly capricious besides, and having to do *something* to support himself while considering how best to obtain the good life, and partly for a lark, and partly to win a thousand-dollar bet, he joined the New York City Police Department.

And discovered there was a market for an intelligent man well trained in police procedure who understood discretion and who was willing to offer his skills on a free-lance basis during off-duty hours, and he cultivated that market – methodically upgrading the socio-economic level of his clients – and was careful to discharge his police duties honestly and conscientiously, while frequently, on his own time, breaking the law, sometimes quite seriously, and making a good deal more money that way than the City paid him. He got a good handhold on the first rung of the ladder he wanted to climb. And then the roof fell on him: one of New York's election-year corruption scandals, a great outcry, a sweeping investigation. Departmental malfeasance was rampant around him. He kept his mouth shut but took no part in it himself, thinking it mean, petty, beneath his dignity, and financially very small potatoes besides. But it was very apparent even to the casual observer that he lived substantially better than a man ought to on a junior-grade detective's salary, and they came after him. He'd been young then, and not as careful as he was now, and he knew that while a probe of any depth would have cleared him of official misconduct, it would concomitantly have been most compromising in the context of his private activities. So he went to the Deputy Mayor, one of the few people of real consequence for whom he'd worked at that time, and that man had the investigation quashed. It was all very vague, the Deputy Mayor alluding only in general terms to a personal service Wylie had rendered him, for which Wylie had been quite well paid, and which, he claimed, accounted for the quality of Wylie's apartment, his clothes, his automobile, and the expensive texture of his social life. Luckily, no one had had the muscle to force the Deputy Mayor to be more specific, which would have meant at least some time behind bars for both of them. But it did cost Wylie his job.

Wylie picked up the phone and dialed Evadne's number. She answered, and he said, 'Baby, I have a Lesley Marecek in my office. Twenty-four years old, long honey-brown hair, brown eyes, nice breasts, good legs, about five six, and maybe one hundred ten pounds.' Lesley gazed at him impassively. 'She's interested in photography.'

'She's straight,' Evadne said. 'I sent her.'

'Who is she?'

'Her father's some kind of composer in Europe. Behind the Iron Curtain. He sent her to school in Paris when she was seventeen. She dropped out after a year, made Costa del Sol, Majorca, Belgrade, St Moritz, landed here two years ago. She's a nice girl, wild and maybe a bit silly, but she's young. She met Victor Lamorena at a party and started dating him for a lark. Do you know Lamorena?'

'I know *who* he is.' Victor Lamorena was, among other things, a labor racketeer, and, among still other things, one of the three people who had been wounded at Malcolm Chasteen's.

'Well, she got involved – there's no accounting for

36

taste; look at how I feel about you, for example – and she's been his mistress since last summer. She doesn't sleep around on him – at least, I didn't think so until she called me this morning. She's real, you don't have to worry about her.'

'Thanks, babe. I'll talk to you, probably tomorrow.'

'Not tonight? Last night was nice.'

'Last night is still tired.'

'Then I'll have to find someone else to help me smoke that fine weed.'

'Bitch.'

She made a kissing sound and hung up.

'Do I pass?' Lesley said.

'Uh huh. Tell me about it, and don't leave anything out. The part you hide may be just the part I need.'

She told him, concisely and without hesitation, and with more intelligence than he'd initially credited her with. She'd stepped out on Victor Lamorena only once, and that was shortly after she'd gone to live with him. With Edward Payne, a Los Angeles scriptwriter who visited New York periodically. She and Payne had slept together several times before Lesley had met Lamorena, and this meeting was more or less a friendly good-bye. Payne had taken a room at the Howard Johnson's motel on Fifty-first Street and Eighth Avenue. One month later a messenger from a commercial service had delivered a manila envelope to Lesley at Lamorena's apartment. In it were half a dozen eight-by-ten prints of her and Payne, and a demand for five hundred dollars. Typed instructions told her where to leave the money. She placed a hysterical call to Payne, who grew no less agitated himself. Payne finally came to accusing her of trying to blackmail him, and slammed down the phone. He had refused to accept further calls, and had not answered the two letters she'd written. Once the initial payment had been made, the blackmailer had settled down to a steady three hundred dollars per month. On the first Monday of each month she received a short telephone message telling her where to leave the money. Finally, three weeks ago, the man had offered to sell her the negatives for twenty-five hundred dollars. She had accepted, paid, and received them as promised.

'And now you learn he has another set and he's starting over again?' Wylie asked.

'No,' she said miserably. Her eyes teared.

'Then what?'

'I got them last night at the fight. I'd given him my seat number, and I was supposed to go to the ladies' room in the middle of the second round. When I did, a little Puerto Rican boy stopped me before I reached the door and gave me an envelope. He told me a man had paid him a dollar to deliver it and that the man had said I'd give him another dollar. I wasn't thinking right. I should have gone right into the bathroom and burned them. But I was so relieved, and so nervous just standing there holding them. I took them out and put them in my cigarette case. It has a little spring plate at the bottom – you can put a driver's license or a credit card under it.

'And then – oh, Jesus Christ! – we went to Malcolm Chasteen's party, and they got – they took – it was a gold case – they stole it in the robbery – oh God, someone else has them now, and I can't pay any more, I can't take it any longer, I just can't, I can't!'

She broke down. Wylie turned in his swivel chair, opened a small cabinet, and brought out a bottle of Remy Martin and a crystal snifter. He covered the bottom of the snifter with brandy and took it around the desk. He rubbed Lesley's neck gently. 'It's okay,' he said. 'It's all right now. Take this.'

She wiped away her tears and fished a handkerchief from her purse and blew her nose, embarrassed. She accepted the brandy. 'Thank you. I'm sorry.'

'You had a good reason.'

Wylie sat near her on the edge of the desk. 'Look, that

robbery grossed better than a quarter of a million dollars, according to the papers. Most in jewelry. Fencing costs are going to cut that down a lot, but each of those four guys is still going to clear twenty to twenty-five thousand. More important, though, they're in for a double killing now, and they're being hunted hard. The last thing they want to do is start dabbling in blackmail. I can just about promise you you'll never hear anything about those negatives again.'

She shook her head. 'The kind of people who did that, the world they live in, they'll know who Victor is, and there have been enough pictures in the papers of me with Victor that someone will recognize me, and they'll try it.'

'A million to one against that, Lesley.'

'I want you to get them for me.'

Wylie straightened a paper clip and reflected on it. 'What does Lamorena mean to you?'

'I know what he is. And everything that has been said about him is true. But there are other parts of him that are nice. Nicer than what you can find in the "right" people. Maybe he will decide to marry me. And I think I would like that. But if he ever sees such pictures, he would never marry me. And he would not simply throw me out – he would hurt my face and my body.'

Wylie went back behind the desk and poured a brandy for himself. There was almost no hope. On the other hand, he hadn't worked in months, and the last job had been a Gibraltar of tedium. He liked this girl, too, a little.

'Find them for me,' she said.

He took too big a drink of the brandy. 'All right. Twenty-five hundred as a retainer. That's against five thousand if I can do it with reasonable effort, ten thousand if it gets messy or means serious trouble. Expenses are on top of that. If I still haven't brought it off at ten thousand, you can decide whether or not you want to up the ante and keep me going.'

Her mouth dropped. 'That's insane!'

'Lesley, the New York City Police Department employs twenty-nine thousand men at an average salary of thirteen thousand a year. Right now the major focus of that department is finding the men who did the Chasteen job. That's twenty-nine thousand cops giving it at least a couple minutes' thought today, and today's payroll will run above a million dollars. Bluntly, I don't have much of a chance, but I'll try it if you want me to. It's your decision.'

'I just don't have that kind of money. I don't.'

Wylie was annoyed. He liked to hold to three or four such jobs a year, and at much higher fees. He thought he'd been generous.

'You put the negatives in a gold cigarette case. I could take you to any jeweler in town and get you at least seven hundred fifty for that emerald ring you're wearing. What kind of money don't you have, Lesley?'

'When Victor gives me presents, he wants to see them. And everything else is charge accounts. I don't have any cash.'

Wylie stood up 'Sorry.'

'You bastard,' she said. 'You stinking bastard.'

'Nice guys don't do this kind of work.'

'When do you want the twenty-five hundred?'

'Tomorrow would be okay.'

'Victor never even looks at the charge statements. His accountant pays all the bills.'

'Right.'

'Try to keep the expenses down, will you?'

'Should I get receipts?'

Lesley went up on her toes and gave him a quick kiss. 'Evadne was right – she said you were a real prick.'

CHAPTER THREE

The emptiness was there again. He felt like the brittle, hollow shells cicadas shed and left clinging to trees and house sides, papery representations of life. It came upon him over several days, a gradual but relentless siphoning, presaged by bloody nightmares and dreams of his own destruction that made him wake trembling on sweat-drenched sheets.

He was grateful for the new job. The hunt did for him what main-lined crystals of methedrine did for others. Soon. But now he was empty.

Russ was thirty-two years old. He had spent two of those years in reform school, and eight more in prison. He had killed men with a variety of weapons, with his hands, and once with his teeth. He had been savaged to the thin edge of death.

A prison psychiatrist had told him that he wanted to die. Russ knew better.

It was simply that he didn't know how to live.

He had a recurrent dream: He was on the street, or at a party, in someone's house – nearly any place – and people were talking and doing business, laughing, drinking, making love, greeting each other, telling jokes, and between him and all of them was a wall of impenetrable glass; he hammered on it with his fists and screamed, but no one ever heard him, no one ever saw him, no one ever knew he was there. When he was a child he had dreamed of arriving in empty classrooms, of deserted playgrounds, vacated streets.

Killing, he had heard his blood's pulse and had known joy. He didn't kill any more – or, at least, rarely, and then with no special emotion – because they would punish him for it now, and he really didn't want to die, not slowly in prison, or quickly by a bullet. And the kill had become superfluous, the hunt itself sufficient. It vitalized him, like a surge of power into a dormant machine.

He was neither happy nor unhappy. He accepted and made do. It was nearly enough.

Perhaps the dogs made it possible. Without them he might not have been able to endure. At times he had a vision. He saw something rising from a dog, a thin warm plait, that would draw something similar from himself, and the two would twine together and writhe in an attempt to merge, but, though of similar stuff, still not the same, and sadly frustrating.

Dogs made him feel good.

When he got home from the school he fed Frank, walked him, and groomed him for a long time while the dog's tongue drooped, his eyes partly closed and the corners of his mouth pulled up in happiness.

Frank was a Rottweiler, a large, big-chested dog of great power, steadiness, and self-reliance. Rottweilers were an old and formidable breed. By day they had driven the cattle herds of Roman armies on the march and, staked around perimeters, had secured the encampments by night. Medieval merchants and travelers had fixed money pouches to the dogs' collars, where they were safeguarded with ferocity. Frank was characteristically broad-headed and droop-eared, equipped with short, punishing jaws, stub-tailed, of a dark mahogany color, and heavily muscled. He was an intelligent and easy going animal.

Russ played with the dog for an hour, tossing a small ball which the animal caught in his mouth, and hauling at one end of a heavy strip of leather while Frank pulled and yanked at the other, emitting mock growls. They wrestled on the floor. Russ batted the dog with his hands, and the dog batted him with his paws.

But Frank couldn't fill the emptiness.

42

Russ stretched out on his back and lit a cigarette. He stared at the faults in the ceiling while he smoked. His eyes drifted in and out of focus. Frank rested his head on Russ's stomach and dreamed. His paws twitched; now and then he gave a stifled little bark. Russ idly caressed the dog's head and shoulders.

He would have been happy to fall asleep too. But he couldn't. So in a while he got up and walked aimlessly around the apartment. Frank watched him and made a noise.

'Nothing you can do, boy,' Russ said.

The dog padded over, sat in front of him, and whined. Russ squatted and roughed his ears. The dog lavished his tongue over Russ's face. Russ smiled and gave him a good scratching. Then he went to the telephone.

Donna danced topless at the Stonehouse, a midtown expense-account bar costly enough to circumvent the guilty embarrassment its patrons would have felt watching young tits bounce in the sleazy joints of Times Square. But one of the late-shift girls had been busted for soliciting, and Donna had to fill in; she wouldn't be getting out until four in the morning. She was sorry.

Women drifted in and out of Russ's life – mostly out. Only Donna had lasted. Russ saw her now and then. She was a nice girl.

Russ stripped off his sweatshirt, washed up, and put on a sportshirt and a blue windbreaker. Excited, Frank went to the door. 'Sorry, buddy,' Russ said. 'Not tonight.'

Frank's head drooped. He walked to the kitchen table and lay down under it, in his favorite brooding spot, and looked at Russ with mournful resignation.

Russ didn't leave Frank often. Even when he ate out, he usually went to local places where he was known and they didn't mind the handsome, quiet animal curling unobtrusively next to his chair. But tonight Russ was looking, and – though Frank, by virtue of being an unusual breed, encouraged people to stop Russ and open a

43

conversation – Russ thought it a cheap and degrading usage of the dog to employ him as bait.

He left the apartment and walked up Morton Street to Seventh Avenue, crossed, and walked the short Cornelia Street block to Bleecker. There he turned right and went east to the intersection of Bleecker and MacDougal, the de facto omphalos of the Village.

Greenwich Village existed in the eye of the beholder. It was a fertile ground of celebration, enrichment, civility, and higher gratification; it was a spiritual leper's colony, the blast area of a psychic bomb. Russ beheld the latter. Noise, and a great hustle. Jammed automobiles blaring horns at each other, noxious fumes compacting. Street people selling chemicals and themselves. Hungry faggots. Milling runaways. Abused and abusive tourists. Dripping noses. Nodding. Fights, gropings, quests for God.

Up to Washington Square and over to Eighth Street and Greenwich Avenue, gradations on a scale of despair. The opportunities were repellent, but soon he'd have to settle. Angling across Christopher to Seventh again. Sheridan Square. Last week, roundups and drug busts here three nights running, but that was last week. The phoenix always rises.

One in bluejeans tied with a rope looked at him without interest, but looked at him. An old green workman's shirt. A field jacket with an 82nd Airborne Division patch. She had a thin, smudged face and lank brown hair. Maybe she was pretty. She approached. Her hand rose indifferently.

'Got any spare change?'

Russ fished three quarters from his pocket and gave them to her. She nodded. It was the moment, but he was too weary to speak to her. He simply looked, then started to turn away. She sensed possibilities, and stopped him.

'You got a place I can crash?'

'Yes,' he said.

She nodded again.

44

They walked back to his apartment. Neither spoke. She might have been twenty; she might have been sixteen.

Inside, she patted Frank on the head. 'You're a nice doggie.'

Frank gave her a courteous lick on the hand.

'You got anything?' she asked Russ.

'No.'

'Nothin'? A little coke, not even some grass?'

'No.'

'Shit, I'm really strung out.'

Russ opened a quart bottle of Dewars, put ice in two glasses, and poured. She shrugged, and drank hers in two big swallows. She poured herself another.

'Are you hungry?' he asked.

'Uh huh.'

He put a pack of frozen corn into boiling water and fried a shell steak with some onions and mushrooms. She ate it all, and a bologna sandwich afterward. She drank three mugs of coffee.

She went into the living room. The rug was brown. A long couch and two oversize club chairs. Blue drapes. One wall stripped down to the brick. There was a color television, a stereo component set with some records, shelves, and a few books.

'Where's the bedroom?' she asked.

He pointed and followed her in. The double bed was fruitwood. A bureau matched it. The room also held a chair, an ottoman, and a small writing desk. She sat on the bed and bounced to test the mattress. 'Hard,' she said. 'Are you weird?'

'Not much.'

'Okay.' She started toward the bathroom. Over her shoulder, she said, 'I'm Beth.'

'Russ.'

The toilet flushed; water ran in the sink. She came out with most of the dirt gone from her face and hands. She unbuttoned her shirt and shrugged it off, dropped it to

45

the floor. She was thin, ribs showing, collarbones seeming swollen. But her breasts were big. One of them was bruised. She kicked her shoes free and bent to pull her socks off. She undid the rope holding up her dungarees and pushed the pants and her panties down her legs, stepping out of them. Her belly was flat, the hair at her crotch sparse. Her hips jutted sharply. Her knees were large. She got onto the bed.

'I have to walk the dog,' Russ said.

He took Frank, returned, and washed up. She was waiting for him on top of the sheets. He turned out the lights before undressing. In a moment Beth switched on the bed lamp.

'Why don't you want me to see you naked?' she asked.

He stood with his T shirt in his hands, a little under six feet tall, slim, muscular, face suddenly hard. Three marks, each the size of a half-dollar piece, ran in a diagonal line across the front of his torso. They were puckered, like tiny meteor craters, and a shiny purple. The first was an inch from his left armpit, the second just below his breastbone, and the third at the bottom right of his rib cage. His back was similarly marked, though the scars there were larger.

'What are those from?' she asked.

'I got hurt once.'

Three slugs from a 7.62 machine gun had passed through his body, nicking the aorta of his heart, collapsing one lung, puncturing his right kidney with splinters from a shattered rib. He should have died.

'They're pretty.'

He finished undressing. She said nothing about the scars on his legs. He turned off the light and got into bed with her.

She had the right movements, but she was mechanical. He took his time, and after a while she began to put herself into it. It became good, and toward the finish she rasped. 'Stick your finger up my ass. Hurry!'

46

Later she said, 'You fuck nice.' Then she rolled over and went to sleep.

Russ dreamed, but the next day didn't remember what about.

In the morning Beth asked him if she could stay. He said she could.

Wylie admired the quality of Evadne's insincerity. He'd bullied her into this party, and she'd been sullen and resentful up to the very moment the first arrival chimed her bell. Now, though she shot him an occasional sour glance, she was moving among her guests with easy, convincing smiles, touching them with her long fingers, laughing, submitting with gracious flirtation to arms looped about her waist, and seeming a successful and thoroughly pleased hostess.

In the week since Lesley Marecek had come to Cerberus, Wylie and Russ had turned up nothing of value. Wylie had obtained a copy of the Chasteen guest list from Al Schattner – Lieutenant Schattner now; it had been Sergeant when Wylie had first worked with him as a patrolman – and among the people at Evadne's party were twelve persons who had been at Chasteen's the night of the robbery. Evadne had selected them on the basis of their intelligence or eye for detail. Wylie had had some small hope of picking up something useful from them.

That hope was growing smaller each moment, but he *had* succeeded in making a date with a tall erotic fantasy from the Danish consulate, and he was having a good time.

Except for Alice Havemeyer, who currently was trapping his wrist with both her hands while he lit her cigarette. Alice Havemeyer had been invited for neither her intelligence nor her perceptive abilities, but because she was the only one of the three wounded who was ambulatory. Alice finally released his wrist, and he dropped his

Dunhill back in his pocket. She exhaled smoke in a thin, authoritative jetstream.

'The guns were loaded with double-o buckshot,' she said. 'That means nine ball-bearing-sized pieces of lead in each cartridge. I mean shell. That's what a shotgun cartridge is called, a shell.' Rhetorically she asked, 'Can you conceive of the destructive power of a single such shot?'

Wylie barely had time to say, untruthfully, 'No, I can't,' before her new ballistics expertise propelled her on.

'Each pellet, under the range of one hundred yards, has the impact of a military rifle slug. They fired four shots that night. That means that the equivalent of thirty-six rounds of military ammunition was directed at us within the space of three or four seconds.'

'Good God!' Wylie said.

'Indeed.'

Alice Havemeyer was the wife of Louis Havemeyer, who was half of Havemeyer & Rustin, the commodities speculators. She had informed Wylie, by discreet innuendo, that she had been at Chasteen's in the company of George Rustin, while Louis had been desporting himself with George's wife, Grace. It was all comfortingly symmetrical.

'You were very fortunate,' Wylie said.

Alice touched the white bandaging on the upper part of her arm and smiled bravely. She wore the bandage like a jewel. 'Yes. It's painful. But it *is* only a flesh wound. Poor Mrs Greer took the full charge. If I'd been standing only a few inches nearer her . . .' She shuddered. 'Louis didn't find out until the next morning, when I was released from the hospital. He went into an absolute panic, and said he would have killed himself if it had been me instead of poor Mrs Greer.' She went up on her toes to spot her husband across the room. Affection settled across her face. 'He's a liar, of course, but he's sufficiently guilty that he's sending me to Rio for a month's holiday.'

'Rio's nice.'

'You've been?'

'Yes. Why did they fire, Mrs Havemeyer?'

'Poor Mrs Greer screamed. It scared *me* half to death. It must have panicked them.'

'Did they say anything?'

'I don't know. There were only guns going off and everyone screaming.'

'Before the shooting?'

'Who can remember? It was all so unbelievable. My mind simply would not accept it when I was shot. It's such an unbelievable thing, being shot.'

'I'd think so. Was there –'

She touched the wide lapel of Wylie's maroon Edwardian suit. 'Is this from Bostick's?'

'Yes.'

'I thought the workmanship was familiar. Louis has all his suits made there, but I didn't know they also did things so . . . bold.'

'It hurts them a little. But they bear up.'

She appraised him, then touched his lips briefly with her fingertips. 'You wouldn't, by any chance, be traveling to Rio next month, would you?'

'Alice!' A woman rushed up and clasped both of Alice's hands. 'Oh, you dear, dear person. I had to take *two* Valiums when Harry called from the office – I never read the papers myself, you know. Does it hurt awfully?'

'It's little enough to endure when I think of poor Mrs Greer. And poor Julius, too, of course.'

'But you could have been killed!'

'Quite easily. Their guns were leaded with double-o buckshot. That means nine ball-bearing-sized pieces of lead in each shell. Can you conceive of the destructive power –'

'Excuse me,' Wylie said.

Evadne's bar was in the corner of the living room, a five-foot span of hand-rubbed wood that cut across the angle formed by two adjacent walls like a support. It contained a small sink for washing glasses, bottles of good liquor pyramided on a multilevel stainless-steel stand, and glasses of various sizes. Russ stood behind the bar in a white jacket and black bowtie. He took Wylie's empty glass, dunked it into the sink, then whipped a towel over it until it gleamed. He dropped in two ice cubes, poured a triple shot of Jim Beam, and added a minuscule amount of water to start the ice melting.

'Thanks,' Wylie said.

'You bet,' Russ said. Polite, professionally noncommittal.

Next to Wylie, a young woman with fair skin, pale make-up, and chestnut hair drawn into a chignon set down her glass and answered some question of her escort, a tanned, athletic-looking man. Her voice was throaty, her hands gracefully animated. Russ emptied the small residue of her drink, cleaned the glass, and made her a fresh Rob Roy.

The girl finished her answer with something that elicited a laugh from the man, then turned and said, 'I'll have a ...' She looked curiously at the drink, picked it up, and tasted it. She raised her eyebrows and smiled at Russ with amusement. 'How did you remember that?'

'Part of the job.'

The girl feigned disappointment. 'I thought it might be something more flattering.'

'That too, ma'am.'

She smiled again. 'Thank you. Bye-bye.'

'How's it going?' Wylie asked when they were alone.

'A big nothing.'

'Me too. Well, we try.'

'I think you got the better end of it.'

'I'm the boss.'

Wylie crossed the gold carpet to Neal Cummings, standing in a knot of people who were strangers to Wylie. Sax Rhomer's new film was the subject. Wylie didn't like

Rhomer. Everyone else did. Wylie remained tactically silent. He nodded sagely now and then. Cummings smoothly commandeered a tiny pause and said to Wylie, 'Hello. Good to see you again.' He made introductions.

Jeffrey Gutmann, about twenty-five, dressed in tight black pants with white stitching up the sides, a hand-blocked Madras shirt, and a black leather vest, said, 'And you're in what, Mr Lincoln?'

'Dogs.'

Gutmann was focused and intense; his eyes seemed to glitter. 'In what way?'

'Training, films, rental, sale. Most every way but breeding. We do breed – but a very particular type of animal. For our own use.'

'What type is that?'

'A specialized attack dog, strongly territorial and not responsive to human company. It does night patrol in warehouses, automobile yards, that sort of thing.'

A bald actor with bushy gray muttonchop sideburns, blearily drunk, said, 'I like dogs.'

The girl who had been at the bar, the pretty girl with the chignon, was named Judy Rukeyser. She asked, 'Are you the ones with the red sign that says "Warning. These premises patrolled by Attack Dogs?" Cer ... Cer something. Cerberus?'

Wylie nodded.

'God,' she said. 'Someone's renovating a brownstone on my block. I've seen your dog being delivered a couple of times. He looks absolutely ferocious. He's beautiful.'

'None of my wives has ever liked dogs,' the actor said.

'How do you teach a dog to attack someone?' Judy Rukeyser asked.

'With caution.'

The actor drank deeply. 'Next time I get divorced, I'm just going to get a dog who doesn't like wives.'

'I mean really,' Judy Rukeyser said. She moved close to Wylie. She was wearing a musk perfume that entered his nostrils as smoothly as an assassin's stiletto slipping through flesh and penetrated to his bowels. 'Do they kill people?'

'They're capable of formidable damage, but no, they don't kill.'

Cummings said, 'The bartender is the fellow who was with you and Vadne at the Garden, isn't he?'

'Yes.'

Judy Rukeyser turned to look at Russ. 'Does he work for you?'

'He's our head trainer.'

'Works all day and works all night?' the actor said. He chuckled, then began to laugh, then between guffaws said, 'Really, Mr Lincoln ... really ... you should ... you should free your slaves!' He pounded himself on the thigh and spilled his drink onto the carpet.

Cummings and another man scowled. Gutmann's mouth pulled into a slight, unpleasant smile. Judy Rukeyser flushed. Embarrassed, the others glanced away or down at their feet.

Wylie sighed to himself: Ah, liberals! You could never attack-train one.

The actor wiped his eyes, still chuckling. He looked around and smiled hopefully. 'Funny? ... No, not funny. Guess not. Well.' He raised his glass. 'Later.' He went listing toward the bar, mumbling, 'Not funny, not funny.'

Wylie let the awkward silence run just long enough for them to be grateful for release, to take up a new subject eagerly. A beat. Another. Then he said, 'I understand Joe Sucher signed with Random House to do the robbery.'

'We'll all be famous,' said a bearded man.

His wife pruned her mouth. 'He's a dirty man. I don't want him even mentioning our names.'

'Two National Book Awards,' her husband said. 'You'll rule your reading club like a dictator.'

'I don't like it. I don't care what they say about him – I say his mind is a sewer. There have to be limits, don't there? Isn't that what civilization means, limits?'

'I read that he tried to jump one of the robbers,' Wylie said.

'Publicity,' a man said. 'He went down with the second shot, the one that killed Julius. The only thing that jumped was his press agent.'

'Julius is the one who grabbed the robber. The first shot went wild and killed Hannah.'

'That bunch with Julius and Hannah tried to make a run for it. That's when the robbers opened fire.'

'Neal, you were right there, weren't you?'

'Yes,' Cummings said. 'But I was lying on the floor with my hands over my head, as we'd been told. I looked up when the shooting began, but I didn't see what started it. Someone told me Hannah Greer fainted and fell against one of them – he thought he was being attacked and started shooting. I don't know if that's true or not.'

'Do you think the police might be holding something back?' Wylie asked. 'They say they don't have good descriptions, but that doesn't seem logical. There were so many witnesses.'

'It seems logical to me,' said a woman in Courreges boots. 'I couldn't even tell you how *many* there were. Most people say four, so I'll go along, but Harriet Adams claims she saw six, and John Sinclair swears there were only three.'

'There was nothing to see,' a man said. 'They all wore black ski masks, black sweaters, black pants, black gloves, and black shoes. Even the guns looked the same.'

The bearded man said, 'Only one of them spoke, the man who met everyone at the door and told us what to do. He was literate, inasmuch as his grammar was correct, but there was nothing distinctive, like an accent.' He shrugged. 'Oh. Yes. And he was polite, seemed to be trying to keep everyone calm.'

'He was not polite,' his wife said. 'He was very threatening.'

Gutmann said, 'People pointing shotguns at you tend to appear threatening.'

'Did they have any odd characteristics or mannerisms?' Wylie asked.

They looked inquiringly at each other.

'They could have been any of ten million men,' the bearded man said.

'But they weren't,' Gutmann said.

'Eventually they'll be caught. Most criminals are.'

'Not the smart ones,' Gutmann said.

'It's dumb to kill people.'

'Everyone dies sooner or later. If you kill someone, you're just making it happen sooner.'

'Poor Mr Greer and poor Mrs Hollander,' Alice Havemeyer said, joining the group. 'I was standing right next to Mrs Greer. I was literally *sprayed* with her blood.'

'How lucky for you,' Gutmann said.

Gutmann was drinking plain Coca-Cola. His pupils were great black holes. His speech was precise and taut. He seemed to be restraining a powerful force within his body. Wylie knew he was up on something.

Alice Havemeyer blinked. 'Beg pardon?'

'It's an excellent social asset, easily as valuable as having lunched with the First Lady. I propose that we canvass the guest list for donations and build a civic monument in the name of Hollander and Greer. We owe them. They did a lot for us.'

'I think that's disgusting,' Alice Havemeyer said.

'Oh, relax your sphincter. You all love me for my nastiness. And I'm not really being nasty now anyway, just the voice of conscience.' He cupped a hand to his mouth and stage-whispered: 'Remember thou art mortal, Alice!'

'You're hardly one to talk about conscience, Jeffrey,' the bearded man's wife said.

'You confuse me with my father. He is Gutmann

54

Munitions, not I. And how can I criticize him? Thanks to him, I will never have to work a day in my life.'

'At the cost of two million dead Vietnamese,' a man said with mild ugliness.

'Not a sparrow falls but that God, et cetera. Father was simply the agent of God, and that is, or at least used to be, a rather commendable function. For my part, if I hadn't been Four-F, I would have fled to Canada. In style, of course.'

Neal Cummings said, 'You've had a bit too much to drink, Jeff.'

'That is the one thing I most certainly have *not* had too much of. And what were you people doing while the poor Vietnamese were being slaughtered? Was anyone here gassed in Chicago, or take a nightstick on the head at a demonstration, or even get blisters from a march?' He raised his Coke. 'Peace with honor, *mes amis.*'

'Really, Jeffrey,' a woman said. 'You do go too far.'

'Laura, that is the first time I've ever heard *you* complain about *that.*'

It had become a tournament, and Wylie would have liked to stay. But you had to give the client fair value. Or something near it, anyway. On the way to see Gordon Tennant, a trial lawyer who had been present that night, he saw Judy Rukeyser at the bar, talking to Russ.

An hour later, she was still there, speaking intensely, gesturing with her hands, wafting her musk perfume at Russ. Russ listened without expression. Now and then he nodded.

Wylie and Freya Helgstrom, the Danish girl, did an awkward dance to pass each other in the narrow hall between Evadne's living room and bedroom as he was leaving the bathroom and she was moving toward it. They collided, and not, Wylie decided when Freya laughed and lay her blonde head against his chest, entirely by accident. He patted her ass and kissed her on the forehead before disengaging.

Twenty minutes later Evadne spilled a bowl of shrimp sauce on him.

'I'm *so* sorry, love,' she said. 'Let me get a towel.' He looked down at his new suit. The red definitely did not go with the maroon. He wondered if shrimp sauce made permanent stains. Evadne came back with a damp towel, patted his ass, and kissed him on the forehead before swirling off.

Sometimes Evadne was a terrific pain.

Jowls hung from Raphaela Bracey's jaw, and long jade pendants from her ears. They shook alike as she danced. She danced with seismic violence, stomping her feet and stabbing out with her elbows, hurling wads of her abundant flesh bulging out with G-force, only to come snapping back with age-weakened but still valiant elasticity. She looked like a frenzied bulldog, and she danced Wylie into the ground.

Gasping painfully, he raised his hands in surrender.

Raphaela grinned and locked him in a bear hug and lifted him from the floor. 'Don't recriminate yourself, son! You lasted longer than most.'

She sat down beside him. The sides of her voluminous striped dress were drenched, and sweat dripped down her arms to her wrists. But her face was dry, and she was breathing with the ease of a long-distance runner strolling to the corner for a paper.

Evadne had introduced them, at Raphaela's request. When Wylie had raised the robbery, she'd said, 'Ha! What they should do, after they catch them, is stuff those shotguns up their asses and pull the triggers.'

She didn't recall a single detail.

'Son, I never saw a real gun before in my whole life. Well, some pistols, yes, but that was when I was much younger and a whole different story. The only thing I remember from Malcolm's is the big black hole at the end

56

of the barrel. I looked down it right to hell and knew it was the end. That's all, son. I've seen it three more times in my dreams, and each time I woke up screaming and made the maid sit with me until dawn.'

Then, to Leon Russell's 'Jumping Jack Flash,' she had dragged him to the center of the room and said, 'Dance!'

She beamed at him now while he regained his breath. 'Very sturdy, son. Half an LP makes most men over thirty look like a coronary's got them. Say, what do you think of spastic children?'

'Spastic children?' Wylie repeated stupidly.

'You know, with the braces, their heads flopping around, that sort of thing.'

'Miss Bracey, what have I ever done to you?'

'*For* me, son. Raphaela Bracey always wants. And it'll be painless. You come to see me Wednesday afternoon, three o'clock. We're going to raise pots and pots of money for spastic children. That is, with a little help from me, *you* are going to do it, and everybody will love you, and you'll feel very moral and good about yourself and all it will cost is a couple of hours, and I'll even buy you lunch at the Four Seasons. Wednesday afternoon, three, right? United Campaigns.' She gave him the address.

After the final guest had left, Wylie sat with Russ and Evadne.

'It was all laid out for us,' Wylie said. He was pleasantly hazy with bourbon. 'We were told every single thing we needed. Unfortunately, I recognized none of it.'

Russ was glum. Evadne teased him about Judy Rukeyser. Usually Russ responded quickly, and happily, to attention from Evadne. Tonight he didn't. He went home, still glum.

Wylie wanted to visit Joseph Sucher in the hospital.

'It's two thirty in the morning,' Evadne protested.

'He works nights, doesn't he? He's not on the critical list, is he?'

'But they won't let you in.'

'No problem.'

Wylie coached her in the cab. They walked through the swinging doors of New York Hospital's Emergency Room and past the dozen persons in various states of injury and discomfort, and two tired nurses, directly to the doors at the rear of the room.

'Oh, my baby, my baby,' Evadne moaned, pulling at a handkerchief.

'He's going to be fine,' Wylie said. 'They told me there won't even be scars.'

They did it again when two doctors came upon them in the service corridor, and once more for the janitor who shared the elevator up to the fifth floor. They got out on the sixth. The hall was empty. They walked briskly toward Sucher's room, careful not to let their heels click against the tile.

A nurse emerged from a room, pursed her lips, and began a frown. Evadne collapsed against Wylie.

'To die all alone, with no one at his side,' she sobbed. 'Oh God. God!'

'Hush now,' Wylie said. 'There was no pain. He slipped off in his sleep. And your mother was here all afternoon.'

'Oh God, I can't forgive myself.'

Wylie held her gently. 'Hush. Quiet now, baby.' He patted her back, and over her shoulder gave the nurse a helpless and apologetic smile. The nurse nodded and turned away. As soon as she had rounded a corner, Wylie and Evadne hurried the rest of the way to Sucher's room.

Joseph Sucher was sitting up in bed with books and newspapers and magazines scattered about him. Clenching a pencil between his teeth, he was finishing a pornographic drawing with quick, heavy strokes of a Magic Marker. The room stank of stale cigarette smoke. Ashtrays overflowed with Gauloise butts, and one was burning on the edge of the night table beside him. He had another wedged between two fingers of the hand that steadied the pad on which he was drawing.

'Baby!' he cried. The pencil dropped from his teeth. 'And...' He squinted. 'Lincoln. Wylie Lincoln, right?'

'Right.'

'Good on names. Lousy on remembering where, but good on names. Kiss, hurry. Not you, Lincoln.'

Evadne kissed. Sucher caught her neck and held her mouth on his making furious sounds in his throat. He let her go and showed her the drawing. 'Have I captured you?'

'Nothing like me.'

'Right. It's my first wife.'

Sucher was a stocky man with bushy cork-screw hair and a harsh face. He believed in neither God nor the devil, but did proclaim the vital existence of Good and Evil; the former resided in the soul, which nestled somewhere above the liver, and the latter is the lower colon. He had once precipitated a riot in Town Hall by throwing a co-panelist, a women's liberation star, across his lap, jerking down her jeans and panties, and whaling away at her bare buttocks with his meaty palm, shouting, 'Naughty, naughty, naughty!' He settled out of court for $175,000, but still insisted that her screams had been cries of sexual delight.

Sucher rifled through two legal-size yellow pads. Each page held a different and obscene drawing. 'They won't let me use a typewriter,' he said. 'It will disturb the other patients. Fuck the other patients! I have a book to write. I said I'd have the goddamn room soundproofed. You'd think I wanted to violate their children. I can't compose in longhand, simply cannot. So here I sit with my brains bursting and I can't have a typewriter and they won't let me out for another five days. It's an atrocity! I've sent telegrams to PEN, the Authors Guild, and the Nobel Committee. How do you like this one?' He showed them a drawing. 'That's the head nurse on the floor. That

thing on her tit is a breast pump. I've got drawings of
every doctor, intern, nurse, and aide, who's been within
twenty feet of this room. They'll kick me out tomorrow if
I have my way. What did you bring me?'

Evadne withdrew a bottle of Metaxa and two tins of
smoked oysters from her bag.

'Marvelous!' Sucher exclaimed. 'You are loves, both.'
He uncorked the Metaxa, drank from the bottle, and
passed it to Wylie. He opened the oysters and began
eating them with his fingers.

Wylie received one possible piece of information.

'The guy who did most of the talking was Middle
America. He had that flat, two-dimensional tone, you
know? English as limp wash. Not the little baffled up-
swing you get in Ohio, or Indiana retard, or Wisconsin
menace, but right in there somewhere, long vowels, com-
pressed r's, the cat syndrome – "naow" for "now." I'd call
it southern Illinois, but it was more controlled than that,
in the way Chicagoans are, you know, when they're aware
their basic tones are woodsy and plainsy and they try to
do something about it. Yeah, a Chicago boy, but origin-
ally from downstate, one of those places like Galena or
Cairo, which they pronounce "Kayro," like the syrup.'

Sucher was on the track of his own whimsies, and once
that happened, he was never turned aside to follow anyone else's.

He pulled up his hospital gown. The blanket did not
quite cover his genitals. His lower belly was thick with
bristly black and white hair which ended in a sharp,
shaved line just below his navel. His upper torso was
bandaged and wrapped with elastic tape.

'Sniff,' he commanded. 'Do you smell that? Pus and
rotting flesh. It's the odor of my own death. It inhabits
me now, like a lover. I expel it this time. It is only a little
death. *Petit mort.* Just like the orgasm, right? But the
French in their stylish foolishness have reversed it. The
orgasm does not partake of death. Death partakes of it.

60

She honked away at my withered little cock, but she didn't get my wad this time. She will, eventually, but it was *my* turn last week – I raped her for knowledge.'

He coursed his fancies through the labyrinths of his mind like a shuddering hound.

'What are guns? Surrogate phalli, of course, of course. Even the NRA can't avoid that one any more. But then: Extrapolate. You shoot your gun – whammo! blow your load. Did you ever see the eyes of those cats on the firing ranges? Bang! bang! bang! Oh, sheer heaven. Watch cops pat their holsters, readjust them. Like a kid fiddling with himself. Sweet Samuel Colt, think of My Lai in those terms! All those late-adolescents with their automatic weapons: Br-rr-rr-rr-p! Br-rr-rr-rr-p! Multiple, rapid-fire orgasms. Certainly we like to go to war. It's meta-sex, one huge orgy.

'So grant me that the firing gun is a jisming cock. Next enquiry, then: What does a bullet do when it hits somebody?' He whacked his fist against the bed. 'Why, it penetrates, it penetrates, by God! *Slusshh!* Ram it in there, man! But why all these surrogates, this symbolic acting-out? Aha, because the real thing can't be managed. You can't get it up, that's why. Or society won't let you do it the way you really want to. Or ... hmm. A kind of rape, is it? Yes, maybe that. But then we must deal with the question of love. Is love possible in that context?'

They continued, or, rather, Sucher continued, until dawn, and the end of the bottle of Metaxa.

Leaving the hospital, Wylie said to Evadne, 'I've got to remember to tell Russ.' He wrote something on the back of a card. 'Got to remember. 'S important.'

'What is?'

'Who we're looking for. Whole thing was done by a gang of impotent Midwestern faggots.'

CHAPTER FOUR

Wylie's first call Monday morning was from Horace Friedberg. Horace was twelve years old. He'd walked into the school a year ago with a showy Sealyham terrier, had asked for the owner, and had grilled Wylie on his qualifications and philosophy of training. Then he'd requested a demonstration. Horace's grave intelligence bemused Wylie, so he'd had a dog brought out and put through its paces.

Horace watched carefully. 'Very good,' he said. He removed a folded five-dollar bill from his pocket, opened and smoothed it, and handed it to Wylie. 'I'd like you to teach me to train my dog. His name is Magoo.'

Wylie had put Horace in a group class – at a loss of one hundred ten dollars. He suspected that he'd been had.

Which was true. Horace was currently training neighborhood dogs, and well, for forty-five dollars, a price no professional could possibly match. Wylie's only consolation was that some people mistrusted Horace because of his age and brought their dogs to Cerberus despite the higher fees.

'Hi, Wylie,' the boy said. 'How's it going?'

'Pretty well. How's it with you?'

'Hectic. I've got more business than I can handle.'

'That's nice, Horace. What can I do for you?'

'There's this guy from Doyle, Dane, Bernback that lives downstairs, and he says he'll use Magoo in a flea-powder commercial if Magoo'll scratch on command. I told him that was simple, and I have to audition Magoo on Thursday. But I tried a couple of things and they don't work and I can't find anything on the routine in my books. So I wanted to ask you how I do it.'

Wylie took the phone away from his ear and made a face at it. 'That kind of training usually isn't worth the effort, Horace. You don't get enough calls for it. You can fake it for the cameras by sticking a paper clip in his coat. That pulls the hair a little, feels like a burr, and he'll try to scratch it out.'

'Very nice,' Horace said. 'Logical and simple. I like it. What's the going rate for TV ads?'

'Figure a hundred for the first hour, fifty for every hour or portion thereafter.'

'Wow! What about residuals?'

'Dogs don't get them.'

'How come?'

'Has to do with Actors Equity and things. It involves a lot of semantic hairsplitting.'

'Hmmm. Maybe I can do something about that.'

'Anything you accomplish would be appreciated by the entire industry, Horace.'

Horace said he'd be in touch. Wylie was sure he would. They said good-bye.

In two or three years Wylie would have to hire Horace, if only to protect himself.

The second call was from Lesley Marecek. She was hysterical: 'I've got the prints in my hand. Right here! Right here! He has another set of negatives. I can't take it. You – him – them! What are you trying to do to me, for Christ's sake!'

Wylie talked her down. He took details from her that he hadn't bothered with before, when the blackmailer had been irrelevant. 'Make the drop,' he told her. 'It'll be the last one.'

'I can't pay any more. I really can't. I'm not conning you. Raising your money was all I could do. It would take me a couple of weeks to get even the three hundred he wants.'

'I'll have one of my people drop an envelope off with your doorman. There'll be three hundred cash in it.'

63

'And how much more is this going to cost me?'

'It's on the house. I'm not getting anywhere with the robbery. This will make me feel productive.'

'Am I supposed to thank you?'

'That would not be inappropriate.'

She hung up.

Russ and Wylie talked it over in the office.

'Three hundred is subway fare,' Wylie said. 'He's small time, maybe an amateur.'

'I lean more on small time. Dumb, too. Real dumb. He's asking to be hit, the way he sets it up.'

'You want to take him?'

'Sure. You're not scary enough for dummies.'

'Don't push it if he has help.'

'Not enough payoff to support a team.'

'If he gets by you, we'll work backward from the hotel. Someone's being paid off. Probably a bellboy.'

'I don't think we'll need that.'

'Okay. So Tuesday at five thirty. The northwest corner of Forty-second and Broadway.'

At six thirty Wylie met Al Schattner at La Trattoria in the Pan Am building. Schattner wore a plain gray suit, with stubborn cuffs on the pants. He had unhappily surrendered white-on-white shirts a year ago, when his daughter had locked herself in her room, weeping bitterly and crying that she would never, *never* bring another friend home to such humiliation again if she lived to be nine hundred years old.

Schattner had a round, benevolent, friendly face. It became skeptical only when he was working, or when he saw Wylie, but even then it remained polite.

He said, 'I promised Hilary I would catch the eight-o'clock train tonight. The mayor can be assassinated and I will still catch the eight-o'clock train. So I have already ordered for both of us. I have compromised to the point of telling the waiter to wait until we have finished one

64

social drink and a plate of antipasto. I have been working too much overtime. Hilary is not happy I am eating with you tonight and she is alone again.'

'Hilary doesn't like me.'

'You lie. Hilary is titillated by you. But she is a faithful woman. So, to ease the pain of her unfulfilled yearnings, she feigns pique.'

'She's a convincing feigner.'

'That is true.' Schattner placed a fat folder secured with an elastic band on the table between them. 'Everything we have is in here,' he said. 'But I am not going to give it to you until you tell me exactly what your involvement is. This is too big for me to take chances.'

Wylie and Schattner often lied to each other, and neither thought much the less of the other for that, but this time Wylie knew that Schattner would not help him without the truth. So Wylie told him.

'You are running a confidence game on this young woman,' Schattner said sadly. 'In the haystack, there is always a needle. Sometimes we find it, sometimes we don't. This is a very big haystack. I do not think we are going to find the needle. And if *we* can't, then...' He shrugged, and shook his head in dispirited stoicism.

'I believe in myself,' Wylie said.

'Pride goeth,' Schattner said.

'Can I have it?' Wylie eyed Schattner's hairy hand, which still lay atop the folder.

'Will you tell me of every tiny crumb you mouse out?'

'I always do, don't I?' Wylie was affronted.

'No, you do not. Frequently you do not.'

'But sometimes I do.'

'And that has been helpful.' Schattner tapped his fingers broodingly on the folder. 'Here.' He shoved it across the table. 'I warn you very seriously, Wylie. There is much emotion and pressure on this one, and many powerful people putting spurs in us. It is not to play with. Everything will be noticed.'

65

'I understand. And I thank you, Al.'

Schattner chewed ruefully on an artichoke heart. 'I don't know why I do this.'

'It's your liberal conscience – aid to minority types.'

'I voted for Nixon. I care who my daughter marries.'

'The rules strangle you. You like to see things happen.'

Schattner shook his head. 'No, I support law and order. I *am* law and order. My whole life is by and for the rules.'

'I saved your life once.'

'It is vulgar to mention that.'

'But you saved mine once, too.'

'I am occasionally heroic.'

'We're friends.'

'That is to my grief.'

They ate, and Wylie paid, and Schattner, rightfully, did not consider that a bribe. Wylie walked him to the train gate.

Schattner said, 'Wylie, in the infinitely unlikely event that you stumble onto something, it is better that you tell me about it and let me do the rest. I will get the negatives for you. You have done things in the past that were not good, and I am afraid that you have done things I have not known about that were even much worse. Wylie, I never want to put you in jail. That would make me sad. But I have learned to live with sadness, and I do what I must.'

Wylie straightened Schattner's tie. 'There should be a law against sadness.'

'If there were, I would enforce it,' Schattner said. Then he smiled. 'Anyway, there is nothing of value in the folder. It has been digested ten times by more brains than there are at Harvard. It only makes for dull, sleepless reading. I would not have given it to you otherwise. Good night, my friend. Thank you for dinner.'

Russ got his windbreaker from the locker at four o'clock on Tuesday and told the receptionist he'd be gone for the rest of the day. He paused to watch Abbie, the new girl, work a male Shetland sheepdog. The miniature collie was lagging behind on the heel. Abbie stopped and said, 'Gilly, sit.' The dog simply stood and lowered his head. Abbie jerked the leash sharply, throwing the animal back on his haunches. He yelped, sprang up, and ran to the end of the leash. Within moments Abbie completely lost the dog; he was in a panic, and the girl herself verged on tears.

'Abbie,' Russ said, 'tell him he's a good boy and take a minute for a break.'

Abbie said, 'Okay, Gilly, okay.' She reached to pat the dog, but he shied from her.

Russ went over and hunkered down on the floor. 'Sit and talk, Abbie.'

'I'm sorry,' the girl said miserably. 'I just can't do anything with him.'

The dog was cowering the full extent of the six-foot training leash away from the tongue hanging out, sides heaving.

'Sure you can,' Russ said. He took the leash and began to pull the dog smoothly toward him, talking to Abbie and ignoring the animal. 'If this were a bull terrier, you'd practically have to club him over the head with a pipe to get his attention. But he's a shelty. Now, while a shelty is a smart working dog, he's also fairly timid and shy.' He turned to the dog. 'That's a good boy. Everything's going to be just fine.' Lightly, he stroked the dog's head. The animal tried to bolt, but Russ held him fast. Russ continued to caress him.

'You have to bellow at a basset sometimes, but just a hint of sternness can make a shelty go all to pieces. He's a soft dog, very soft, like cotton candy. When, say, a shepherd, or even a Yorkie, wants to argue a point, you're going to need a hard correction, but not with a shelty. He'll work like hell for you, but you've got to be featherlight with him.'

The dog was lying down, submitting to Russ's fingers, which touched his head and chest.

'This one already knows how to sit, right?'

'That's what threw me, he learned so fast. Today I was just starting corrections, and suddenly he acted like he'd never heard of the sit, and then his heeling fell apart.'

The dog gave Russ's hand a tentative lick.

'What we're going to do is break a lot of rules. Abbie. We're going to repeat commands, talk to him too much, heap praise on him until he forgets himself and starts jumping around, and give corrections that will be mostly coaxings and placings. It will all be terribly wrong, but it'll work, and we can phase it out in a day or two.'

The dog snuggled closer to Russ and rolled over onto his back so Russ could stroke his stomach.

'Another little point,' Russ said. 'I noticed that he's hypersensitive to his name. His emotions get all in an uproar when he hears it. That blocks his concentration. So we'll drop his name and just give him the command. Okay?'

Abbie nodded, looking only slightly less unhappy.

Russ stood, and Gilly sprang up in alarm. Russ rubbed and patted him and assured him he would learn to love this sort of thing.

'Heel,' Russ said, and started off. The dog braced against the leash and was pulled forward, stumbling. Russ hung his left hand low and rubbed his thumb and forefinger together. 'Come on, boy. Heel. Right here. Heel. That's good.' He touched the dog lightly, walked a few steps in silence, and encouraged the dog again. The dog licked his hand nervously. Russ slacked the leash, and Gilly held position. Russ withdrew his hand for a few moments. Gilly looked up anxiously, but continued at Russ's side. 'So good, so good. What a *good* boy.' Russ executed an easy turn, and the dog followed without the leash tightening. '*Terrific!* Good boy, *good boy!*' Gilly's next turn was sharper. 'Oh, superb. *Good* dog.' Gilly's tail wagged. Russ stopped and tightened the leash smoothly, without tugging. He pressed the dog's croup gently down. 'Sit, good boy. Sit, good dog. Sit.' Trembling, Gilly sat.

The praise Russ lavished on the animal would have flattered God.

Within five minutes Russ had the dog heeling and sitting without need of placement, and had halved the flow of his initial encouragement. He turned the leash back to Abbie and watched her. She was a little awkward, and the dog did not trust her at first, but Russ saw that it was going to work.

'That's great, Abbie,' he said. 'You'll make him a pro in two weeks.'

Abbie smiled. Then she went delirious with joy over a successful sit, and the dog joined her.

Russ left. Outside, Kenroy was standing in the gutter with the corgi who was in for housebreaking. The animal's vulpine, intelligent, friendly face was focused on Kenroy.

'You may not shit on the carpet,' Kenroy was saying. 'You may not piss on the desk, or the chairs, or the lamps. You may shit in the street. You may piss on the curb and the fire hydrants. You *will* shit in the street. You *will* piss on the curb and the fire hydrants. Do you understand me, Kong?'

'Rowf!' the dog said.

Russ got out of the cab at the Sixth Avenue and Forty-second Street corner of Bryant Park, behind the gray mass of the Fifth Avenue Public Library. It was five o'clock. Precursors of the vast horde of office workers imminently to discharge onto the streets were walking through the park, taking forty seconds' green respite from midtown's harsh stone and metal geometry, their version of the commuter's club-car gin-and-tonic. Tall, sweet-wine black men with gray hair and whiskers stood by shoeshine equipment and masked their despair with hazily jocular come-ons. Pigeon feeders scattered largesse

69

and believed that the clustering birds loved them. Half a dozen draggled and stinking derelicts sleeping on benches were ignored, and thus, through the will of the passer-by, were made not to exist.

Russ walked on the south side of Forty-second one block west to the triple intersection of Seventh, Broadway, and Forty-second. He looked across to the north-west corner. The metal waste basket was three-quarters full, and surrounded by a welter of poorly aimed debris. A few persons were loitering; many were moving by. None held his attention, seemed more likely than any other. He walked to Eighth Avenue, crossed to the north side of Forty-second, and returned to Seventh, hands stuffed in his pockets.

Times Square was a wet rectal chancre. The building façades were defeated and grimy, the streets and sidewalks littered, stained. Pizza and hot dog and hamburger shops abounded, with greasy counters, napkins and paper plates on floors smeared with mustard and catsup, crumpled cups, sticky spilled coffee and soda. Music lashed concussively from speakers mounted over the doors of record shops, and camera and audio wares were jammed in display windows under bright paste-boards crying SPECIAL, CLOSEOUT, DISCOUNT, CLEARANCE, GIANT, BARGAIN, WHOLESALE. Marquees jutted above the sidewalks like the jaws of ponderous imbeciles and offered six-year-old movies and hard porn in color. Brown paper opaqued the windows of endless narrow storefronts, ADULT MATERIAL. Live shows, massages. A pinball arcade with the soul of a moray eel. Novelty shops; hundreds of tiny Empire State Buildings, statues of little boys that cutely pissed, long knives with points thrust into blocks of styrofoam. A miasma nearly as palpable as the gas bursting the belly of a bloated corpse, and through it insinuated the living droppings of the city. Anything could be bought here: a fragmentation grenade, a body living or dead, a maker of bodies, the powder of poppies, the honor of judges, an

70

eater of feces, a consecrated host, beginnings and interludes and ends.

It was needed, else it would not exist. The city did not attempt to purge it, only to contain it, and the city was made restless in sleep by dreams of rupture in the encircling membrane, seepage and metastasis. Times Square was weak and vicious, a flayer – like its people, who could not wholly believe in their own existence.

Russ hated it. In its mirror, he too frequently glimpsed parts of himself.

He spotted Lesley Marecek at five twenty-five as she rounded the corner of Eighth and Forty-second and started toward Seventh. She was wearing tight white pants and a short red plastic jacket, like the companion of a Honda rider in an advertisement. She carried a magazine under her arm. Russ fell in behind her.

She did not know there was a Russ Turner in the world. He thought about that as he followed her. It depressed him, though he didn't know why.

She reached the corner and flipped the magazine into the wastebasket without breaking stride, turned left on Seventh, and disappeared. A man in back of her dumped a container with a half-finished fudge sundae into the basket. The liquefying ice cream and brown fudge oozed across the magazine. An envelope was taped inside the magazine, and in the envelope were six fifty-dollar bills.

Russ pulled a handful of dimes from his pocket and stopped at one of the open telephones a few yards away from the basket. He dialed the number of the phone he was speaking from.

He said hello to the busy signal.

He answered questions, and he listened a lot; he shook his head or nodded assent; he gestured.

A crumpled pack of cigarettes went into the basket; a pizza crust; a wad of wet Kleenex. Additional junk missed.

A balding man reading a newspaper walked abstractedly toward the basket, bumped into two people and mumbled apologies, closed the paper, and threw it into the basket.

Russ felt happy.

'Look,' he said into the phone, 'we were supposed to have settled all this last week. So how come ... yeah ... uh huh.'

The balding man stopped abruptly after a few steps, made a chopping motion as if he were angry with himself, then turned, retrieved the paper, and walked off, moving his finger down a column and scrutinizing the print intently.

Russ hung up.

Lesley's magazine was no longer in the basket.

The balding man wore a brown sport jacket. Russ followed him around the corner and down the steps of the subway kiosk. Rush hour was in full swing. Russ took off his blue windbreaker and carried it in his hand. He wore a tan pullover sweater. Changing clothes was the simplest efficient method of keeping cover.

The man went through a turnstile. Several persons behind, Russ followed, walked a short distance across the concourse, and descended behind the man to the downtown local track of the IRT.

Russ admired the dumped sundae. Gooing the magazine had eliminated the chance of a scavenger's picking it up. The newspaper routine had been done pretty well, too. On the other hand, working alone hurt the man – a mistake to handle the sundae *and* the newspaper himself. And while the basket drop at first scan seemed a good idea, it was a liability in the end. He'd had to retrieve the magazine too fast in order to keep it from being buried. That hadn't give him enough time to look for surveillance.

The train came noisily into the station, aflame with graffiti. There was a rush of pushing at the doors. The corner of an attaché case gouged into Russ's back. His toes were stepped on. Pretty girls turned ugly, elbowing their way in. The balding man entered through the car's first door, Russ through the middle. The train lurched into motion. Russ stared at an advertisement; from the corner of his eye he saw the balding man examining the other passengers, but apparently at ease.

Crowds were good for losing a tail, but only when you knew you had one. Otherwise they worked against you: too many faces, too many bodies – hard to isolate the one that appeared and reappeared.

The man left the train at the Eighteenth Street station. So did a dozen others – not enough to make Russ comfortable. He hesitated in the door, then hooked an attaché case with his foot and slid it forward. The case's owner, one hand on an overhead grip, the other holding a folded *Post* before his eyes, didn't notice.

The balding man was walking slowly toward the exit, surveying the others who'd gotten off.

Doors hissed shut along the length of the train. But the attaché case jammed the set in front of Russ, gapped them three inches.

The doors wrenched open and slammed shut again. Then a third time. The intercom distorted the conductor's irritated voice: 'Watch the doors. Clear the doors, please!'

The balding man reached the stairs, looked about him one last time, and started up.

'Watch the doors!'

The doors opened and started to close instantly. Russ kicked the attaché case away and sprang onto the platform. The joining doors plucked at his sweater. The train pulled out.

Russ removed his sweater. Beneath it he wore a plain gray shirt. He came out on Seventh Avenue and saw his quarry walking downtown half a block ahead. Russ followed the man to Fifteenth Street and turned west after him, keeping to the opposite side of the street. The blackmailer mounted the stairs of a five-story building, paused to glance around, then went into the lobby. The building was a narrow walkup.

Russ debated a moment. He crossed the street quickly, slipping a plastic credit card from his wallet. It was worth a try.

There were ten mailboxes in the lobby; 5-A read *H. Carter*. Russ slipped the credit card between the jamb and the door, which was fitted with a cheap key-and-buzzer-release lock, and sprang the lock easily.

He heard his man walking across the second-floor landing. He tossed his windbreaker and sweater behind the stairs and waited until the blackmailer was halfway between the second and third floors. Then he began to whistle, loudly, and went up the stairs two at a time. He overtook the man just below the third-floor landing. The man stiffened.

Russ smiled broadly. 'Hi. Can you tell me, is Carter on four or five? I forgot what I was told.'

'Uh, I think five. Yeah, five. In the front, I think.'

'Terrific. Thanks.' Russ went on by, no longer whistling; he covered the landing in quick steps and started for the fourth floor. Midway up the stairs, he stopped and listened. In a moment he heard a key in a lock. He came soundlessly back down the stairs. The man stood before the door of the rear apartment, his back to Russ. He took his key from the top lock, put another in the bottom and turned it, then opened the door.

Russ was behind him instantly. Using the force of his lunge, he hammered the bottom of his balled fist against the back of the blackmailer's skull.

The man was driven through the doorway and went stumbling into the kitchen, falling to his hands and knees. Russ slammed the door shut, seized the man by both ears, and yanked him to his feet. The man screamed. Russ hurled him against the refrigerator. The man struck hard and bounced off, turning, hands reaching feebly for

74

failing balance. Russ kicked the small of his back. The man fell face down on the linoleum floor, with a sound of agony.

Russ ripped the cord from a lamp on the table. The man was trying shakily to rise. Russ kicked him in a kidney, and he collapsed with a gasp. Russ knelt on the man's spine with one knee and tied his arms behind him with the lamp cord. He stripped a shoe and sock from one of the man's feet, pulled the man's head back by the fringe of his remaining hair, and stuffed the sock into his mouth. He tied the sock in place with a soiled dish towel from the sink.

Then he went through the man's pocket's: wallet, comb, a couple of benzedrines, cigarettes, change, subway tokens, a ring with car and door keys.

The driver's license said the man was Walter Maloney. Maloney, according to business cards in his wallet, was a photographer: WEDDINGS, PORTRAITS, & SPECIAL ASSIGNMENTS.

Maloney was sweating. His eyes were wide and frightened, and his cheeks were turning red. He made muffled sounds.

Russ slapped him. 'Shut up.'

Russ removed the cord from another lamp, tied Maloney's ankles, dragged him to the door, secured a lock, and lifted Maloney's legs off the floor and fastened the end of the ankle cord to the doorknob.

The apartment was a kitchen, a living room, and a bedroom. Small. The furniture was cheap. The rugs were clean and the floor borders dusted, but the windows were nearly opaque with gray film. The paint on the walls was yellowed and cracked. The only decoration was a big photograph of a naked girl sprawled on her back atop a Harley-Davidson.

Maloney was a horseplayer. There were dope sheets everywhere, bet stubs, handicap lists, pages of lined white school paper with a system being worked out for a dozen

75

horses, tear-outs from newspapers listing schedules at tracks around the country.

There were two cameras on Maloney's bureau, a Nikon with a 50-mm. lens and a beat-up Pentax with a 125-mm. lens. Four rolls of exposed film. Beneath the cameras and film, a manila envelope addressed to Mr William Fulweiler. In the envelope were eight-by-ten black-and-white prints of a chubby, middle-aged man in bed with a young girl. The shot's weren't posed.

He found a Beretta .32 automatic with a full clip and a box of cartridges beneath a pile of underwear in a drawer.

There was nothing else.

He returned to Maloney and kneeled beside him, holding the Beretta and a pillow he'd taken from the bed. Maloney's breath whistled through his nostrils. He trembled. Russ pulled the Beretta's slide back and released it, throwing a shell into the chamber. He made a fat glove of the pillow, with the pistol enclosed. Maloney's bowels voided themselves. Russ pressed the pillow and the gun to Maloney's temple. Maloney jerked his head back and twisted his body. There was a muted liquid sound. Maloney's face turned scarlet; his eyes grew grotesquely swollen. Brownish fluid seeped from his nostrils. Russ untied the towel and pulled the sock from the man's mouth, which released the surge of vomit on which he'd been strangling.

'Where are negatives of Lesley Marecek?' Russ said.

Maloney gagged. 'Please, for God's sake, please don't kill me!'

'I want the negatives.'

'You can have them! You can have everything. It's all in my studio. Anything you want. I'll give you money, I can raise money, I got friends who'll give it to me!'

'Where's your studio?'

It was a Canal Street address.

Russ jingled Maloney's key ring. 'Where's the car?'

'On the street. This side. Two or three down from Eighth. A sixty-nine Chevy, gray two-door. Take it!'

Russ slipped the man's other sock off and used it to gag him again. Maloney groaned. Russ pulled him into the living room.

'We're going to be here awhile,' Russ said.

Maloney squeezed his eyes shut. He was still trembling.

There were forty or fifty paperback books and several years' back issues of *National Geographic* in a bookcase next to the couch. Russ went through the *Geographics* and put a few to the side.

Then he left Maloney to rummage through the kitchen. He opened a can of soup and made a salami sandwich and brewed some instant coffee. He ate and made another cup of coffee and carried that back to the living room. He read a piece on a man who had tamed a killer whale and could play with it like a porpoise. He read about Alaskan musk oxen and about Hsing-Hsing and Ling-Ling, the two giant pandas given to the U.S. by China, who now resided in the Smithsonian Zoo. Then he read a long story on chimpanzees by Baroness Jane van Lawick-Goodall. It fascinated him, and he searched through later editions until he found an ad for the Baroness's full-length book. He tore out the coupon and put it in his pocket.

It was still too early, so he turned on Maloney's television and watched the eleven-o'clock news, and after that most of an old movie that wasn't too bad. He turned off the set at one, before the movie was over.

He squatted next to Maloney, dangling the Beretta. 'I'm going to let you loose. You can clean up and change your clothes. Then we're going to your studio and get the negatives. Now, here's a truth: I don't care whether you live or die. I don't have any special reason to kill you – if I get one all of a sudden, it'll be because you gave it to me. You understand that?'

Russ removed the gag, and Maloney blurted, 'Any-

77

thing you want. I'll get it for you, I'll do it for you. Just please don't –'

'If I ask a question, you give me an answer. Otherwise, I don't want to hear anything from you.'

Looking fearfully at Russ, Maloney got out of his fouled clothes, washed himself, and put on clean garments.

Russ opened the door and folded his arms over his chest, concealing the Beretta in his armpit. 'Remember,' he said. 'You're the one who makes yourself dead.'

In the lobby he retrieved his windbreaker and sweater. He stuck his right hand and the gun into the windbreaker pocket.

They drove to Canal Street and parked across from a four-story warehouse building close to Chinatown. Russ questioned Maloney about the layout. The narrow stairway leading up to the second-floor studio was windowless. The windows of the studio proper were sealed, and no light could escape.

They got out of the car. 'Direct and easy,' Russ said. 'You're a man going into his own property to pick up some equipment he needs.'

There weren't many people on the street: a quartet of Puerto Rican juveniles, a couple, a drunk, a few solos. Traffic was light. The juveniles cast speculative predators' eyes at Russ and Maloney, but passed by, and no one else paid them any attention.

The studio was a big room, some fifty feet square, and high-ceilinged. A double bed surrounded by arc lights stood in one corner, with a 16-mm. camera on a tripod at its foot. There were sheets of hanging no-seam. In front of one was a pillory like a dead snake. An open stand-up wardrobe held costumes of feathers, fur, transparent materials, leather, and rubber. Toys and beach equipment, varieties of furniture, swaths of carpeting lay about. A trunk with instruments of bondage and punishment. An eight-foot false wall on casters with a window and shade in its center. Crushed cigarette butts and wadded delicatessen bags on the wall. A heavy work bench was bolted along one wall. On it were developing trays, bottles of chemicals, a light board, an enlarger, a contact printer, and a film editor. Above it were shelves of canned 16-mm. film. Five four-drawer filing cabinets were ranked at its end.

'The Marecek negatives,' Russ said.

Maloney opened a file drawer. He chewed his lip as he rifled the folders. He withdrew one and dropped it, which scattered the negatives and a sheaf of prints. Hastily he picked them up and gave them to Russ. Russ flipped through the prints. He held the negatives up to a light.

'This all?'

'Yes, I swear.'

'How'd you take 'em?'

Maloney looked at his feet.

'Come on!'

'I, I got this thing with a guy at Howard Johnson's uptown. Two rooms side by side with a slot through the wall. When he gets probables checking in – young chicks, or guys or chicks who look like they're with someone they shouldn't be – he puts 'em into one room and keeps the other clear for me. I got a couple of customers that can only get off on candid stuff. You know, like peepers. And I put the shit into the regular markets, too. Once in a while, when we can finger somebody for sure, we – we . . .'

'You what?'

'We squeeze 'em,' Maloney whispered.

'How'd you get on to Marecek?'

'I seen her picture in the *Daily News*.'

Russ burned the negatives and prints in the sink.

'I swear to you,' Maloney said urgently. 'I won't even go near Howard Johnson's again.'

Russ washed the ashes down the sink. 'I don't give a fuck about that.'

He had Maloney sit down where he could watch him. He began pulling one-gallon and five-gallon tins from beneath the workbench, unscrewing the caps and sniffing. He set aside two of the larger cans and one of the smaller.

Maloney looked on in growing apprehension.

'You got any tools here?' Russ asked.

Maloney pointed to a cabinet.

Russ took a hammer and a crowbar. 'The windows on the side, what do they look out on?'

'An air shaft.'

'Rip the plywood off two of them.'

When Maloney had cleared and raised the windows, Russ had him open cans of movie film and build a pile against one wall.

'Please don't kill me,' Maloney said softly.

'You haven't given me any reason to yet.'

Russ sloshed the contents of a five-gallon tin and the one-gallon tin over the film and the nearby wall and floor. He placed the remaining tin atop the film. Maloney wept quietly and shook his head from side to side.

Russ lit a cigarette, puffed it to a fiery point, positioned it in a full pack of book matches, then set the pack with care at the edge of the film.

'Let's go,' he said.

They waited in the car with the engine running. There was a dull, deep *whummph!* A small shudder ran through the car, and across the street the wood masking one of the windows split. The glass cracked and fell to the sidewalk, and a long tongue of yellowish fire licked out.

Russ nodded, and Maloney put the car in gear and pulled away from the curb. He drove west to the end of Canal and stopped at the entrance ramp to the West Side Highway. The streets were dark and empty.

'Get out,' Russ said.

'Please. Mary Mother of God, don't do it!'

'Just get the fuck out before you mess yourself up.'

Maloney's hand trembled on the door handle. Then he

yanked it up, pushed the door open, and dove out. He hit the pavement rolling and came up running. Russ watched him zigzag away.

Russ slid behind the wheel. He turned off the highway a little later at Twenty-third Street and continued until he passed Sixth Avenue, then parked. He removed the clip from the Beretta and jacked the shell from the chamber, putting it back in the clip. He set off on foot toward the school. On the way, he stopped to stuff Maloney's pistol deep into a garbage can, and again, a block later, to do the same with the clip.

Frank was waiting patiently in Cerberus's darkened front room. The dog shivered with pleasure, and washed Russ's face. Russ hugged and scratched it. The animals in the rear began to bark. As Russ was leaving, the lights went on. A sleepy-eyed Kenroy appeared in the door with his hand on the switch. A big Doberman stood stiffly at his side, ears pricked forward.

'Oh,' Kenroy said. He looked down at the Doberman. 'It's all right, Tank.'

The dog relaxed.

'Sorry to get you up,' Russ said.

'Sure. 'S okay.'

They said good night.

Walking back to his apartment, Russ stopped in Washington Square to throw a stick for Frank a while, an apology for having left him cooped up in the school. Frank was appreciative.

Beth was asleep when Russ arrived. Deeply, making a sound in her throat that bordered on a snore.

Russ didn't wake her up. He got into bed, and was soon deep asleep himself.

CHAPTER FIVE

Ahab leaned against Wylie. It was four in the morning, and Wylie was sitting cross-legged on the living-room floor in the center of piles of photographs and Xerox copies of depositions, reports, interviews, analyses, and summaries. He was now reading the coroner's post mortem on Mrs Hannah Lewis Greer, female, Caucasian, age sixty-two, formerly of One Sutton Place. Shotguns were very messy.

Ahab bunted Wylie's elbow with his nose.

'Good boy,' Wylie said abstractedly.

Ahab dropped a plum silk ascot on the coroner's report and pushed his head between Wylie's arm and side, looked up with his ears laid back and an expression that was both mildly guilty and hopeful.

Wylie picked up the ascot and held it before the dog's face. 'No, Ahab. You know better. Shame. No.'

Ahab squeezed his eyes shut and withdrew in contrition.

Ten minutes later he was back, with a calfskin slipper in his mouth.

'No!' Wylie said, taking it. 'Bad dog.'

Next time it was one of the batik pillows from the bed, held gently between the spikes of his teeth.

'No,' Wylie said, but not forcefully.

Ahab hung his head and peeped up shyly. His heavy tail struck once, tentatively, against the floor.

'Oh, all right,' Wylie said. He stood, stretched. 'Settle for a walk?'

The dog's jaw dropped in a grin, and his tail swished the air.

Wylie hung a light jacket over his shoulders, and they

went down in the elevator, across Fifth, and into the park.

Ahab had done in a chair leg once, and a Russian icon, but he'd been five months old then, and shedding his puppy teeth. He was not a destructive chewer. Nor did he carry or drag things around the house. But now and then, when he felt that he had been ignored beyond reasonable limits, he would begin to seize prohibited articles and bring them to Wylie and drop them at his feet until his existence was acknowledged and some measure of attention paid him.

The park was thinly misted. It was chilly, and pleasantly solitary. Ahab danced about Wylie, growling. Wylie got down on his knees and wrestled with him. Wylie's pants became wet with dew. The wrestling done, Ahab went quartering across a field. He found a scent he liked, and set off on the trial. Wylie ambled along behind, mentally reviewing the material from Schattner.

The police had been meticulous and thorough, and Schattner no less so in assembling all their goods for Wylie. Schattner had even appended notes of his own with information not included in the formal paperwork – for example, Chasteen's dog, a big Irish wolfhound, had been kenneled that night so that it wouldn't be in the way of guests; George Emsley, the ex-con who worked for the caterers (and whom a subsequent probe had cleared) had at first been thought an inside man, and had been worked over by two eager patrolmen, an embarrassment covered up by the patrolmen's senior officer; the seventeen-year-old son of the people who owned the brownstone behind Chasteen's, Peter Ferenbach, had been busted twice for drugs, and the second time had resisted the officers with violence. Peter had been cleared, too, but his name had been expunged from the investigation, Schattner's note read, at the request of someone in the Mayor's office.

Schattner was right. Depressingly, the police had over-looked nothing.

Ahab collapsed his front legs and drove his shoulders against the wet grass. He flopped over onto his back and wriggled happily. The dog sensed the imminence of snow, and was already anticipating it.

Wylie arrived at Cerberus at twenty past nine. Russ wasn't there yet.

Russ had little sense of ease, and even less of frivolity. His concept of indulgence was to sleep an extra half-hour in the morning. Once, in an orgy of self-pampering, he had bought himself a custom-tailored shirt. And he felt he was entitled to such treatment only when he'd accomplished something difficult.

So Wylie assumed he'd gotten the negatives.

Russ came in just after nine thirty. Frank and Ahab postured and assured each other that each was still the most fearsome creature to have tread the earth, and then retired to neutral corners. Russ and Wylie went to the small office in the back.

Russ gave Wylie the envelope with the three hundred dollars and told him what had happened.

'You burned the goddamn building?' Wylie said.

'If he *was* holding something out, he doesn't have it any more. And it made him take me seriously.'

Wylie nodded uneasily. Once, the aftermath of Russ's work had made Wylie vomit. He said, 'Well, we have this for Lesley. It does make us look quick and efficient. There was nothing in the stuff from Al. Rather, there was pretty near everything. It'd cheer me up if they had missed something. If they did, I'm right behind them. I'm going to try Finn this afternoon.'

'I'll cruise the dives. It's there, somewhere.'

'I'm glad you have faith.'

'It's always there. It's just a matter of looking long enough.'

'I can think of one or two hundred philosophers who'd like to talk to you about that.'

Russ shrugged. 'Sometimes you don't live long enough to find it, but that doesn't mean anything. It's still there.'

Raymond Finn's office was on the twenty-fifth floor of 666 Fifth Avenue, indicated by nothing more than his name on a small brass plaque on the door. Wylie pressed the bell stud. A female voice addressed him through a tiny speaker in the frame: 'Who is it, please?'

'Wylie Lincoln.'

'Just one moment, please.'

An attractive, groomed woman admitted him. The windowless room was illuminated by concealed lights, the walls were covered with thick planks of old hand-hewn chestnut, there was a desk and a single lounge chair. The woman stepped to her desk and did something to the console there. She glanced down to see the response.

'Mr Finn will see you now, Mr Lincoln.'

She led him around her desk to a door behind it, which was opened by Raymond Finn, and closed by him after Wylie had stepped through. It was an impressive door. It could not have been breached by anything less than an oxyacetylene torch in the hands of someone with a lot of time.

Finn was a white-haired blue-eyed man of medium height with a pragmatically trim body and a stately face. He shook Wylie's hand. 'It's pleasant to see you again. May I offer you tea?'

'No thanks, I've just eaten.'

The room was comfortable, walls textured with woven fabric, the carpet dense. At one end was a small marble table with a silver tea service and two Queen Anne chairs. At the other was Finn's desk, intaglioed rosewood and teak. There was nothing on it save a telephone, a leather-bound note pad, and a silver fountain pen. An authentic Rembrandt hung behind it.

At Finn's invitation, Wylie took a chair facing the desk. Finn sat down behind the desk and clasped his hands over his note pad. 'What business is of mutual interest to us, Mr Lincoln?'

Wylie took a paper-clipped list from his breast pocket. 'I'm trying to find item twenty-one, but information on any of these would be helpful.'

Finn looked at the top sheet, glanced at the one beneath it, and dropped the papers on his desk. 'This is a listing of the material stolen from the guests at Malcolm Chasteen's party.'

'Yes,' Wylie said.

'There was murder done there. You were at one time a policeman.'

'I've worked for you, too.'

'That employment did not involve murder.'

'I have no interest in this other than the recovery of item twenty-one.'

'Why is that item significant?'

Wylie told him.

'People can be ugly.' An anthropologist's detached observation.

'Can you help me?' Wylie asked.

'*Can* I is a question of capability. *Will* I, assuming the capability, is a question of self-interest: Which way would I benefit more?'

'Nothing else is reasonable.'

Finn tapped a finger on the papers. 'There is very little here to interest me. It is nearly all contemporary jewelry.'

'I was told, in a confidence I've never violated, that you were once seriously engaged in plans to ... acquire the *Mona Lisa,* and that you stopped simply because your client became frightened and withdrew his offer.'

A smile slipped briefly across Finn's lips. 'A charming story.'

'*Will* you help me?'

86

'I will tell you that I have neither seen nor heard anything of this material.'

'If you should, I'd be greatly in your debt if you'd inform me – providing that it doesn't conflict with your self-interest, of course.'

'I will remember that.'

'Thank you. You can keep the list for reference, I had it duplicated.'

Finn handed the papers back. 'I already have a copy.'

Russ was downstairs in the big chain-link enclosure, applying lotion to the shaved haunches of an area guard with a case of eczema. The compound consumed the rear fifth of the basement, and was sometimes used for territorial work. School policy required that when an area guard was out of its kennel, it be tight-leashed by its handler or secured in the compound.

Cheryl came down the stairs. The dog hurled itself against the fencing. It snarled and bit at the chain. Area guards were taught to look upon everyone but the one or two persons who handled them as enemies to be driven off, or, if they penetrated the dog's territory, to be attacked.

'Good boy,' Russ said. 'Good *boy*.'

Russ arched his eyebrows in question at Cheryl. The other dogs kenneled in the basement began to bark. Cheryl signaled that Russ was wanted upstairs. Russ took hold of the dog's leather collar and snapped a short leash to it.

'I'm going to have him run you off,' he shouted.

Cheryl nodded.

The animal's lips were skinned back from his teeth. Russ opened the pen. The dog barked furiously and lunged out, raking the concrete floor with his nails. Cheryl fled to the stairs and disappeared. Russ stopped the dog's pursuit.

'Good boy! Terrific puppy! You chased that old witch

87

away. Good boy!' He thumped the dog affectionately.

He interrupted his growls to lick Russ's hand. He was still making rumbling sounds in his chest when Russ closed him in the kennel and went to the stairs. Cheryl was waiting for him halfway up.

'I do not enjoy being referred to as "that old witch,"' she said.

'Part of the training,' Russ said. '*I* think you're very sweet.'

Cheryl sniffed. 'There's a "lady" for Mr Turner. A "Judy" for Mr Turner.'

Judy Rukeyser was waiting in the front area. Her chestnut hair was loose about her shoulders, softening the patrician austerity of her pale skin and fine features. She wore suede pants with patch pockets and a bright red blouse with long collar tips; over that, a long-sleeve wool Peruvian jacket. There were gold hoops in her ears.

'Hello, Miss Rukeyser,' Russ said.

'Judy.'

Russ nodded.

'And I'll call you Russ.'

'What can I do for you?'

She smiled widely.

Cheryl took away the schnauzer she'd been working. Abbie, waiting out a Weimaraner's long down-stay, glanced covertly at Judy.

'Evadne told me you were in the Army. In Vietnam. How come you didn't mention that at her party?'

'My father was a carpenter of sorts. I didn't mention that either.'

'It's not quite the same thing.'

'Sure it is.'

'You're very much,' she said. She pushed some papers over on a desk top and sat on the edge of it. 'You wouldn't say much about attack dogs at Evadne's. So now I'm here, where it's the one thing you should talk about. Tell me about them.'

'Are you in the market?'

'Oh, most definitely.'

'Look, I'll give you a couple of good books on the subject.'

'Reading is such a bore. I can't stay awake more than two or three pages. Do you train them to go for the throat?'

'No,' he said with annoyance. 'It's theoretically possible. But just barely. And on a practical level it's not possible at all. They hit the arm. Or the leg, if you're kicking them. Or the buttocks, if you're running. Or any piece they can reach if you go bananas and jump on one.'

'But they can do a lot of damage.'

'Yes.'

'How much?'

He looked at her a moment before answering. 'That depends on circumstances. Figure ten or fifteen stitches per bite, on the average.'

Judy stroked her long, delicate throat with the fingers of one hand. 'What's the worst thing any of your dogs have ever done to someone?'

'Try three severed fingers, Miss Rukeyser. Or an entire triceps muscle chewed up beyond salvage. Or a crushed kneecap. Do you like any of those?'

'My. They really are aggressive, aren't they?'

Cheryl returned with a golden retriever. The dog had just completed an obstacle trick course and was awaiting pickup tomorrow morning. She said, 'Sit, stay,' and continued until she'd crossed half the room. Then she whirled and made a hoop of her arms. 'Sunny, hup!' The dog bounded forward and leaped cleanly through her arms, landed, reversed itself when she called, 'Hup!' again and bent at the waist, and sailed over her back. 'Stay,' Cheryl said. She put the tip of an unsharpened pencil between her teeth. She snapped her fingers. The dog came fast, went up into the air, took the pencil in its own mouth without touching the girl, brought it back, and sat in front of her, holding it until she took it.

Russ sat down and propped his feet atop the desk on which Judy was sitting. He watched with a pleasant expression while Cheryl put Sunny through several routines. The dog executed them stylishly. Finished, Cheryl praised the animal and patted its shoulders, roughed its fur, and submitted to its kisses. Looking at a point somewhere between Russ and Judy, she smiled over its shoulder.

Judy took the lapels of her jacket in hand and slowly removed it. She cast it on a nearby chair and leaned back, her arms extending behind her, her palms against the desk top. The thin fabric of her blouse lay against the sweeping contours of her breasts like a glistening film.

A small tic pulled at the corner of Cheryl's eye.

Abbie said, 'Let's go for a walk, boy,' to the Weimaraner and took him quickly out the front door.

'I'd like to see one of your dogs attack,' Judy said. 'And what I'd like is, I'd like to wear the protective gear and have him attack me.'

'No way,' Russ said.

'That's a terrific idea, ma'am,' Cheryl said. She hurried over. 'There's no other way to really *understand* what an attack dog can do. You've got to face one and feel the emotions a criminal would before you can realize what protection a dog can be. It's an excellent idea, ma'am, and don't let Mr Turner talk you out of it just because you're a woman. All us girls here work as agitators sometimes.'

'You're sweet, dear,' Judy told her.

'While you get into a sleeve,' Cheryl said, 'I'll go downstairs and bring up a dog.'

'No,' Russ said.

Judy picked a brochure from the desk and tapped its cover. 'It says right here "Demonstrations upon request." And that's what I'm doing, requesting.'

'It's just what the lady needs,' Cheryl said to Russ. 'I'll be right back.'

'Which one you thinking of?' Russ asked.

Reluctantly, Cheryl said, 'Bumpy.'

'Thought so.'

Bumpy was a crazy. Two years ago a gang of five men had invaded the auto lot Bumpy patrolled and had broken his shoulder and three ribs with baseball bats. The dog had still managed to inflict more than four hundred stitches of injuries upon them, and had held them trapped on top of cars until his handler had arrived in the morning.

'We'll use Frank.'

'Talk him into Bumpy,' Cheryl appealed to Judy. 'He's a real sharp dog.'

Judy patted Cheryl's hand. 'We can't have it all our way, dear.'

Cheryl left the retriever with Pat, the receptionist, and went with Russ and Judy to one of the back rooms. On wall pegs hung a leather jacket, a torn raincoat, two burlap sacks, a club of light styrofoam, a couple of leashes and collars, and a massive sleeve which would protect its wearer from shoulder down to fingertips. The sleeve was torn, and stuffing bulged out.

Russ sent Cheryl to the locker to get another. 'The new one from Germany,' he said, 'the reinforced one.'

'Why not a suit of armor?' Cheryl muttered as she left.

Russ told Frank to go to the corner and lie down. The dog obeyed, but kept his head up and watched intently as Russ helped Judy into the sleeve Cheryl had brought and fastened the support strap over her other shoulder.

Russ became all business. 'Face the dog with your right side,' he said. 'Plant your feet apart and bend your knees slightly for balance and leverage. No, pull your right foot in a little. If it's too far out, he'll reach your leg before your arm. Lean slightly and extend your arm, bent at the elbow. We want him to take your forearm. Good. That's how you'll do it when I tell you. Okay, relax until we're ready.

'Now listen. There are two offense commands. The first is an alert; essentially, you're telling the dog to get ready to fight. Some dogs are taught a quiet alert – they stiffen up and focus, maybe growl a little, but they don't move. Others, like Frank, learn a more active version. The advantage of the first is its subtlety; it won't panic anyone and push the situation into unnecessary action. The point of the second is to convince a skeptic that the dog really does mean business; that's almost always enough.

'The actual attack command pulls out all the stops. The dog hits with everything he has, and if he's a good one, you can cut him apart with an axe but he'll keep coming until he's dead. He'll also stop on a single command from his handler, or if you show him by ceasing to resist that you've surrendered, or if you pass out from shock or loss of blood.'

Judy was staring at Frank.

'Frank hits hard, so keep your head and watch your balance. I don't demonstrate him much. A demo dog who does this over and over either begins not to take it seriously, which makes people think he's not very tough, or he grows frustrated and starts trying to go under or over or around the sleeve to get at the real stuff. When I signal, raise a fist and threaten me, and then get set to take him. Do you have all that?'

Without removing her eyes from Frank, Judy nodded.

Russ fastened a wide leather collar around Frank's neck, which would distribute the force of his lunges over a broader area; using the choke chain would have cut off his breath.

'Careful not to slip, ma'am,' Cheryl said.

Judy ignored her.

'Stand,' Russ said to Frank.

The dog rose, watching Judy. Russ patted him in the shoulder. 'That's a good boy. Cool now.'

Judy ran her tongue over her lips.

'Go ahead,' Russ told her.

Judy clenched her left hand and raised it. 'Come on!' she shouted. 'Come on and try me, you big bastard! Yaahhh!'

Frank took two rigid steps forward, mouth opening, brow furrowed.

'Pass auf!' Russ said in a low urgent voice.

Frank sounded a deep *arruuhh!* The dog lunged against the leash and went up on his hind legs. He did not bark, but emitted a continuous wavering roar. His paws flailed the air, and spittle was flung from his mouth.

Judy was transfixed.

'Set up,' Russ said over the noise of the dog. 'Damn it, set up!'

Judy did. Her face twisted, and she screamed back at the dog.

'Fass!' Russ commanded.

He played slack into the leash, and the ninety-five-pound animal surged forward, with Russ running behind. His teeth sank into the sleeve. Snarling, he threw the powerful muscles of his dense chest and shoulders against Judy and yanked her forward. She tried to pull back. The dog jerked his head from side to side and staggered her, tore at the sleeve, jaw muscles swollen, chest thundering, spinning her around, savaging the three-ply leather, slipping his bite for an instant and slashing in again, finally stumbling Judy to her knees.

'Aus!' Russ ordered.

Frank released his hold immediately, went quiet, and stepped back from Judy.

'Heel,' Russ said.

The dog returned to Russ's side and sat. Russ put him in a down-stay.

Judy was still on her knees, arms hanging limply at her sides. She saw nothing but Frank, and was only minimally aware of Russ helping her up. Her face was flushed and sheened with sweat. Her mouth was open and slack, her lips puffy, her eyes hazed.

'Are you all right?' Russ asked.

'It ... was ... beautiful,' she whispered.

'Here. Give me the sleeve.'

She watched the dog and said softly, 'May I touch him?'

'Frank, friends,' Russ said. Then, to Judy, 'Go ahead.'

Judy's hands stroked the hard muscles of the animal's shoulders and chest, drifted slowly down his sides to his loins. 'How lovely you are,' she murmured. 'How lovely and terrible and frightening. How sweet and deadly, and, God, so beautiful.'

Cheryl left the room in embarrassment.

The decorator had striven for a single effect with the offices of United Campaigns, to say: *This was incredibly expensive.*

'Nothing attracts money like money,' Raphaela Bracey said as she linked her arm through Wylie's. 'Rich people don't trust poverty.'

She toured him through the suite, helloing a staff of highly attractive girls. The lone male was a young man with wire-rim glasses, a charcoal-gray suit, and a regimental tie. His name was Christian Wright. He was courteous and well-spoken. Raphaela ended the circuit in her own spacious office. She dropped her mammoth body onto a long, curved brocade couch, the arms of which embraced a chrome table with a glass top. There were decanters of liquor on it, and glasses and an ice bucket. Raphaela poured a bourbon neat for Wylie and straight gin on the rocks for herself. She kicked her shoes off and dug her stockinged toes into the deep shag of the white rug.

'They won't spring for a dime unless they think you understand money. So you show them that you do, and that you know how to spend it. The girls help, too. Most rich men are old men, you know? I won't hire a girl who's not qualified, but I won't hire one either who couldn't make it as a two-hundred-dollar-a-night hooker if she wanted to. They don't have to ball anybody, but they damn well better not get prissy about a few pats and pinches. Christian is our heavyweight, our reassurance factor. That boy knows nothing of the milieu of money, but there's nothing he doesn't understand about its *méthode*. When I hired him, he was actually *buying* some emerging African nation for a Texas cartel. You know what he does for entertainment? On computer analogs, he builds and wrecks national economies.'

'We're all children at heart,' Wylie said.

'The hell we are. Do you mind?' Raphaela, wearing a green velvet pants suit, resembled nothing so much as a mobile mountain in summer plush. She opened the jacket and the first two buttons of her blouse and reached within to swab her armpits with a handkerchief. The jacket was sweatstained. 'Bloody nuisance. All my life I've gushed like a geyser. It offends my vanity, but it won't much longer. I'm going to Copenhagen in December. They have this new technique where they smear iodine on your armpits and cover them with a special paper. Then they mark where the sweat comes trickling through, and they slice the little sweat buggers right out. Four-in-five chance for success. Pray for me. Where was I?

'Oh yes, children. Have another bourbon and pour me a slug of gin, will you? Thanks. It's so nice to have a down-home boy to talk to. One thing about the rich is they're boring. And of course you always have to lie to them. Anyway, I had a Dun and Bradstreet run on you, and some other digging done, and Christian went over it all, and he tells me you have way, way too much money for what's visible, I mean your dog school. There's no question, he says, but that you're into something besides dogs, and since whatever it is has obviously been con-

95

cealed, then we simply must assume it's something naughty. Some day we should talk about it. I'm always interested in other people's games.

'I live in a lovely co-op. It's a duplex – you'll have to visit some day – and it cost me a hundred thirty-five thousand dollars. The monthly maintenance is seven hundred fifty. I have a cute little Ferrari for scooting about in myself, and a charming silver Bentley with a Japanese chauffeur for occasions of state. And the appropriate servants, of course. It's all quite necessary, money to attract money, but I do take to it like a skunk to garbage. It's very satisfying for a li'l ol' Virginia girl who turned her first trick when she was barely fifteen. Last year our operating expenses were roughly forty percent of our gross collections. United Campaigns is good to us, bless its tax-deductible heart.

'Now, the thing about a really *fine* hustle, the whole secret, is to give your client more and better than anyone else can give him. That way your client never objects to you taking your piece, right? Long as everybody gets theirs, no one complains. That's the difference between fraud and a hustle, a hustle always delivers. Now, here's what you and I are going to do. I have this little contract to raise money – they're hoping for a fifty-thousand-dollar gross – for a spastic children's clinic in Mount Vernon. I don't have to tell you about spastic children, do I? I mean, hell, your heart goes mushy without having to hear all the distressing medical details. Okay, two months should give us enough time.'

She consulted a date book. 'I can give you the afternoon of November fourteenth, seventeenth, or eighteenth. Let me know what's best. We're making personal contact with a hundred seventy-five selected *grandes dames* in Boston, Philly, D.C., and local environs, and we're projecting an eighty-five percent acceptance. A luncheon show at the Sheraton. At five hundred dollars a plate, we're going to gross seventy-five thousand dollars.

That's thirty thousand for United and forty-five thousand net for the spastic people, which is substantially more than they expect. Terrific, eh?'

'It's entertaining, Miss Bracey,' Wylie said. 'But I don't trust people worth a damn who volunteer the kind of information you just have.'

Raphaela beamed. 'Of course you don't. But you're some kind of ringer, son. Evadne wouldn't tell me a thing, only that I'd get burned if I tried to fuck with you. Evadne doesn't make statements like that without good reason. So I'm laying it all right out. I want to hustle you a little, dear, and the best way to do that is to tell you exactly what the hustle is.

'Obviously, *you* are the show. Our *mondaines* are all animal types: SPCA, Fund for Animals, Bide-a-Wee, and that sort. The cause is right, and the show is right. You give them a nice talk on dog psychology, assuming dogs have psyches, on proper care, on training, and you show them one of those Seeing-Eye dogs, a police dog, a trick dog, a ... hell, I don't know – you're the expert, you set it up. Just be sure to give them a question-and-answer period and allow for an hour's social mingling. It'll be a smash.

'Christian tells me we can receipt you for a fifteen-hundred-dollar contribution. Doing the show can't cost you more than a couple of hundred, and with the receipt you'll come out well ahead on the tax deduction. And you'll have roped in fifty big ones for a good cause. Pour me another, will you?'

'Three thousand,' Wylie said.

Raphaela's hand went to her monstrous bosom. 'My dear man!'

'A tax receipt for three.'

'Oh. Good God, you appalled me for a moment. But I'm afraid that's still not possible. Perhaps I could get Christian to see his way up to seventeen fifty.'

'Have him see up to three. It's not all that much farther.'

'Two. But even for that, he'll have to be very clever.'

'Miss Bracey.'

'Ah well, three. But it's going to hurt.'

'And I'd like the name and telephone number of the doctor in charge of the clinic.'

Raphaela pouted. 'You don't trust me.'

'I just have a mania for details, that's all. And you'll owe me a favor, right?'

'That *is* the customary mode.'

'I think we have an agreement, then.'

Raphaela refilled Wylie's glass and toasted him. 'Good. We'll be working on you, you know. Thorough files can be very helpful in securing donations and getting things done.'

Wylie raised his glass. 'To your files.'

'You wouldn't know anyone in the FBI who wants money, would you? God, we'd love to get at their stuff.'

Wylie didn't. They finished their drinks, and Raphaela showed him out and said she'd send one of her girls around to interview him for a pitch letter.

CHAPTER SIX

When Wylie returned to the school, Kenroy, Gene, and another handler were loading area guards into the Cerberus panel trucks for delivery to the stores, car lots, construction sites, and warehouses they would guard through the night.

Harold was walking the Welsh corgi in the gutter several yards away. 'Kong,' he said, 'there are thirty million dogs in this country, all of whom once felt the way you do now. But they managed to learn, even though they're not half as intelligent as you. Do you want people to think that all those run-of-the-mill mutts are your superiors? I'm sure it's just a simple misunderstanding. We can work it out. What do you say? Will you try it once outside, just for the experience?'

'Rowf!' the dog said.

Inside, the school was being closed down for the day. Surprisingly, Russ was already gone.

'He left with some *lady*,' Cheryl told Wylie.

Twenty minutes passed before Cheryl signed out. In that time she got into an argument with Pat, and another with Harold, who was as easily provoked as a loaf of French bread.

Wylie ran through the list of calls that had come in during the afternoon. He checked most, including two complaints, for tomorrow morning's attention, and began to return the remaining half dozen. He waved good night to people as they left, without breaking the rhythm of his conversations. He ended with Horace Friedberg.

'I got my money for Magoo,' Horace said, 'but I couldn't do anything about residuals.'

'They're a problem,' Wylie agreed.

'I think what we should do is organize about a dozen trainers and hire a lawyer. And maybe open discussions with Actors Equity about an animal division.'

'Mmmm,' Wylie said.

'Let's talk about it in a week or two. But listen, this guy from Doyle, Dane is doing a spot that he needs a couple of sled dogs for, huskies or malamutes. I told him you were the best in the business and not to think about anyone else.'

Wylie was genuinely pleased. 'Thank you,' he said.

'So if he calls you and you get it, it's like I was your agent, right? That's a ten percent commission. You can mail the check to me.'

'We'll discuss it, Horace.'

'Okay. Incidentally, the paper-clip routine worked all right, but I found the clip comes off too easy and the dog stops scratching. Try a little tab of Scotch tape, it's much better.'

As Wylie said good-bye, Kenroy came up from the basement and asked, 'You going to lock up?'

'Uh huh. Do you have a couple of minutes? I'd like to rough out a charity show.'

'Sure. Stay for dinner. Kathy's makin' spaghetti.'

They went upstairs to the apartment over the school in which Kenroy lived with his wife and baby. Susie was two years old, and Cerberus's mascot. She sat on Wylie's lap, as imperiously comfortable as a cat, while Wylie read two books to her. Kenroy repaired an electrical outlet, and Kathy made a clam-and-garlic sauce. Then Kathy took Susie off to bed. Kenroy brought beers into the living room, and he and Wylie worked out a preliminary program. Dinner was good. They drank most of a gallon bottle of Seggesta with it. Wylie helped clear the table. He played a game of Crazy Eights with Kenroy and Kathy, then stayed another hour more in pleasant idle conversation.

He was cheerful when he left the school. Twenty-fifth

Street was dark and empty, and Wylie let Ahab walk free. The dog snuffed about, reading a tapestry of scents, pausing frequently to lift his leg and stake off territory. Wylie lit a cigarette and walked leisurely, the dog a few yards behind him. A car engine turned over. A jaywalker paused for a speeding cab to pass, then crossed the street and sidled between a parked car and a Volkswagen bus and gained the sidewalk behind Wylie.

'Excuse me,' he said.

Wylie turned. 'Yes?'

The man showed Wylie a snubnosed pistol, then slid it back into the pocket. 'The Buick across the street,' he said. 'Nice and easy.'

'Are you a pro?' Wylie asked. He watched Ahab padding up behind the man, tail stiffening with interest.

'All the way. Move, friend.'

'Then you want to keep your eyes on mine, and don't move at all, and make very sure that gun doesn't go off.'

'And why is that?' Beneath the mocking tone lay an edge of wariness.

'*Pass auf,*' Wylie said.

Ahab braced and growled behind the man.

The man shoulder's hunched up.

'Because otherwise you'll have a hundred and five pounds of killer dog on your back,' Wylie said.

Ahab's rumble loudened.

'Okay,' the man said phlegmatically.

'Clasp your hands behind your back,' Wylie said. 'Slowly.'

As the man complied, Ahab escalated his growl to a snarl, but didn't break position. Wylie removed the gun from the man's pocket, masked by the Volkswagen bus from the eyes of whoever was across the street.

'How many in the Buick?' Wylie said.

'One.'

'What's his name?'

'Danny.'

'What's yours?'

'Hop.'

Wylie took off his jacket and hung it loosely over the gun in his hand. 'Hop, we're going over to see Danny. Keep your hand in your pocket and stay five steps in back of me. Act like you've got it all greased in. If you make one bad move, the dog'll take you from behind and I'll put a bullet in Danny.'

Hop nodded.

'Ahab, *aus!*' Wylie said. The growling stopped.

Wylie commanded the dog to stay, then preceded Hop around the Volkswagen bus and across the street. Danny watched them come with an indifferent face. He released the parking brake as Wylie opened the back door. Wylie slid onto the seat, dropped his jacket, and pressed the muzzle of the pistol against the base of Danny's skull.

'This is your friend's thirty-eight,' Wylie said quietly. 'Put your hands on the top of the wheel ... good. Where's your gun?'

'In a shoulder rig, right side.'

Wylie removed a Walther .380 automatic from him, and told Hop to get in the front seat.

'How the fuck did he take you?' Danny asked.

'He had a friend,' Hop answered sourly.

Wylie called Ahab from across the street and into the car.

'Hey, man,' Danny said. 'Don't let that mother near me! They scare the shit out of me.'

'Just keep being a pro, and the dog will too,' Wylie said. 'What do you dudes wants?'

Danny and Hop glanced at each other, looked away, sat in silence.

Wylie waited. Then he said to Ahab, '*Gib laut.*'

It was only a command to speak, but when the dog barked – near deafeningly in the confines of the car – Danny flung himself over the wheel and screamed, 'No! Hold him back, for God's sake!'

'Talk,' Wylie said.

'We're supposed t' bring you t' Mr Lamorena,' Danny said, shaken.

'Victor Lamorena?'

'Yeah.'

'Where?'

'His office if we could o' got you during the day, his apartment now.'

'Let's go.'

Danny looked at Hop. Hop shrugged. Danny put the car in gear. They drove to Park Avenue, then uptown to Sixty-eighth, and turned right. They parked in front of a fire hydrant.

The Walther was tucked into Wylie's waistband beneath his shirt. He carried Hop's .38 in his hand, covered by his jacket. He walked into the lobby a step behind Danny and Hop, with Ahab at heel. The doorman said good evening to the two white men.

Lesley Marecek opened the door of Lamorena's twelfth-floor apartment. She said, 'Hi,' to Danny and moved her eyes over Hop with recognition but no interest. Then she saw Wylie, who was standing behind the other men. Her eyes widened. She choked. Wylie scowled and shook his head *no*. He nudged Hop in the back with the .38. Danny and Hop entered the apartment grudgingly.

'Where's the bosss?' Danny asked.

Lesley was pale. 'In the living room.'

The living room was done in stark, almost hurtful whites, with black iron accoutrements and woods of unnatural colors. At the far end a spiral staircase rose to the floor above. Lamorena sat on the couch in powder-blue pajamas, over which he wore a maroon dressing gown, watching a western on a big color TV. He was chunky, muscled, and about forty. A density of black whiskers showed through the talc on his shaven cheeks. His leg, in a cast from hip to foot, was extended straight before him, its weight supported by a white leather ottoman.

His stubby toes peeped out of the plaster like embedded sausages.

When Lesley called, he turned off the set with a remote-control instrument and said, 'Come in, Mr Lincoln.' To Danny and Hop he said, 'You can take off now, boys. Don't forget Donetti's tomorrow.'

'Uh, Mr Lamorena,' Hop said. 'He ... uh ... he's got our pieces.'

Lamorena stared at them.

Wylie leaned out from behind Hop, smiled at Lamorena, and waved hello with his free hand.

'I want to see you guys here tomorrow morning at eight thirty,' Lamorena said. 'Now get out.'

'Yes, sir,' Hop said.

Leaving, Danny looked as if he wished to do murder, or fall down and sob.

Ahab followed Wylie into the living room. Lamorena eyed the dog with distaste. 'They get hairs over everything,' he said.

'Not if you keep them brushed.' Wylie pulled a captain's chair close to Lamorena and said, 'Down,' to Ahab. The dog lay down, tested the air with his nose, and looked about, weighing this place without alarm.

'You don't send men with guns unless you want someone shot,' Wylie said, unloading the pistols. 'Is that what you wanted?'

Lamorena sipped from a brandy glass. 'I told them to bring you here. I didn't say to point nothing at you.'

'You've got to make these things clear.'

'Maybe. But the point is, you took 'em even with their heat. Jerks and meatballs, that's all I can get these days,' he said with disgust. 'It's not like it used to be.'

Wylie dropped the loose cartridges and the Walther's clip into his pocket and handed the guns to Lamorena. 'They were pro enough to know it was no good. Only amateurs and crazies try to cowboy it through. And they don't live very long.'

Lamorena held the guns by their barrels. 'Lesley! Put these goddamn things away some place.'

'Next time telephone,' Wylie said.

'Yeah,' Lamorena said. Lesley took the guns. 'What are you drinking?'

'Bourbon. Neat, please.'

'Fix for him, will you, honey?'

'What do you want from me?' Wylie asked.

'You've been nosin' around the Chasteen thing. I want to know why.'

Lesley brought Wylie a drink. She sat down beside Lamorena.

'What's your interest?' Wylie said.

Lamorena rapped his knuckles on his cast. 'It took eight hours on an operating table to give me back something that looked like a knee. For the rest o' my life I'm gonna walk like Gregory Peck in that whale movie. I want to have a discussion with those shitsuckers. I sent people lookin'. And I found out there's this spa – this guy Wylie Lincoln lookin' too. And some other Russ Turner guy. And it turns out this Russ Turner is an ex-con that works for this dog trainer. And this dog trainer is Wylie Lincoln, and this Wylie Lincoln used to be a cop that got caught on the take, or juicin' some politico or somethin', and got pushed off the force, and his name comes up after that, too, with no real stories as to what he's doin', but in some very curious connections with some very curious people that wouldn't know a dog from a goddamn buffalo, so you can see how I began to grow very interested in what this Wylie Lincoln has to do with four punks who boost plushes in townhouses and shoot my kneecap to pieces in the process. You can see that, can't you?'

'It does pose intriguing possibilities,' Wylie admitted.

Lesley finished her martini and went to the bar to mix another one.

'So I ask you properly, like a gentleman of second generation Italian extraction, would you do me the honor of explaining to me just why you present these intriguing possibilities.'

Standing at the bar, Lesley drank her new martini straight off, and mixed another. She returned with the cautious unsteadiness of a boozy cleric at dinner in a parishioner's home, praying that a merciful God will help him bring it off.

Wylie shrugged. 'One of the guests lost something of sentimental value in the robbery. He hired me to get it back.'

'Who?'

Wylie waggled a finger and shook his head. 'Uh uh. Professional ethics. You know, the sacred trust.'

'So what did he lose?'

'A piece of the True Cross,' Wylie said gravely.

'That's not funny. Jokes about religion aren't funny. You might just find the whole Cross, and get yourself nailed to it.'

'You get offended by religious jokes, okay, I apologize. *I* get offended by threats and men with guns.'

Lamorena reflected on this a moment. 'All right ... I apologize too.' It was difficult for him.

Wylie nodded. 'It comes simply to you looking for them, and me looking for them. Me, I could use help. Have you turned anything up?'

Lamorena guffawed. 'You're a pisser, man, a real pisser. Nothin'. How 'bout you?'

'The same.'

Lamorena's face lapsed back to dour. 'If you do, you call me.' Exercising will, he refrained from adding, *Or I'll have your legs broken with baseball bats.* 'You help me out, maybe I can help you out in something.'

'Good enough. And maybe I can do the same for you if you turn a lead my way.'

'Outside o' the knee-shooters, the only help I need is with the tax case the Feds got goin' on me.'

'You guilty?'

'Jesus Christ, does the Pope live in Rome?'

'*Always* pay your taxes,' Wylie said. 'The government couldn't care less how you make your money – they just want their piece.'

'Great: I, Willie Sutton, report an income of one hundred grand last year from boosting banks.'

'No. I, Willie Sutton, report an income of one hundred grand last year from my five dry-cleaning stores and my two restaurants.'

'I got as many o' those as I got wings.'

'Me too. Except on paper. It explains the extra money, and if you get a good man with books, he can figure the deductible overhead high and now and then declare a loss on one of the places. Keeps the taxes reasonable.'

'Goddamn!' Lamorena said. 'What's your man's phone number?'

'He's fainthearted. He won't touch it if the suit's already under way. Do they have all your paper yet?'

'No, but my lawyers can't hold 'em off much longer.'

'You know Raphaela Bracey?'

'I met her once or twice. So?'

'She has a superboy working for her. You do a little something for her, maybe she'll lend him out to you.'

'No shit. Hey, that's terrific. Thanks a lot.'

'It's a hard world.'

'I really am sorry those meatballs flashed metal.'

Wylie stood. 'It's okay. I've got to be getting on now.'

'You'll let me know if you find anything, right?'

'And you'll do the same for me. Well, take care.' Wylie nodded to Lesley. 'Good night, ma'am.'

Lesley rose and said she'd show him out. She wasn't walking very well. At the door Wylie said good night to her again.

She had trouble focusing her eyes. 'Yes,' she said.

After two drinks, Russ told Judy Rukeyser he had some things to do and that he'd have to say good night. She pouted. She had wanted him to take her to dinner. She'd even been willing to fix dinner for them at her apartment.

'But if I acted insulted,' she said, 'I don't think you'd care. Next time we'll set it in advance, and then you won't have any "things to do."'

He didn't answer. Outside the bar she pressed her body against his and put her tongue in his mouth. Then she said, 'The least you could have done was to get a little bit of a hard-on. You're not very gentlemanly. Bye now.' She turned and walked to a cab that was discharging its passenger.

Russ went up to Seventy-seventh Street to talk to Vic Scannapico. Scannapico weighed three hundred pounds. He was a newspaper vendor, and he peered out from his small green stand at the passing world like a gross and pulpy mollusk from its shell. He was also a message drop for pros and small-timers who weren't affiliated with the Organization. If he knew a man and was certain of him, he would monger gossip with all the passion of an adolescent boy sliding his hand up and down his shaft in a darkened room.

'This is a very bad one,' he told Russ. 'Every stoolie in town has had his ass whipped by his private pig, and the ones shootin' pig powder have been put on half ration. The Man is shuttin' down pussy palaces, closin' high-roll games, raidin' books, bustin' dealers, violatin' paroles, lockin' bars, and sweepin' the streets. Whatever's happenin', the Man is stompin' on it. And the true and hard word is, there ain't nothin' goin' t' loosen up until those cannoneers are in the jug. The street is hurtin', and there ain't a bad boy in the city who wouldn't point the finger t' get out from under. What's your in?'

'Got a client. I just want to find something that was lost there.'

'You ain't alone. Aside from the whole goddamn police department, there's insurance snoops, five private dicks,

108

that I know of, and some of Vic Lamorena's people. He got shot up, you know. I wouldn't want t' be those boys now. But they're hanging tough so far. Maybe they'll pull it off.'

'Maybe,' Russ said. 'If you hear anything, let me know – I can lay some of my action on you.'

Scannapico nodded, the doughy flesh of his face quivering.

There were other people to see, and places to sit and drink and listen. But Russ couldn't face them; he'd barely been able to finish with Scannapico. *Was a knife as intimate as they said?* Judy Rukeyser had wanted to know about prison and Vietnam, about killing. *Did blood feel hot on your hands?* About killing. *Did men who died violently die with erections?* Killing. *Was it like getting high? Did ...*

Russ's head was pounding. His stomach was souring. Barriers were rising between him and the people he passed. He quickened his steps, trying to flee the faint cries of the past and the memories of frenzy that ghosted through him.

At Fifty-ninth Street he turned abruptly into Bloomingdale's. He measured the image of Beth against the salesgirl and guessed at the size. He bought her a blouse and a pair of slacks. He was perspiring, and breathing with difficulty. The salesgirl was relieved when he left.

He took a cab from Bloomingdale's to the school and had the driver wait while he went inside to get Frank. Seeing the animal, the driver protested. Russ handed him a five-dollar bill. 'That's over the meter,' he said, and gave the Morton Street address. The driver pocketed the money, but warned that he would dump them if the dog caused any trouble, and that if it vomited Russ would have to clean the cab.

Once inside the building and walking down the hall to the stairs at the rear, Russ began to calm down. His apartment was partly a sanctuary; in it he was somehow safe from himself.

He smelled hash when he opened the door, a thicker and more pungent odor than grass. Beth was on the couch with her bare feet tucked beneath her. She held a thick-stemmed plastic steamboat pipe. She smiled loosely at him and nodded.

He set the Bloomingdale's package on a chair. 'How'd you get the stuff?'

'Just went out and found someone and spent some time with him and rapped and everything and he gave me some, and the cute little pipe, too.' Her voice was soft. She held up the steamboat. 'Take a hit.'

The blackish nugget in the wooden bowl was out, and still mostly intact, a powdering of white ash on one side. 'No thanks,' he said.

'It's very sweet. It sort of wiggles underneath and lifts you up very gently. It's floating hash.'

Russ had smoked a good deal once. He rarely did now – because it tended to wash him back to those times. And Judy Rukeyser had sent him too close already.

Beth lit a match, held it over the nugget while she puffed, and filled her lungs. She set the pipe down and lay her head back. She sighed. A thin wisp of smoke curled up from the bowl for a few moments, before the stuff went out again.

'I got you something,' Russ said.

'You did?' Her eyes lit with wonder and pleasure.

He gave her the box: a gray crepe blouse with a long collar, tiny white nub buttons, and full puffy sleeves, and beneath that blue velvet slacks with a low rise, flared from the knee down.

'They're beautiful,' she said. 'I'm going to cry. No, I'm going to be happy without crying.' She held the blouse to one cheek and the pants to the other and rubbed them against her skin. 'God, they feel so good!'

She stood, opened her shirt and shrugged out of it, took

110

off her jeans, put on her new blouse and the slacks, and pressed her hands over them. 'Oh, wow!' She ran to the bedroom to look at herself in the mirror. She stared a long time. Then she picked up Russ's brush and began pulling it through her hair. She struck knots and winced, but brushed with determination. In a few minutes her hair lay softly about her shoulders; she'd even managed to impact a dull sheen to it. She put her hands on the bureau top and leaned forward on braced arms to peer at herself. 'I'm pretty,' she said at last.

'Yes, you are,' Russ said.

'I really am.' She moved her body, feeling the pull and slide of the fabric against her skin. 'Sooo good!' she breathed. She faced him. 'You don't want to fuck me now, do you? I mean, if you do, okay, but I'd really like to ride just like this for a while.'

'That's all right,' Russ said. 'Go ahead.'

He went into the kitchen and poured himself a Scotch. She came up behind him and rested her hands lightly in his shoulders and kissed him on the ear. 'Thank you,' she said.

'You're welcome.'

She moved around in front. 'You know what I'd like to do?' He shook his head, and she said, 'Go out to dinner. Go out and have Chinese food at a restaurant – noodles and snails and curries and peanut soup and all that. Can we? Please? Please?'

The pants fit snugly. The blouse was a trifle large, but that simply made her more appealing, in a pixyish way. She was making Russ feel good. 'I'd like that too,' he said. 'We'll go through the whole menu and order everything that interests us, and not give a damn if all we take is two bites from each dish.'

'Do you mean it? Oh Jesus – heaven!' She went to the living room to take out one last hit of hash. To keep going, she said, to make this the longest, scrumptiousest meal she'd ever eaten.

111

They went by cab to Chinatown, getting out at Mott and Canal and walking up Mott to Bayard Street, where, one of Cerberus's handlers had said, there was a new and good restaurant. They held hands. Beth got him to skip a few paces. She laughed. He felt foolish, and he was pleased to feel that way.

The waiter brought them three varieties of soup and eleven separate dishes, and, as the domed servers began to multiply on the table, Beth responded as if she were witnessing the miracle of the loaves and fishes. Their waiter disapproved. So did some of the people around them. But Beth was happily oblivious to them. One man's comments to his wife grew louder and more pointed. Russ caught the man's eyes, held them, and thinned his lips. The man turned his attention to his plate and said nothing further. They ate voraciously, and at least a part of everything, but a hopeless abundance still remained.

Beth began to feel guilty. 'Do you think we could take it home in doggie bags?' she whispered.

Russ had the waiter pack it up.

Outside, Beth announced that nothing would do but that they play Monopoly. They flagged a cab and rode to Sheridan Square, where Russ bought a set at the cigar store. They walked down Seventh Avenue to Morton Street and home. Beth opened the game on the living room floor while Russ took Frank for a walk.

When he came back the board was ready and she had the pipe going again. She offered it. 'Come on, there's enough here for four.'

'No, I ...' He felt so good; he wanted to feel better. 'Oh, what the hell,' he said. He took the pipe.

'That's my lover! I'm going to be the cannon. What do you want to be?'

'The dog.'

They played a long time, Beth intent and bursting into paroxysms of delight, Russ laughing, both taking occasional hits from the pipe, the movement of the game grinding slower and slower, each marveling at the line drawings on the Community Chest and Chance cards of the mustachioed little capitalist, losing themselves in the tropic bands across the top of the property cards, and finally disregarding the game entirely and becoming engrossed with each other's fingers. Russ lay down on his back. Beth stretched out on her stomach beside him. One of her hands played idly with his hair and caressed his scalp.

He filled with intense pleasure. He lost himself in reverie. Soft moans rolled up within him and spilled through his lips as long exhalations.

He floated into death, and he saw that it was there. It was neither frightening nor lovely, it simply was. He did not understand why it had ever upset him. He forgave Judy Rukeyser. She was innocent. Everyone was innocent. Even him.

'I'm not a bad person,' he said with surprise.

'No,' Beth murmured, 'you're not.'

'You have to see it,' he said. He had evaded Judy's questions. He had never talked about it to anyone. But he understood now that he could be forgiven. And with forgiveness possible it suddenly became an urgent need.

'Listen,' he said. 'I never got a birthday present in my life. My mother split when I was a baby, and it fucked up my daddy's head. He boozed a lot and smashed things up. I'd come home and say, "Hey, Pop. Isn't it my birthday this Wednesday?" and he'd wrinkle up his forehead and say, "Naw, that's a couple months from now." He could never remember the date, so no matter when I asked, it would always be a couple of months from then.

'He was a carpenter, but he finally got too drunk to work. One afternoon when he was soused almost blind he cut the end of his thumb off on a bench saw. He couldn't figure out what to do, and he just sat down on the floor with blood squirting all over and cried like a baby. I picked up the piece of his thumb and brought him to the hospital with it. He didn't come home much. When the school or a neighbor told him I was getting in trouble, he'd beat the hell out of me and stick around a couple of days, but that was all. I got arrested for burglary when I was thirteen. He broke three of my teeth and hurt me so bad I couldn't get out of bed for five days. From then on we hardly said hello without screaming at each other. I wired a car when I was fifteen and took off for California. I piled up in Nevada, and they sent me to reform school. That's where I learned when my birthday was, because they let me out on the day I turned sixteen.

'I knew I was just going to get my ass in a sling again, so I told my father I wanted to join the Army. He helped me forge my birth certificate. The night before I left he blew fifty bucks on dinner for the two of us. We boozed all night and ended up putting our arms around each other and crying, and then in the morning he took me down to the induction center and said good-bye, and that's the last I ever saw of him.'

Russ was no longer sure whether he was speaking aloud or simply thinking quietly to himself. He looked into Beth's face for a clue, but he couldn't see anything there, so he closed his eyes again. Sometimes he thought he heard his voice, a hazy thing confounded by itself, and other times, though there were words in his mind, his straining ears registered nothing but silence.

'They were just starting this new cadre, Special Forces, and I went into it right after basic training. It was like I'd never been alive before. I was dropped a year later by parachute into a hill village in Vietnam. That's when it was a rinky-dink country the newspapers didn't even know how to spell yet.

'It was like going back a thousand years in time. The tribe I lived with was still telling stories about ancient battle heroes around the fires at night. Fighting was their way of life. It was as natural as fucking. For me it became

– no, it didn't become anything. *I* became *it*. I turned into a hunter. I breathed, I lived, to kill. They thought I was crazy, but they loved me, because I helped them kill so many enemies. And everyone who wasn't them was an enemy. We didn't fly any flags. Anything would have served: the Cong banner, the American flag, the skull and crossbones. They fought because there were others who weren't them, and I fought to kill. When we lost weapons we killed with old black-powder muskets and shotguns. When we ran out of ammunition we used axes and clubs. We killed with punji stakes and deadfalls. We killed with stones and with our hands. We took heads, we cut bodies, we painted our faces with blood. But then the war changed. Aircraft started bombing the hills around us. Troops penetrated our area. Not tribesmen, but real soldiers from other places. A helicopter began bringing an officer once a month to evaluate our activities. We didn't like it. And then I got caught in an ambush and chewed up by an automatic weapon. I didn't know anything for three weeks. They told me in the hospital that my people had refused to hand me over and had wanted to kill the crew and burn the helicopter. The pilot finally convinced them I'd only die if I weren't evacuated. He promised them a replacement, but they still wouldn't let him take me until he swore he'd bring me back as soon as I'd recovered.

'The doctor said I was as close to dead as you could get without being put in a coffin. They did pretty good – sometimes I get winded, and rain makes certain things ache, is all. But they forced a medical on me anyway, and they put me back on the street.'

In his mind Russ saw the crippled twenty-year-old trapped in the alien city, a damaged predator shrieking its baffled anguish, maddened by its chains. But now, at this moment, he felt no horror of that creature, only a sad and affectionate compassion, and a kind of peace. With his eyes closed and his cheek upon the rug, and one hand resting in security upon a part of Beth's warm and passive body, he talked, or he thought, about himself.

'I worked half a dozen jobs in as many months. I couldn't talk to anyone. I locked myself in my apartment for days at a time and ate out of cans and sat in the dark. I got a gun and I held up a liquor store. And then another one. And it was all right then, I was living a life that almost seemed real. But they busted me on my fifth job, and the best my lawyer could get was three to ten on a plea bargain. I did three, was out a year, then went back in for burglary. I did five that time, and I knew that if I dropped again they wouldn't let me out till I was an old man. But that's what I was headed for, I still couldn't make it. Then I took a job at a dog school, and...' His hands moved and cupped a few inches apart, as if he were touching a dog's head. 'I found something in me that would work. This thing with dogs. I train them. That's what I do.'

'What?' Beth murmured.

'I said that's what I do.'

'What do you do?'

'I train dogs.' He opened his eyes.

Beth was looking at her hands, smiling at some inner self. She moved her eyes to him. 'That's truly wonderful,' she said with love.

Russ laughed. She did too. I'm getting by, Russ thought. It's all right.

They spent the night in a half sleep, lyrical and seemingly endless, touching each other with their hands and bodies, and once Russ thought he had entered her, but wasn't sure, and even if he had it was merely an extension of their touching, and when he was coming awake in the morning he felt cleansed and renewed, and he kissed Beth very gently because they had made love, real love.

By the time he reached the school, that had vanished, and what he remembered of the long night made him feel foolish and ashamed, living dope dreams, and he was irritated with himself.

Cerberus would handle emergencies at any time, but tried to schedule most of its interviews and consultations on one day, at intervals of two and three weeks. Training programs were explained, prospective owners were drawn out in detail as to what they wanted in a dog, and suitable breeds were suggested to them, behavior problems discussed, breed and show advice given, general maintenance covered. It was depressing how little most people knew about the animals with whom they shared their lives.

Today was a consultation day. By early afternoon Russ had done seven interviews and Wylie six. Three more were on the books, and one of these had already arrived and was waiting.

Wylie was currently engaged with a Mrs Gardner, a pretty pleasant woman in her mid-thirties with graying hair. They were seated at one of the desks in the front training room.

'Does Mutzi destroy anything when she's on the furniture?' Wylie asked.

'Oh no.'

'Good. She doesn't urinate or defecate on anything, does she?'

Mrs Gardner was offended.

'Some do,' Wylie said in a conciliatory tone. 'They're spoiled. Before you're five minutes out the door, they're up on your bed, soiling it. We call them revenge ... uh ... piddlers.'

Mrs Gardner shook her head, placated. 'Not Mutzi. She just likes to snooze when we're gone. On the bed, on the couch. I wouldn't really mind if it didn't get everything dirty and scatter hairs all about.'

'Does she have a towel or a blanket that she knows is her own bed?'

117

'Yes, but she ignores it when we're not home.'

'You and I probably would too. A couch is definitely more attractive. What we have to do is convince her otherwise. I want you to buy six mousetraps. When you and your husband are leaving the apartment, set the traps and place them on the couch and the bed before you go.'

'But she'll set them off!'

Wylie nodded. 'That's the idea. Don't worry, she won't be hurt. It feels about the same as a medium-strength pinch. It's the surprise, the startlement, that we want. Since no one's around to stop her, we have to create a piece of furniture that will stand up for itself, one that fights back.'

Mrs Gardner laughed.

'If your couch snapped at you every time you tried to sit on it, what would you do? Mutzi's going to come up with the same answer. Try to arrange to go out four nights running, more if you can, and put the traps out every time. You can't teach a dog anything if you're inconsistent. It's cruel, too, because a dog can't make any sense of a sometimes "yes" and sometimes "no" situation. It only confuses and eventually depresses him. You have to convince Mutzi the furniture will attack her *every* time she tries to get on it. Even if you think the first experience or two have cured her, keep setting the traps for a solid month. That's enough for ninety-nine out of a hundred dogs. If she's that one hard-nose holdout, stick at it for another two months. She'll learn to love sleeping on the floor.'

Wylie had to reassure Mrs Gardner that the mousetraps would not injure Mutzi before she thanked him and left.

Pat told him, 'You've got Mr Elmer Hochner waiting for a consultation on a guard dog. A writer from *New York* magazine called. He's doing an article on urban dogs and wants to talk to you. And a Mr Raymond Finn's office called, please call back.'

'Ask Hochner if he can wait a little longer, will you? Apologize and tell him we're jammed up. I'll be with him in about ten minutes.'

Wylie went to the soundproof office in the back, pushed the button on an open line, and dialed Raymond Finn's number. Finn's secretary put him through.

'Mr Lincoln,' Finn said. 'Will you by chance be free to perform a service for me three or four months from now? It would involve a week, perhaps two, but no more, of your time, and a trip to the West Coast.'

'Possibly,' Wylie said. 'It's difficult to predict my schedule that far in advance.'

'I would like to know now. Complicated planning revolves about the question. Incidentally, I've obtained some information concerning that matter we discussed.'

'Terrific,' Wylie said. He paused. 'Thumbing through my book, Mr Finn, I *do* think I could arrange a free week or two for you.'

'I'm delighted. I may take that as a commitment, then?'

'Assuming the design of your project is sound, yes.'

'Excellent. I hope it will be helpful to you to learn that one of the items on your summary was recently sold. A rather lovely seventeenth-century Hungarian brooch of rubies and chased gold.'

'Who was the seller?' Wylie asked.

'A professional salesman. Ethics prohibit me from naming him, but I can tell you that he acquired two other items from the same consignment. Unfortunately, neither was the one you are interested in. He sold the brooch without knowing its provenance. When he discovered it, he became very disturbed. He has destroyed the other two items.'

'Can you at least tell me in what part of the country he's located?'

There was a moment's silence. 'The Midwest.'

Wylie tensed. 'Chicago?'

'The Midwest, Mr Lincoln, the Midwest.'

'Thanks, Mr Finn. You've helped me.'

'Would you like the name of the buyer?'

Wylie decided he did not particularly care for Raymond Finn. 'Yes, I would,' he said.

'She's a former client of my own. We had a disagreement four years ago, and as a result she retained some merchandise I had given her to evaluate, but she refused to pay my bill. It was large, and still remains uncollected. Happily, I give you Grace Tennant.'

'Thank you.'

'Certainly. Why don't you call my secretary soon and make an appointment. I'd like to discuss my project with you.'

'I will.'

'Very good. Good-bye, Mr Lincoln.'

'Good-bye, Mr Finn.'

Wylie hung up. He lit a cigarette, looked at the phone, and thought.

CHAPTER SEVEN

Wylie finished the cigarette, dialed United Campaigns, and asked for Raphaela Bracey.

'Hi,' he said. 'Just called to let you know that the seventeenth would be good.'

'Wonderful. We're firm for the seventeenth. You're a dear.'

'I've always thought so. Can you tell me something about Grace Tennant?'

'Eminent counsel, the wife thereof?'

'That's the one.'

'Yecch. They're a pair. He wanted to defend Charles Manson and was upset that the poor boy couldn't afford the fee. His lady is a charmer; she has a steel trap for a cunt.'

'How does she feel about jewelry?'

'Why does that interest you?'

'Don't ask questions, you owe me a favor.'

'And this is it?'

'You've got to be kidding. This is five percent of it.'

'Ten,' Raphaela said.

'Ten,' Wylie agreed in exasperation. 'Now give.'

'I really don't know, dear. She doesn't wear much. But I'll have one of the girls pull her file. Hang on a sec.'

She put him on hold, came back in a moment, and said the file was on the way. They chatted. She told him Victor Lamorena had called.

'He wanted to hire my Christian. He's a very evasive man, Mr Lamorena, but I sensed he's in desperate need of creative bookkeeping. He doesn't see Christian till I get the whole story. And you can bet your ass that if Christian works any miracles for him, Mr Lamorena's union is

121

going to adopt a pet charity. I think an educational complex for Pacific Northwest Indians would suit them, don't you?'

The file came, and Wylie could hear Raphaela making neutral little noises as she read, and the sound of pages being turned.

'Ah yes,' Raphaela said. 'She *is* a jewelry freak. Not for wearing, collecting. Exclusively antiques. Her collection has been variously estimated at three hundred thousand, half a million, and one million two. Dear, dear, the pastimes of the idle rich. Is that what you wanted?'

'It's good enough. Thanks.'

'My. Enter jewelry collectors and labor racketeers into the life of Mr Lincoln. What *is* it that you do?'

'If you ever need a dog trained, I'll show you.'

'Your file is growing thicker, but it's still not providing any answers. When I get them, Wylie, I have the feeling that you're going to be mine.'

'That would be extortion.'

'Accommodation, dear.'

Wylie laughed. 'You should be in jail.'

'I was once. But that was during my flaming youth, and under another name. Bye now, baby.'

Wylie checked to see who wasn't busy, found Harold between dogs, and sent him up to a nearby bookstore. Mr Hochner owned a cocker spaniel bitch that, to the embarrassment of the family, was always sitting and then dragging her genital region across the carpet. Wylie told him this action was not sexual, but usually an attempt to relieve pressure from clogged anal glands. An infestation of certain worms might also be responsible. Mr Hochner should take his pet to a veterinarian, who could eliminate the problem speedily and simply. Cerberus never refunded consultation fees, but when a problem was resolved in a few minutes the remaining time was devoted to any aspect of training or care the client wished to discuss. Wylie and Mr Hochner talked about vitamin supplements and corrective measures for his cocker's hole-digging, which had made his back yard look like a battle-field.

Afterward Wylie spent ten minutes leafing through the two Joseph Sucher novels Harold had brought back. It confirmed what he'd remembered: Sucher was a master of regional dialect and idiom.

Finn's information, supported by Raphaela's file on Grace Tennant, had some of the Chasteen take in the hands of a Midwestern fence. Sucher had asserted that one of the men had a Chicago voice.

Chicago, then. Wylie began to hum the 'Toreador Song,' which he frequently did when he thought he was about to close his fingers around a key.

Charlie's was a grubby bar on Hudson Street. The tin ceiling had been painted white and was peeling. The floor was dirty. The long bar itself belonged in a museum. A constant slip of shoes kept the brass footrail gleaming. No one was ever pressured to drink up and reorder, and everyone was known to the degree that the other patrons were confident he wasn't a fink. Strangers were not welcome.

A good fight broke out an hour after Russ had sat down. Johnny Keogh and some ironheaded truck jockey started bludgeoning each other like big farm boys under the eye of a city scout. They broke a table. Betting was heavy. Jay Beel, the quiet, tattooed bartender with heavy arms, came halfway around the bar and watched them mordantly. The jockey backed Keogh to the bar and caught him in the groin with a knee. Keogh doubled, but managed to move his head enough so that the next knee only grazed him instead of smashing his nose. He straightened up gasping, with a knife in his hand. The jockey stepped back. Keogh poised for a slash. Jay Beel slipped a weighted leather sap from his back pocket, moved quickly, and tapped Keogh behind the ear.

Keogh collapsed. The jockey rushed to stomp him, but Beel interposed himself between the two. 'It's all over,' he said.

The jockey sized up Beel and balled his hands into fists. Beel waited, loose and relaxed.

A man at the bar said, 'Don't try, Tom. Believe me.'

The jockey hesitated, then lowered his hands. Beel put the sap away. He picked up Keogh's knife, and pocketed that, too. He righted the broken table.

'A new top is twenty-nine fifty,' he said to the jockey. 'The base is okay. So your share is fourteen seventy-five.'

'Why the hell should I –'

'Your share is fourteen seventy-five,' Jay said.

The man looked in the bill compartment of his wallet and showed it to Jay. 'I only got the eight bucks.'

Jay took the wallet, went through the photo shields, and removed the man's union card. 'I'll keep this,' he said. 'You can bring the bread tonight or tomorrow night and get it back. Now, split and cool down.'

The man nodded. 'But she wasn't, was she?'

'Who wasn't what?'

'Ida Lupino. A dyke. He said she was.'

'I don't know,' Jay said.

The jockey left with a friend. Jay went through Keogh's pockets and took fourteen dollars and seventy-five cents. He had two men carry Keogh into a back room, where he would stay until he woke up.

The bar settled down. Bill Hamling, who managed a Times Square massage parlor, resumed his conversation with Russ.

'So I figure it had to be niggers that did it,' Hamling said. 'They haul ass back to Harlem and dig in, and there's *no* way you're going to find 'em. Half them jiveass young bucks don't even exist. They get born at home with no record or under a fake name in a Welfare hospital, they never register for the draft, they never get a Social Security, and they don't pay no taxes. Man, there must be a hundred thousand spookin' around with no face, no number, no name. Had to be niggers. They're the only ones that can disappear like that.'

Later someone else told Russ that he *knew* the men were trained Cuban exiles up from Florida, trying to bankroll raids on Castro. And after that an old con whose big joke was to bite into an apple or a sandwich and leave his three false front teeth sticking there said it had been off-duty cops who'd learned about the party when Chasteen had asked that the area patrol car check periodically on the expensive cars that would be parked along the street.

From Charlie's Russ went to a shooting gallery on Delancey Street and sat talking with Larry Payne and Larry's friends, who drifted in and out and were openly contemptuous of the customers. It was a busy night, and Larry kept leaving the conversation to tube off arms, to slip the needle in and ease the plunger down. Larry was a vulture. He lived on panic, selling his powder by the single spike at double the street price. When the junkies ran out, or missed their buy, or their contacts had vanished, they'd try other ways first, but sooner or later their mouths would dry and the shakes would start, the turkey's first cackle, and then they'd come to Larry. In many the big arm veins had collapsed, and they shot in the legs or between the fingers. One, with a hawkish parole officer who frequently checked for tracks, had to take it in the inner flesh of his anus. Most left then, but some went to the mattresses on the living room floor. Once when Larry was hung up in the bathroom, Russ shot up a fortyish Spanish guy with a faded Pachuco tattoo on his hand.

At Larry's he was told: 'It was Washington Willie. He's only twenty-one, but a smooth planner and mover. The problem is, he's some kind o' crazy. He wigs once in a while, and pistol-whips somebody or cuts 'em. Last June he pushed his best partner out of a car at seventy miles

per and splattered him all over the road. It was Willie –
that same sharpness, and then that crazy shootin'.'

Larry didn't think so. 'Those dudes are at the bottom
of the river. Whoever fronted the bread and planned it,
he freaked over what happened. He put those boys down
to protect himself. Gonna be a long time before he goes
adventurin' again.'

Russ left when three of Larry's friends decided to
gangbang a sixteen-year-old from Queens who was so
spaced on a mattress that all she could do was smile and
dribble spit.

He went to the One-Eye Inn on Avenue B. A numbers
runner told him that Washington Willie had been shot
to death in Pittsburgh last month by the girlfriend of the
guy he'd thrown from the car.

Tommy Bernstein, who'd done two falls for jewel robbery himself, said, 'Man, that was nobody but Pete Itzler.
I worked with him a couple of times, and that was his
style all the way. Poor bastard, he must've teamed with
some speed-eater that blew apart and opened up. Pete
knew how to use artillery for effect, but he was too smart
to blow away a solid and have the big bitch hanging over
his head the rest of his life. These fuckin' kids and their
chemicals, they'll get you screwed every time.'

Russ didn't get home until two. He'd picked up several
leads, but doubted that any would prove out. He didn't
make the circuits much any more, only enough to keep
his channels open. The night had depressed him.

Beth was watching television. She looked up and nodded, but didn't say anything. She was wearing the crepe
shirt he'd given her and her old jeans. The suede pants
were crumpled in a corner. Russ sat beside her and gave
her the box with the boots he'd bought earlier in the day.
She looked at the box several moments before she opened
it. The boots were soft brown leather, shin high.

'Thanks,' she said.

'You want to try them and see if they fit?'

'Okay.'

She put them on and walked across the room and back without taking her eyes from the television. She sat down again. 'They're all right.'

'What's wrong?' he asked.

'Nothing. I just want to watch this.'

'Look,' Russ said. 'I'm going to be working the next couple of nights, and I won't be home for dinner.' He gave her thirty dollars. 'So here. Pick up some food for the place, or eat out if you want.'

'I don't need your money.'

'We're pretty low on stuff. There's only some cans left.'

She took the money and stuffed it into her pocket.

'You're sure there's nothing wrong?'

'Hey.' She gestured at the television. 'I'm right in the middle of this. Do you mind?'

'I'm beat,' Russ said. 'I'm going to sack out, okay?'

'Right.'

'See you.'

'Right.'

Russ and Wylie caucused in the back office on Friday.

'I still have Frank Trajewski and Herman Gainor to run down,' Wylie said, 'but I don't think they'll be worth any more than the others were.'

'You get word on that Badillio guy?'

'He's been locked up in Danbury for the last eighteen months.'

'Fuck, he sounded good to me.'

'All we have is Chicago.' Wylie tugged at his ear in annoyance. It was bothering him to have come up with so little. He was beginning to take it personally, which was not a good thing to do. 'Schattner's package didn't have the out-of-towners – they hadn't come in yet. If I ask for the Chicago list, he'll freeze us out and be on his way.'

'A list wouldn't help, anyway. These guys don't have priors, at least not for this kind of job. They'd have been run to ground already if they had sheets. We have to work backward from the fence.'

'I pulled some names on that. But even if one is our man, he won't spill unless we really stick it to him.'

'I've been slogging through so much shit these last nights, I'd like a chance to kick some out of the way.'

'That won't work with this guy. He's big enough to have the money and contacts to come back at you, and you can't watch your back seven days a week.'

'Maybe. But first we have to find out *who* he is.'

'You know anybody in Chicago?'

'One or two, I think. I'll check.'

'You might have to go out there.'

'Okay.'

'There's still something wrong about this one,' Wylie said. 'But I can't get hold of it.'

'Sooner or later. In the end we all get eaten by the same worms.'

Wylie looked at Russ. 'You came down on Gene pretty hard about that beagle.'

Russ shrugged. 'He was handling it like it was a cow.'

'Not that bad.'

Russ didn't answer.

'Why don't you lay off over the weekend and relax?'

'I got a couple of places to try tonight. But then I'll cool it until Monday.'

'Good. Shack up with that Rukeyser chick or something.'

Russ frowned.

'Hell,' Wylie said. 'It's no secret, is it? She's been calling you twice a day.'

'She's a killer groupie. She likes blood.'

'Oh. Well, there are some good movies around.'

'Maybe I'll go to the country. Any of the school cars free?'

'Take the Ford.'

'Okay.' Russ stood. 'You're probably right about Gene. Maybe I'll talk to him.'

After work Russ went with Frank to Entry House, on West Eighteenth Street. Entry House had been founded by veterans of the Fortune Society and Esalen; it was a halfway house for released convicts, a shelter and mutual-support group while they made the transition back to society. Russ had served time in Attica with one of the directors.

A dozen men were lounging in the living room. Russ mentioned the Chasteen robbery and triggered a round of speculation and argument.

'Professionals mah ass!' said a black man with a shaved head. He went to his feet and strode up and down the room, glaring at the others. 'Professional don' never start shootin' unless he get cornered by the Man. Even then, he most always lay down his piece and take his time. Professional goin' t' gun-whip a dude who smarts off, or fire a load into the ceiling an' start the shit runnin' t' prove he the man on the highchair, but he *ain't* goin' t' off no citizen. Not if he a pro, he ain't.'

Russ's hand moved over Frank's broad head for several moments. 'Clover,' he said, 'you are one hundred percent right.'

'You bet your lily white I am.'

Russ left and took a cab to Wylie's. The driver told him about the two Irish setters he had at home. If a New York cabbie stopped for you when you had a big dog in tow, and failed to demand extra money or threaten to sue you if your dog so much as farted, then you could be sure he owned a dog himself, and would talk about it with all the enthusiasm of a man describing his favorite grand-child.

Russ asked the doorman to ring Wylie and tell him Russ was on his way up. He heeled Frank to a corner of the lobby and dropped his keys on the carpet. 'Place,' he said. Frank lay down; he'd hold his position until Russ returned, even if that were not until the next morning.

Wylie opened the door in bare feet. He wore tight brown pants and a linen shirt open several buttons down. He held a bourbon in his hand. 'What's happenin'?'

Ahab pressed his nose against Russ's leg. He sniffed deeply several times, then growled and circled the small vestibule. The armed truce between Ahab and Frank did not extend to each other's homes, their inviolable caves.

Russ walked in. 'We've been coming at this thing from the wrong direction. It wasn't a –' He smelled perfume. 'You have company?'

'Yeah. Go on into the kitchen. I'll be with you in a second.'

Satisfied that Frank was nowhere about, Ahab returned. He accompanied Russ into the kitchen and sat down beside him. He pawed at Russ's leg, wanting his chest scratched. Russ hunkered down and massaged the animal's heavy chest. Ahab flattened his ears. His mouth opened, and his tongue hung out. The dog liked Russ, and didn't hold his unfortunate association with Frank against him.

Wylie appeared, closing the door behind him. He'd brought a Scotch for Russ. They sat at the table.

Russ sipped, then said, 'Listen, man. It wasn't a jewelry score – it was a hit.'

Wylie's forehead creased.

'That's why it's been so off the wall.' Russ told Wylie what Clover had said. 'I thought about it, and the dude was right. Part right, anyway. They were pros, but they were *contract* pros. Everyone's been looking in the wrong place.'

Wylie fooled with the thin water ring his glass had left on the table. 'I like it. I like it a lot. This way we'd have the boost as a decoy. Too big and too well-planned for it to occur to anyone that it was something other than a boost. And hell, the take was enough to meet the price, or sweeten it up a lot.'

'Nothing went wrong. These people knew exactly what they were doing. That's why we get fifteen different versions of how the shooting started.' Ahab pawed Russ, who resumed scratching the dog's chest. 'Pros *don't* shoot – unless they're professional shooters. If something *had* rattled them, one corpse would have been enough. But they kept banging away, and that leads us to –'

'Right. With one person down, some flashy cop is liable to say, "Hey, let's be wild and try it out as a murder." So you get yourself two bodies and three wounded. No one sees murder in that. On the other hand, we have four hit men. That's overkill, and expensive, too.'

'Call it one, maybe even two. The rest are dressing. Bona fide jewel men without records. Guys who thought it was a straight score. You don't have to pay them. And they'd be so tight after what happened, they'd just take their cut and run. Get out of the country.'

'Better,' Wylie said. 'Let's play with it. We have Hollander and Greer dead, but maybe the boys missed the kill, and one of the wounded was supposed to be the dead one – that's Havemeyer, Sucher, or Lamorena.'

'Or maybe someone who didn't pick up any lead at all.'

'Too depressing. There were nearly eighty-five people there.'

A knock sounded on the kitchen door.

'Yes?' Wylie said.

Freya, the blonde from the Danish consulate, looked in. 'I thought you were going to be only a few moments.' She was pouting prettily.

'The UN Chief of Building Security called,' Wylie said. 'I'm sorry, baby, but he wants four guard dogs by Monday, and we have to work a few things out.'

'How long will it take?'

'Not too long. But a while yet.'

'What am I supposed to do?'

'How about taking Ahab for a walk?'

'In the park?'

'Sure.'

'It's dangerous at night.'

'Stay to the lighted areas. But not with him it isn't. Here.' Wylie slipped a leash from a hook on the door, fastened the snap to Ahab's chain, and handed the looped end to Freya. He placed a hand on Freya's shoulder and said, 'Ahab, protect her!'

Ahab cocked his head quizzically.

'Would he really?' Freya asked.

'Tear their arms off and eat their heads for you.'

'Don't I have to give him a command?'

'He's a specialist. He knows what to do.'

Ahab would attack automatically if Wylie were assaulted, but under all other circumstances was a command-only dog. Were Wylie to tell him, 'Guard,' he would guard whatever he had been told to – golf club or human being – but his only emotional involvement would be to please Wylie. Wylie was damned if he would send the dog out with Freya cocked and ready to go off. It was like giving someone a hand grenade: Sooner or later some fool would detonate it. Besides, he had no real concern for Freya's safety. Ahab's massiveness and confident manner were sufficient to discourage trouble.

Freya left, pleased and flattered. Ahab looked ruefully over his shoulder at Wylie as he walked out with the girl.

Wylie poured fresh drinks. They sat in the living room. 'Mrs Radford Greer,' Wylie said. 'Why would you want to kill her?'

'She's an ugly old bag, and she won't give me a divorce. My twenty-five-year-old mistress drives me out of my senile gourd, but she's threatening to leave unless I marry her.'

'Or I'm an anxious heir, and I know *Mr* Radford Greer

doesn't have long to go, so I'm clearing the competition.'

'Or I'm that crazy forty-year-old faggot kid of hers who dumped the soup bowl over her head at the mayor's birthday. I've finally gone completely psycho.'

'I'm the maid, and I've been stealing securities from the wall safe and she's going to turn me in.'

'I'm Radford's first, second, or third wife, and I hate her because she's got him now.'

'Julius Hollander.'

'I got something big on one of my partners.'

'I'm standing in the way of a raiding cartel.'

'What's that?' Russ asked.

'A group that buys companies, sucks out the assets, and leaves them in ruins. The stockholders get jigged. I lost twelve thousand dollars in one company that way last year.'

'Or I'm his wife and he's a miserly bastard and I'm tired of an allowance and want the whole works.'

'Or he's going to divorce me and I don't want to lose the pie.'

'He's one of your raiders. I was wiped out and I'm getting revenge.'

'I borrowed a million from the Organization, made the wrong moves, and couldn't pay it back.'

They put in another quarter-hour on Hollander and Greer. 'How about Lamorena?' Russ said. 'He's a natural – a power struggle in the Organization. They can call on the talent for this kind of job.'

Freya returned. 'He's wonderful,' she said, patting Ahab's head. 'How much does such an animal cost?'

'Five or six thousand. More if I campaigned him on the show circuit.'

'*Mein Gott!*'

'You can get a stable, very-well-trained one for fifteen hundred to two thousand.'

'I could buy a car for that,' Freya said unhappily.

Russ and Wylie retired to the kitchen again. Freya

didn't bother to conceal her displeasure.

Wylie said, 'Gang war sounds good, but try this. Lesley Marecek is fed up with him, but knows he'll never let her go. Somehow we're dupes in the scheme. It's very baroque.'

'Sometimes you have too much imagination. Leave it at a gang war for now. How about Joseph Sucher?'

'I'm a long-haired crazy who thinks he's a false prophet selling out the Revolution. Or I'm a oil millionaire protecting the beacon of capitalism from that Jew-commie-bastard. Or a crew-cut ex-Marine preserving democracy and the American way.'

'Or any one of his six ex-wives, especially the one he threw off the balcony in Los Angeles.'

'Or God's Avenger striking a Christian blow for morality. On Sucher, it's open season.'

'What about this Havemen, or whatever it is?'

'Havemeyer, Mrs Alice. She was at the party with someone else's husband. You might make a case against that guy's wife, or her own husband. But those two were in bed together the same night, and everybody seems happy with the arrangement. An esthete might take her off simply because she's in bad taste, but I don't know anything else about her.'

They went back to Hannah Greer and started again. They were interrupted some time later by Freya, who banged open the door without knocking. She had her coat in her hand.

'I understand why you're such a good trainer,' she said to Wylie. 'It's because you are a dog yourself. I do not thank you for your hospitality. Good night.' She walked out.

'Wait, Freya!' Wylie went after her.

Russ petted Ahab. Ahab lifted one leg slightly so Russ could scratch a spot the dog particularly liked.

'You're a good fellow,' Russ said fondly. 'What do you make of all this, huh?'

Ahab sighed.

Wylie returned. 'I have just received a detailed analysis of my monumental male-chauvinist piggery. I prostrated myself with repentance, which satisfied her, but I promised I'd only spend another five minutes with you.'

Russ shrugged.

'So in effect,' Wylie said, 'we have five people who don't invite murder much more or much less than most other persons do. Barring Sucher's capacity to give people ulcers, and Lamorena's occupational hazards. We can look at the obvious – mates, heirs, and business rivals – but unless it's right on the surface, I don't think it's worth much. Too broad a field.'

'I'll check the local shooters for one who disappeared after the job.'

'And any out-of-towners who were noticed around. Particularly Chicago men.'

'Uh huh.'

'Grace Tennant banks at First National City. I know a guy there, and I might get a look at her account. Not smart to pay a fence by check, but people like her don't use cash much.'

'Give me the stuff on that con who works for the caterer.'

'He came through clean.'

'Yeah, but he's still a con, and we're running a new game. I want to look at that junkie kid, too.'

Behind the door, Freya called, 'You have thirty seconds left.'

Wylie opened the door and kissed her nose. 'And I don't even need them,' he said.

Frank wriggled his stub tail when Russ stepped out of the elevator. Russ said, 'Okay!'

Frank sprang up and bounded to him. Russ petted him. 'Good boy.' Catching Ahab's scent, Frank raised the hair on his back. He walked around Russ, sniffing, and went to the elevator doors. Russ let him satisfy himself that

Ahab was not lurking about, then said, 'Keys. Take.'

Frank trotted to the keys, picked them up, and brought them to Russ. 'Good goof.' Russ scratched the dog's ear. 'Thank you.' Russ habitually thanked dogs, excused himself to them, and explained things to them. He extended identical courtesy to men and dogs, but thought dogs worthier of it.

He walked Frank through the park to the West Side, where there were more gypsy cabs. Gypsies hustled harder than yellows, and weren't so finicky about picking up dogs. The few people he saw in the park were walking German shepherds, Dobermans, Great Danes, or other big dogs. No one else felt comfortable there at night.

The superintendent's door was on the first floor, adjacent to the stairs. Approaching, Russ heard the peephole cover sliding back. A chain rattled; there was the sound of a police bar-lock being removed. Mrs Lewandowski, who was as much the super as her husband, opened the door. She beckoned to Russ, her face troubled.

'Mr Turner,' she said. 'You're a good tenant and a nice boy. I don't know how to say this. This girl you have in your apartment, she's doing bad things.'

'What do you mean, Mrs Lewandowski?'

The woman clasped her hands. 'Ah. Ah. My husband and me, you know we're not nosy, we don't care. We live our lives, and we let others live theirs. So long as everybody respects everybody else's privacy. It's a nice clean building here. Everybody don't bother nobody else. But this girl, she had *five* different men to your apartment today. Five that I know of, after Mrs Moskowitz upstairs complained and I started to watch. And the sounds that went into the courtyard!' She shook her head as if to cast them from her memory. 'We can't have that going on in this building. But I don't want to do nothing myself, just talk to you. You're a nice boy. I know you'll fix it.'

Russ felt weary. 'I'm sorry if it caused you any trouble. I'll straighten it out.'

'I got nothing against her. We all do what we have to, and she can live here if she wants. But just she shouldn't bring the men in here.'

'It'll be all right.'

'I'm sorry to have to talk to you like this.'

'I know. It's okay. Don't feel bad.'

'Thank you, Mr Turner.'

Russ went upstairs. Beth was in the living room, listening to the phonograph. She was wearing a gray bulky-knit sweater and black ski pants. There were half a dozen new record albums on the couch, and around them shreds of the cellophane with which they'd been sealed.

'Hi,' Russ said.

'Hi.'

He sat next to her on the floor, and leaned against the couch. Frank lay down beside him. He stroked the dog's back.

'The super's wife stopped me in the hall,' Russ said. 'She told me you ran a series of guys through here today.'

'What business is it of hers?' Beth said.

Frank rolled over, and Russ scratched the dog's stomach. 'How come you did that?'

She turned off the phonograph and took the record from the turntable and put it back in its jacket. 'Okay,' she said. 'So I'll split.'

'I just asked you how come you did it?'

'I needed some stuff.'

'I would've gotten it for you.'

'I don't want anything from you.'

'Why not?'

'Because I don't want to owe anything to any*body*.'

'You wouldn't owe me anything.'

'Sure. I know that. But after a while you'd start thinking I did. Everyone does.'

'Look, you don't have to do this.'

'You bet your balls I don't. I don't have to do a single

thing. But I pay my own way, and nobody lays a claim on me.'

'If you want some bread, I can get you easy work at a fancy kennel I know. They have a dog-walking service, and they like to hire pretty girls.'

'What would I owe you for that?'

'Nothing.'

'If I walked out of here, you'd still get me the job, right? My ass.'

'I'll pay you,' Russ said. 'You can do the cooking and the cleaning up, shop and take the laundry out and stuff.'

'You didn't mention fucking. Aren't you going to pay me for fucking you?'

'No,' Russ said. 'I'm not.'

'But if I stay I have to fuck you, huh?'

'No.'

'You're telling me that I won't owe you anything.'

'Just don't bring guys up here, that's all. That messes up where I live, and I don't want to go looking for a new place.'

'But we each do whatever we want. No holds.'

'That's right.'

'I'll think about it.'

'Do that.' Russ stood.

'Where are you going?'

'I have some work to do.'

Russ went into the bedroom and sat down at the desk with Schattner's material. Peter Ferenbach, the adolescent junkie, didn't show Russ anything. He was reported to be on methadone maintenance. Russ thought that worth verifying himself. It wasn't hard to beat a methadone program, and if the kid was doing that and his habit was big, someone could have pressured him. He returned to Emsley, the ex-con.

Beth came into the room. 'I think I'll go out to a movie,' she said. 'You want to tag along?'

'Not particularly.'

138

She was surprised. 'Really?'

'Have a good time,' he said.

She looked at him curiously before she left.

Russ closed his eyes. He rested his head in his hands, elbows on the desk top. He didn't think about anything. Frank set his jaw atop one of Russ's shoes. Russ petted him and went back to Emsley.

George Emsley did look clean, but Russ wasn't interested in that. He only wanted a way in to the man. He found it on the third page. Emsley played poker regularly on Tuesday nights. He played at Terry Butler's apartment, on West Seventy-First Street. Russ knew Terry a little from the bars.

He got Terry's number from Information and dialed it.

'Yeah?'

'Hi, Terry. Russ Turner.'

'Hey, Russ. What's happenin'?'

'Pretty much the drill, a little somethin' here and there.'

'That's what keeps it goin'.'

'Uh huh. Listen man, I'm in a game that's fallin' apart, and I'm lookin' for somethin' new. I heard at Charlie's that you got one goin'. Any empty chairs?'

'We got a group of regulars, but there's a little room sometimes. It ain't a high-roller's play, though – half, one, and two.'

'So who's got more these days?'

'Baby, sometimes I ain't even got that.'

'What kind of cards?'

'Pure. Five draw, five and seven straight. No wild cards, no high-lows.'

'Any bet limits?'

'Yup, top of a dollar until there's a picture showing or until after the draw. No more than three ups on a bet. Sandbagging's okay.'

'Sounds cool.'

'No sharps in here, Russ. This is a clean game, and we're keepin' it that way.'

'Sharp isn't my style.'

'Just wanted to let you know.'

'Can I get in?'

'Well, I don't know for this week. It depends on who shows and how the cards run. You can drop by and sit and see if it opens. We play on Tuesday, seven-thirty.'

'I'll be there. Thanks, man.'

'Sure thing. See you.'

When Beth returned from the movie, Russ asked her if she wanted to drive to the country with him tomorrow.

'Not particularly,' she said, echoing his earlier words.

'Really?' he said.

'Have a good time,' she said.

They smiled at each other.

Russ rose at five Saturday morning, cabbed to the school with Frank, and picked up the Ford. The sun was bright, and the throughway nearly empty. He was in Woodstock a little after eight. Few of the shops were open yet, but Mill Stream Road, the main thoroughfare, was already thick with kids: shaggy, shabby, sexual, life as style. He turned right at the two-centuries-old Dutch Reformed Church, was on Byrdcliffe Road in a few minutes and drove to the summit of Meade Mountain. He pulled off onto a small area that had been cleared of brush. Cerberus had trained a guard dog for a Woodstock realtor three years ago. A good, solid working dog. The appreciative realtor had offered Wylie and Russ blanket access to the big, undeveloped forest tract he owned any time they wanted to break away from the city and relax. Russ had camped there three or four times.

He roamed the woods with Frank until late in the afternoon. Frank was ecstatic. He raced, leaped deadfalls, plunged into brush, barked wildly. They stalked small game together. Russ removed his shoes and socks and rolled up his pants legs and splashed with the dog until his feet and ankles were numb. Then he sat on the bank and smoked and watched Frank make a fool of himself trying to catch minnows in shallows. The dog grew indignant and outraged over the elusive silver flashes. They were both tired by the time they returned to the car. They drove home in contentment.

Beth wasn't there. Russ fed himself and the dog, then stretched out on the living room floor and listened to music. Frank nestled against Russ's side and snored peacefully. Russ stroked the dog. At eleven, he took Frank out for a final walk. He soaked in a hot tub for half an hour. He went to bed and fell asleep immediately, and didn't wake until twelve hours later, when Beth, sitting on the edge of the bed and holding a cup of fresh coffee, for him, shook his shoulder.

Beth was in good spirits. She'd scored some grass last night and had already smoked a thin joint this morning. Humming, she cooked bacon and eggs for him, cleared the table when he finished, and washed his plate and silverware and put them in the drainer to dry.

She offered him a joint, and he declined. 'Man, you have got to loosen up,' she said.

She sat on his lap and played with his hair. 'Would you like to go to the planetarium with me? And if I say *please*, will you say something besides "Not particularly"?'

'The planetarium?'

'It's supposed to be an absolutely astral trip if you do it stoned. They've got this kind of show in a big dark room where some machine puts stars all over the ceiling, and zap! you're in outer space. Please?'

'Okay, but I'm not up to getting stoned.'

'Then just hold my hand while we're there, huh?'

Beth put herself where she wanted to be before they left the apartment. The show overwhelmed her. She sat through it slouched deep in her seat, her head hanging over the back, eyes wide and unblinking, mouth open, tiny gasps of wonder exploding past her lips.

She was subdued and quiet on the subway back home, and remained that way for several hours. She smoked more. Sometimes she came to Russ and leaned against him or held him, and once she took his face in her hands and brushed his lips tenderly with her own.

In the evening he sat on the couch, and she lay down and rested her head in his lap. He stroked her hair and massaged her temples, feathering her cheeks and closed eyes with his fingertips. He tried to get her to talk about herself – because he had talked to her, even if she hadn't heard, and it had made him feel better.

But she said, 'Yesterday's gone and tomorrow isn't here yet, so they don't mean anything.'

Later, but still before they had removed their clothes and gone to bed, with her hands lovingly upon him, he said gently, 'The only time you become affectionate is when you're stoned, do you know that?'

'I know,' she murmured. 'God, I know.'

CHAPTER EIGHT

Cheryl detached herself from Abbie and Pat, who were standing by Pat's desk, and came to Russ, giggling. Behind her, Abbie and Pat tried unsuccessfully to suppress smiles. Russ was furious.

'She –' Cheryl burst out laughing. 'She's on the phone again. Oh yes, she really is, as purry as a cat.' Hilarity seized her. When she had recovered, she said, 'Any message?'

'None. Don't bother me,' Russ said tightly. 'The next one of you who says anything, I'm going to feed you to Attila.'

'She says she knows you're here, and now she's going to start calling every fifteen minutes, and then ten, and then five.'

'I'm still not here.'

'Okay.' Cheryl walked away, grinning.

Judy Rukeyser had called at nine. Russ had told Pat to tell her that he was out of town. She called again at ten, at eleven, then noon. Then at twelve thirty, and every half-hour after. The girls at Cerberus were merrily taking turns informing him that '*Judy*' was on the phone again.

Russ glared at Pat when she approached several minutes later. Pat held up her hands. 'No, no. The phones are dead.' She leaned on Russ's desk and lowered her voice. 'The guy with the schnauzer?'

Russ looked over Pat's shoulder at a slim man who was making a show of looking at the photos mounted on the wall. 'Uh huh?'

'He came in about training, but he wouldn't talk to me. He couldn't get his eyes off his feet, and he turned beet red. He said it had to be a man.'

143

'Okay.' Russ got up and introduced himself and asked if he could help.

'Tom MacDonald,' the man said, shaking Russ's hand. MacDonald was pleasant looking, in his mid-twenties. He glanced at the girls. 'Uh, could we go over to your desk?'

They did, and sat, and MacDonald moved his chair closer to Russ. He told his dog to lie down. It obeyed promptly. 'I ... uh ... I've only been in New York for a month,' MacDonald said in a low voice. 'I came from Ohio, a small town outside Cleveland. I've got this ... well, I've got this kind of problem with girls.' He flushed. 'I can't, I mean I don't know how, I mean I've never been able just to walk up to one and say hi ... and I don't know anyone in this city. And I wondered, I mean, is there a way you can train a dog to run up to someone and ... and ...' He looked away.

'And make a big friendly fuss over them?'

MacDonald nodded. 'Yes, that's it.'

Across the room Abbie was holding up a sign she'd lettered with a marking pen: SHE'S ON AGAIN.

Russ shut his eyes a moment. 'Sure,' he said to MacDonald. 'It's a routine you have to do for films occasionally. And we get maybe forty requests a year from private owners, too.'

'Really?'

'At least,' Russ said. Actually, the average was three or four such calls; but the inflated figure softened the embarrassment people like MacDonald felt. Russ smiled. 'Hell, I even have my own dog trained for that.'

MacDonald returned Russ's smile, and the tension fled his body. 'Son of a gun!'

Russ nodded at the dog. 'What's his name?'

'Ivan.'

Russ hung his hand a few inches from the dog's head. 'Hey, Ivan. How's the dog, how's the good boy?'

The schnauzer sniffed Russ's hand and licked it. Russ patted the dog's head. His tail wagged.

'Temperament's good?' Russ asked.

'Terrific. At least, I think so.'

'Has he ever been trained?'

'Yes, I taught him basic obedience and a couple of tricks.' Talking about his dog, MacDonald became confident and animated.

'I'd like to see him work a little – to get an idea of how much of a job it'll be.'

MacDonald unsnapped Ivan's leash, which surprised Russ, since the layman's usual idea of a trained dog was one that didn't struggle too much against being hauled around on its leash. Ivan was peppy and had good concentration. He took pleasure in his work, and he performed smartly.

Russ said, 'You did a very nice job.'

MacDonald was pleased. 'Thanks.' He petted Ivan. 'He's a good dog.'

'We won't need more than a week. We'll have you work him with our girls. How are your hours – can you bring him in once a day?'

MacDonald glanced toward Pat's desk. 'That would ... uh ... that would be kind of tough. Those girls, they'd, you know ... I'd have to face them with them knowing what I was doing.'

'Okay. We'll board him and have one of our people handle him.'

They agreed on a price. MacDonald pumped Russ's hand. He roughed up Ivan and told the dog to behave and that he'd be back for him soon.

By four thirty, Cheryl and Abbie and Pat were in a state of near-constant laughter. Judy Rukeyser was a woman of her word: She was calling the school every five minutes.

'Tell the bitch to hold,' Russ said. He stalked into the soundproof office, punched the illuminated line-button, and picked up the receiver. 'What the goddamn hell do you want!' he spat.

'You,' Judy's voice answered sweetly.

'You got me. So run your mouth, then get off this phone.'

'I could almost come just listening to you talk like that. Welcome back. Did you have a nice trip?'

'I was mutilated in a plane crash.'

'You're a love. I called your apartment when the school said you weren't in. A charming little thing told me I could reach you at work. So it was just a matter of persistence. She really does have a lovely voice, your cleaning girl. Or is she your roommate? I'm making trout amandine and I have a bottle of Dom Perignon chilling. Seven o'clock would be fine.'

Russ didn't say anything.

'I'll worry if you're late,' she said. 'I'd have to start making phone calls again.'

'Seven o'clock,' Russ said. He hung up.

Judy lived in a condominium on West Twelfth Street. The foyer floor was rock-maple parquet, the walls paisley fabric. She wore a palazzo pant suit, and was naked beneath it. Deep perfume.

She kissed Russ lightly on the lips. 'I simply couldn't resist your advances any longer.' She held out a hand. 'Coat?'

Russ took the neck of her suit and ripped it down to her waist, exposing her mounded breasts. They were tipped with cherry-red nipples. She pulled in a breath. Her hands fluttered uncertainly. Then her eyes narrowed, and the tip of her tongue appeared between her lips. Her nipples engorged under Russ's eyes. Ferality suffused her face. She put her hands on his shoulders.

'You want to be whipped, or for me to shit in your mouth, or what?' Russ asked.

'Wh – what?'

'You like tongs, you have shackles here? You want the marks not to show, or doesn't it make any difference?'

Judy pressed the back of her hand to her mouth.

'Come on, cunt. If I have to pay to get you off my back, then let me know what the price is.'

She stepped back. She shook her head. 'Stop it!'

Russ scowled.

Judy's mouth trembled. Her eyes teared. 'You rotten bastard. You cocksucker.'

'No more games,' Russ said. 'I want to get it over with and get out of here.'

'Get out now!' she screamed.

He looked at her with contempt.

'Yes!' she cried. 'Dangerous men turn me on! Violence makes my cunt wet! I can't help that. I didn't ask for it that way, and it makes me ashamed. But it doesn't mean I have to be debased and hurt, you twisted prick. I'm not a filthy toilet or a slobbering animal. I'm a human being, you freak! Just a goddamn human being in pain. What makes you such a lofty – get out of here!' Tears etched dirty lines of mascara down her cheeks. She seized a book from a small marble table and threw it at him. It whipped by his head, pages snapping, struck the wall, and fell to the floor. 'Get out!'

'Hey,' Russ said, shaken. 'The questions you asked, the way you were with Frank ... I'm sorry, I mean I didn't, you had all the signs –'

'Get out!' she shrieked. 'Get out!'

She rushed him and clawed at his face. Two of her nails broke his skin. He caught her wrists. She kicked his shins. It hurt.

'I'm sorry,' he said.

He let her go and turned, opening the door. She stood with her face buried in her hands. He stepped into the hall and eased the door shut behind him. He paused, and he heard her sobbing. He walked slowly down the hall. He pushed the elevator button, lit a cigarette, and dropped the match into the gray sand of a standing ashtray. A tic snagged the corner of his eye. The door before him rattled as the elevator came hissing up. His throat was dry. The car arrived. It was bright and clean. Russ stared into it. He lifted his leg, cocked his knee across his body, then drove the outside edge of his shoe against the thick column of the ashtray. Sand sprayed across the carpet; the silver rim popped off. The heavy stand rolled until it came up against a wall. The riveted seam had burst. The metal was deeply dented.

Russ stepped into the elevator. He rode down with the cigarette cupped in his hand, the hot tip resting against the skin of his palm.

Tuesday, Wylie went to lunch with the *New York* magazine writer. He was young and wore his hair tied back with leather thongs. The tight braid hung to the center of his back. He was writing on dogs in the city. The mike from a battery-driven cassette tape recorder rested between his shrimp scampi and Wylie's veal and mushrooms.

'Most people come in,' Wylie said, 'and tell me: "I want a dog that will love my kids, that I can train in a couple of days, that won't be shed, that doesn't eat much, that only barks when strangers come to the door, that won't chew the furniture, that isn't hard to housebreak, that will wrestle on the floor with me, that doesn't need to be walked much, that will protect me on the street and massacre burglars, but not growl at anybody else, that will come when I call him, and that's easy to handle. Now, what kind do I want?" Man, what they want is the Dog-god. It makes me sad, very sad.

'Look, there are more than thirty million dogs in this country, better than half a million alone in New York City. But you can't find one out of three hundred owners who has a gnat's ass of an idea of what a dog is about. A dog is not a dog, is not a dog. First, you have very big differences between the six groups that pure-breds are divided into. The physical ones are obvious, but the differences of temperament, character, instinct, and intelligence are just as extreme. The hounds aren't like the working dogs, who aren't like the terriers, and so on. Then you get internal variations, breed to breed. Dobermans and collies are both working dogs, but they're sure as hell not the same kind of animal. Then you have the dog-to-dog differences within the breeds. Any three Dalmatians will share a lot of characteristics, but they won't be interchangeable.

'Problems with dogs are rarely simple matters of bad luck. It's the owner's ignorance. People purchase dogs mostly on impulse – a neighbor's bitch has a litter, there's a cute pup in a store window, a cousin's got a pretty malamute, the kids are nagging you, that kind of thing. Then zap, a couple of months and you have this thing on your hands that's driving you crazy, you don't have any idea what it really is, why it acts the way it does, how to handle it, what to – oh hell, it goes on and on. Look, you buy a dog as a pup, and either it gets to be too much and you haul it down to the SPCA, where it's summarily executed after a few days, or you keep it, which means it's going to be with you for roughly the next ten to twelve years. That's longer than you'll have your car, your house, your apartment, and maybe even your wife. Now, *that* should require a little consideration...'

Wylie was pleased to have a forum – etiquette and restrictions of business usually prevented him from sounding off – and the writer was pleased with Wylie's volubility. They went to a bar after they finished lunch, and they continued the interview past the writer's supply of cassettes, the man scribbling notes in hurried longhand on a yellow pad. In the end they made a dinner date for the following week to talk over collaboration on a dog book.

Cheryl had Kong in the street when Wylie returned to the school. The corgi was alertly watching a group of pigeons clustered around a sandwich bag several yards away. 'Kong,' Cheryl said. The dog looked up at her and wagged its tail. 'Kong, we have a very specific purpose in being out here, and it has nothing to do with birdwatching. You have achieved your goal: You hold the school record for sheer willfulness, and you have gained our sincere respect. But you have also made it a matter of principle for us. The combined expertise and cumulative experience of Cerberus is aligned against you. You cannot possibly succeed, and further stubbornness is a meaningless gesture. Instead of admiring your fortitude, we will begin to look upon you as simply pigheaded. Your reputation is at stake here, Kong. You're not going to destroy it, are you–'

'Rowf!' the dog said.

Russ was working a brindle boxer bitch inside. She didn't like the down, and she was about to show her teeth. Wylie watched Russ's hands on her, fluid and easy, rubbing the base of her ears, touching her chest, stroking the muscles of her shoulders. Russ's voice was firm and sympathetic, and his eyes were intense, as if he were trying to merge his own consciousness with hers. He was oblivious to everything around him. Gradually the dog began to acquiesce. Russ transmitted his appreciation through his hands. The bitch licked his wrist. She began to concentrate on him, surrendering her resentment of his command and now working to comprehend it, to please Russ.

Wylie didn't understand Russ. He doubted that anyone did. It was likely that Russ himself knew only the shoals of his own being. Russ had been particularly fine with the dogs today, but distant and blunted when not working with them. It was as if he and the animals formed a corporate living cell that was adrift in a sea of emptiness.

When the boxer had gone down on command happily and willingly four consecutive times, liquid eyes turned up to Russ in anticipation of praise, Russ terminated the lesson. He hugged and petted the animal and took it back to its run.

He was dulling again when he returned. The first three members of a new group class had arrived, and were squirming in helpless embarrassment as their dogs barked and lunged at each other. Russ motioned Wylie to a corner. Over the noise, Kenroy was trying to explain to the owners that it was anatomically impossible for a dog to bark or bite if a firm hand was clamping its jaws shut, so if you would please snub your animals in and quiet them, I'll use the silence to explain a couple of quick easy ploys to bring your pets under temporary but immediate control. Then we can proceed in a more effective manner.

Wylie bent his head to Russ, and Russ said, 'I got word on the Ferenbach kid this afternoon. He lifted a grand from his parents and took off for Spain. No attempt to hide – he booked the ticket in his own name and used his own passport. Spanish Customs busted him for a hash smuggle, and he's in the can on a three-year knock. I don't think we want him – he's too dumb, and he's not showing any bread – but I'll check out some people who knew him.'

'Did you get anything on Emsley?'

'Going to see him tonight.'

'Grace Tennant's checks drew a blank,' Wylie said. 'And it cost me a friend to take a look. He wouldn't go along, so I blackmailed him. But what the hell, that's what friends are for.'

Kenroy had succeeded in having the dogs restrained; muzzles locked by hopeful fingers, the best they could manage was indignant little squeaks.

Russ was staring out the window at nothing. 'I talked to Gene,' he said vaguely. 'I told him I was sorry for jumping on him Friday.' He turned to Wylie. 'I really didn't mean to hurt him.'

'Forget it. You didn't stick it to him all that bad.'

Russ looked back to the window. 'Yeah,' he said. 'Maybe.'

The game at Terry Butler's was decent and seriously played. But the seven men around the table were drinking too much, and the play was loosening. Two players were declining, and weren't likely to last the hour. Russ sat out, patiently waiting for an opening, nursing Scotches with lots of water.

Terry was banker, skimming 5 percent from each pot, but the deal rotated. Two packs of cards were on the table, one always shuffled and ready; new cards went flicking out beneath the hooded light even as those from the hand just finished were still being reassembled.

Aside from Terry, Russ knew two others slightly. The rest were strangers. George Emsley was a fortyish man with black hair so thin it did little more than shade the pink of his scalp. His face was round. He had a gold tooth and washy gray eyes. He played well, and was an emotional blank while a hand was in progress. But when he lost a close one, he swore and pouted, and when he won he baited the others and tipped his chair back and slapped his stomach smugly. He was one of the heavier drinkers.

By ten thirty there was more than eleven hundred dollars on the table. The biggest loser dropped out with a sigh and made his good-byes. Russ took his place and bought a hundred dollars worth of chips from Terry.

Alcohol was steadily eroding the game – not with gross stupidities, but with small mistakes: misremembered cards, attempts to improve upon faulty foundations that should have been folded, clumsy bluffs, and occasional suicidal betting. Russ's chips began to multiply.

Russ was a better-than-average player who won more often than he lost, but not brilliant, and at least three of his opponents were of superior skill. That he didn't care whether or not he won, and that he'd brought six hundred dollars in cash that he wouldn't be upset to lose, gave him a helpful confidence and freedom.

Russ didn't believe in money. He understood its usage, but beyond that it was only numbered scrap paper to him. He had four savings accounts, two registered under his real name, and together they represented a sizable amount. He didn't spend much, and he never thought about the rest. Someday he would do something with it, if he ever discovered something he wanted to do.

A second man dropped.

Two players working in secret consort can ravage a poker game. One, working for the benefit of a second who has reasonable ability, can not exercise the same control, but can be effective. Russ wanted George Emsley to win, and big, because Emsley was increasingly pleased with himself as he won, and he drank more and talked more, and Russ wanted him drunk, happy, and garrulous by the end of the night.

At one in the morning only Russ, Terry Butler, Emsley, and a man named Vic remained. Russ was ahead by two hundred dollars. Emsley was up by several hundred, and in an expansive, liquory mood. Terry sat behind a comfortable stack of chips. He played too conservatively to win big, but he made slow, consistent gains, and, win or lose, he still took his percentage from each pot; the weekly game was his prime source of income. Vic was the biggest loser of the night. He was a sandy-haired thoughtful player with cupped ears, the best of them all. If Russ hadn't been throwing the game to Emsley, Vic would have won the lion's share. By nature, or discipline, Vic was a casual and relaxed player who was difficult to read. But his losses had confused him, and he'd tightened up too much. Russ knew that he was now trying to decide whether to take his beating and quit or to risk more and attempt to recoup.

Russ needed him in the game a while longer. So in the next ten hands he managed to throw three big pots to the man. Vic shifted in his chair, caught his lip in his teeth momentarily, then poised himself again and took the next pot with an excellent bluff. The deal passed to him, and he paused to light a cigarette.

'What do you guys say to making the game a little more interesting?' he asked offhandedly.

Emsley tipped his chair back and folded his arms across his chest. He grinned like Sherman pausing at the Georgia border. 'What you got in mind, my friend?'

'Oh, I don't know, maybe we could up the stakes to, oh, say one, five, and ten.'

'Well,' said Emsley, slapping his stomach, 'I do believe a man should be allowed to dig his grave just as deep as he wants to. I'll be pleased to shovel along with you. Russ, you in?'

Russ pushed his chips around a moment and made a show of looking in his wallet. 'I've been pretty much walking in place,' he said. 'What the hell, maybe it'll get me movin'.'

'I'm gonna bury you both,' Emsley said happily. He tossed off his drink and refilled his glass from the bottle beside him. It was the last in the house, and was almost empty. 'Terry?'

'It's all yours, people. Too heavy for me.'

'You deal for us?' Emsley said.

'If that's the way you all want it.'

Vic and Russ nodded.

While they were cashing in chips to clear the board for the new stakes, Russ asked Terry if there were any place around where he could pick up another bottle.

Terry looked at his watch. 'The liquor stores are closed, but there's a bar on the corner, Johnny's Place.

The guy behind the counter is Ed. Slip him an extra five and he'll fix you up.'

Emsley handed two twenties to Russ. 'Get a pair,' he said. 'On me. Georgie-boy is his mother's darlin' and one pussy-jumpin' goddamn gracious son of a bitch of a winner, and you can tell that to the world.'

'First chance I get,' Russ said. He told them to stack him up with five hundred's worth.

As he was leaving, George yelled, 'Buy the good shit, baby!'

Russ brought back two quarts of Ambassador 12-Year-Old. His chips were stacked neatly at his place. The ash-trays had been emptied. Terry was reading a magazine, and Vic was cleaning his nails with a tooth-pick. Emsley was playing acey-deucey with himself, and laughing hugely when he won.

'Count 'em,' Terry said.

Russ eyed his chips and said, 'It's okay.' He gave Terry five hundred dollars. He opened a bottle and poured himself a drink, a bigger one for Emsley. Vic had switched to black coffee, and Terry was drinking beer. Russ set the bottle next to Emsley's glass, opened the second one, and stood it near his own.

Terry riffled the cards. 'Call your game in turn, and I'll deal 'em.'

Emsley finished his drink and sloshed another into his glass. 'Seven stud,' he said. 'Ante with ten, and hang on to your asses.'

Vic shouldn't have been in. The big stakes worried him too much and broke his game apart; he went down four hundred dollars in twenty minutes. He put his elbows on the table, closed his eyes, and massaged his temples for a few moments. Then he stood and gave them a sick smile. 'That's the bottom, friends.'

'Rest in peace,' Emsley said. He made the sign of the cross at Vic.

Vic nodded, put his coat on. 'Night,' he said.

Terry frowned. 'Night, Vic,' he said. 'Next time, man. Next time it's yours.'

'You bet,' Vic said. 'Stay loose.'

Emsley filled his glass with Scotch. It spilled over the top and wet the pile of green bills next to his chips. He looked at the money perplexedly. 'Should ... dry them off,' he said. He took out his handkerchief.

Terry Butler sat looking at the cards he was shuffling and reshuffling.

'Call your game, Russ,' Emsley said, thick-tongued.

Terry began turning cards over to no particular purpose. 'George,' he said. 'You've cleaned just about everybody. Why don't you call it a night?'

'What the hell? What the hell? 'S a man here with gelt 'at wan's t' play cards.'

'George –'

'Deal, baby!'

'Five draw,' Russ said.

Russ lost a couple of hundred over the next hands. Emsley was swaying in his chair and chuckling. Spit bubbles blossomed between his lips and slicked his chin. He could barely read his cards.

Russ tossed a losing hand in. 'That's it. I've got to save a couple for the landlord.'

Emsley couldn't add up his chips, so Terry counted them for him. Emsley grinned. 'Boy. Oh boy! What a goddamn night. Boy!'

'Which way you going?' Russ asked.

Emsley had to think about this. 'Down,' he said. 'Eighteenth Street.'

'Share a cab with you,' Russ said.

'Sure, ol' buddy. An' I'll pay it. 'S least I c'n do.'

Terry finished his count in silence and paid Emsley off. It came to a little over two thousand dollars. Emsley stuffed the bills into his pockets and went off, swaying, to the bathroom.

'I wouldn't like it that anything happened to George,' Terry said.

Russ looked at him without expression.

Terry held the base of a deck and flipped the card tops with the thumb of his other hand. 'He's a nice guy, a little dumb, but okay. You bought whatever you're lookin' for, so you're entitled. But go easy.'

'Sure.'

'I don't want you in again.'

'It's happening all the time, Terry. Put down in your book that I owe you one.'

'Who you owe is the other guys that were playin'.'

Russ shrugged.

Emsley couldn't manage his legs properly, so Russ looped one of the man's arms over his shoulders and half carried him down the stairs to the street. They walked slowly toward Broadway.

'Bad night,' Russ said. 'Bad goddamn whole month. Started off wrong when the cops came down on me for that Chasteen score. Christ, I never worked stuff like that.'

'Bastards!' Emsley said. 'Stinkin' pigs! Lemme tell yuh, I was *there* at that grab.'

'Jesus,' Russ said. 'That was *your* action?'

Emsley flailed the air with a hand. 'Nah, nah. I do my square thing for a caterin' outfit, and we had this job, see? Christ, I pissed my pants when them cannons went off, an' that's no shit, man. But after it's over the place is crawlin' with pigs, right? An' this one prick makes my face – I did ice once, and pulled seven in Dannemora for it. So him an' this big nigger pig, they wanna make sergeant an' they figure me for an inside man an' they haul me down t' the basement and put me up against the wall. The first one's got his club over my throat an' leanin' on it with both hands while the shine's usin' his to hit home runs on my balls. They left me on the floor in my own puke.'

They were moving down Broadway, with Emsley leaning on Russ. Emsley didn't notice the empty cabs that passed. He was muttering viciously about cops.

'Yeah,' Russ said. 'If they treated a guy like he was a man, maybe they'd get some place. Bet there *were* a couple o' things you could o' told 'em.'

'Nah,' Emsley belched. 'It was first-class work. They didn't do nothin' that would tag 'em.'

'I can see the straights being blind, but a guy who's been inside and knows how to look? That's hard to chew.'

'I tell yuh, buddy, that's the front an' back of it. Nothin'. A big zero.' He screwed up his face. 'Well ... there was this one thing.'

'Yeah? What?'

'I don't know. Just ... I don't know. They split through the back, the kitchen, yuh know? I was tied up in there. An' this one guy trips an' he sticks a hand out. He falls against a table an' breaks a water pi'cher. An' then it's like he goes crazy. He drops his piece an' grabs his hand to his chest an' starts moanin' an' cryin'. One o' the other dudes has t' shout at him an' finally slap him a couple o' times before the guy gets straight again an' picks up his blaster an' makes the run.'

'So he got cut bad, huh?'

'Nah. It couldn't o' been much more'n a scratch. There was only a drop or two o' blood. That's why it didn't make no sense.'

'And the pigs wouldn't believe that was all you had for 'em.'

'Hell, I didn't even have that for 'em. Them bastards get nothin' from me, nothin'. I wouldn't give 'em the shit from my asshole.'

They walked three blocks more, but Emsley had nothing else to offer. Russ hailed a cab.

Wednesday was hectic. Harold phoned in with the flu,

158

and Ernie, who was new to Cerberus, got his thigh ripped by an Afgan. The dog was a fear biter, and of the worst kind. Outwardly calm, it had exploded in snapping terror the moment Ernie had taken the leash from the owner. No one at the school sympathized with dog bites. People who truly knew dogs were rarely bitten, not because they engendered love or confidence in the beasts, but because they respected the animals' capacities and didn't take stupid chances. Ernie had brought it on himself by not bothering to evaluate the dog properly or ask the owner for his idea of the dog's personality and quirks. Luckily, the Afgan had backed off after one slash. Ernie had needed only five stitches, and he'd be back at work tomorrow. But now the schedule was heavy.

Russ and Wylie couldn't get together until late in the afternoon, and even then it was only to go over a list of German shepherds Russ had reviewed for the police department of Pritchett Bay, Long Island. The department was organizing a small canine unit – four dogs – and had hired Cerberus as consultants. The school's first responsibility was to locate suitable animals. A police dog that was anything less than faultless was a liability.

'I think Kellerman's will be okay,' Russ said. 'But I'd like to bring it in and work with it a couple of days to be sure. Beckhardt's, like always, are pure quality. She's got two I'd love to have, but she's already promised one. I bought the other. He's only fourteen months, but he'll go the distance. None of the rest panned out.'

'Harvey Crippen didn't have anything?'

Russ shook his head. 'All kennel dogs, no socialization history. They're fine with each other, but not too good with people. I think we ought to pull him from the files. He's too much into volume, and his dogs are going downhill.'

'Okay. We're still two short, three if Kellerman's doesn't make it.'

'It probably will. I have a couple to look at tomorrow,

including one Beckhardt recommended. We should have them all by Monday.'

'Good enough. Did you get next to that guy Emsley last night?'

'Yeah. Another blank. He gave me a footnote that Schattner didn't get, but I couldn't make anything out of it.' He told Wylie what Emsley had said.

'Russ,' Wylie said, 'there's an Eric Hall from Pyramid Food coming in about ten minutes. That's the pup commercial. Will you handle it? I'm going to be in the back office for a while.'

When Wylie came out, nearly an hour later, he was whistling the 'Toreador Song.' He handed Russ a notepad sheet on which was written 'Eugene Perry – 1108 S. Albine – Park Ridge, Illinois.'

'Who's he?' Russ asked.

'I think he's a man with a shotgun.'

CHAPTER NINE

Russ went to the back office with Wylie. He was tense. Perspiration slicked his palms. He could feel his blood. Spoor found, he was quickening.

Wylie put his feet up on the desk, pleased with himself. Russ shifted his weight from his heels to the balls of his feet and back again. His hands moved at his sides, touched his hair, picked at his shirt.

'How did you find him?'

'Why does a man go bananas when he cuts himself? Why does a guy who's got to move for his life drop his gun and suddenly become paralyzed over a scratched hand?'

'I don't know,' Russ said impatiently. 'Come on.'

'Because the sight of his own blood terrifies him more than anything else in his life – because he's a hemophiliac, a bleeder, a guy who's lived every day of his life like there was a crazy on his back with a gun pointed at his head. Because every time he nicks himself he hears that gun going off and he thinks he's dead.'

'Okay, maybe he's a bleeder. How do you find him?'

'What do you do at one A.M. when you think you're dying – you haul your ass in a panic to the nearest hospital. And that's where I found Eugene Perry, hemophiliac, at one fifteen the night Chasteen's was knocked over, shaking to pieces in the Roosevelt emergency room. They checked him in and had him two days.'

Russ shook his head. 'No good, man. He's just gunned down half a dozen people, he's not going to spell out his name and address on a bunch of hospital forms.'

'For God's sake, who's ever going to look for a connection between a bleeding out-of-town hemophiliac and a gang of shooters? Why not try visiting epileptics with seizures, or astronauts with vertigo? What the hell? Remember, this is a guy in the grip of absolute horror. A bad bleeder can be unconscious in half an hour, and dead not much later. If our man goes comatose and the hospital hasn't got his real name and can't reach his doctor for his history and procedural information, then the crazy is already squeezing the trigger. Our man wants to wake up, and that's all he can think about.'

Russ reserved judgment.

'It's him,' Wylie insisted. 'Joe Sucher said it was a Chicago twang. Finn said a brooch was sold through a Midwestern fence. Perry lives in Park Ridge – that's a Chicago suburb. Emsley gives us a guy who's probably a bleeder. And forty minutes after the hit we get a bleeder in Roosevelt. He's scared out of his gourd he's dying, and he plugs them into the registry. It's his only hope if he starts to go down. He's our man.'

'Which one of us goes to find out?'

Wylie pulled a quarter from his pocket, flipped and caught it.

'Heads,' Russ said.

It was tails.

'When are you leaving?' Russ said.

'Tomorrow.'

Russ nodded. Energy stormed within him, filling him and threatening to rupture the thinning bag of his skin. He sucked breath and tightened muscles, trying to dissipate it, a caged animal watching with trembling anticipation as the walls of its prison began to collapse.

Wylie deplaned at O'Hare Airport in the early afternoon. He walked down the corridor to the nearest bank of telephones, took Perry's number from his breast pocket, dropped in a dime, and dialed. An operator cut into the line to tell him that Park Ridge was a toll call, please deposit ten cents more.

'Hullo.' A dullish female voice.

'Hello,' Wylie said. 'This is Joseph Lewis from the Cook County Board of Appraisal. May I speak with Mr Perry, please.'

'From the whut?'

'It's in reference to property taxes.'

'Oh.'

'Is Mr Perry home, please?'

'No, he ain't.'

'Is this Mrs Perry?'

'Uh uh.'

'May I ask to whom I'm speaking, then?'

'The day maid.'

'What time are Mr and Mrs Perry expected?'

'Miz Perry took the chil'en t' see they gran'ma down t' Sprin'fiel'. Mistuh Perry ain't goan be home 'til ten t'night or so.'

'I see . . .' This one was lucky if she could remember her way home from night to night. Might as well ask. 'My information says the family dog is an Airedale. Is that right?'

'Ain't no kind o' dog here.'

'Oh. I'll have to correct the form. There won't be any message. I'll try to reach Mr Perry later. Thanks very much. Good-bye now.'

'Uh huh.'

Nice about the dog. One thing about being a trainer was that you understood that no dog in the world had any reason to give two shits about your expertise when you first encountered it. Not even Lassie's trainer could sweet-talk a strange dog down if it decided its home or master needed defending.

Wylie was carrying an attaché case and a calfskin overnight bag with side pouches. He stored the bag in a coin locker and walked to the commercial island in the center of the major causeway. He looked at the toy displays. It was criminal how realistic some of the model handguns

163

were. He brought his face nearly into contact with the glass, but still he would not have been able to differentiate between one of the reproductions – a short-barreled Smith & Wesson .38, the Chiefs Special – and the legitimate article if they had been laid side by side. The muzzle was a menacing black hole; even the dullness of the lead slugs in the cylinder chambers had been accurately simulated. Wylie shook his head in sadness at a society that could so willingly produce and consume such toys. He bought the model for three dollars and twenty-five cents.

He'd applied for a pistol permit after his resignation had been forced from the department. He'd received it, but six months later it had been revoked; there had been, and still were, people in that department with power who did not like him. He owned half a dozen handguns, none legally, and carried and used them when necessary. But he'd have been nailed in an airport security check if he'd tried to bring one today. Skyjackers had made life difficult for a lot of people.

He had the model gift-wrapped, and he put it in his attaché case. He idled fifteen minutes over the paperback-book racks, then went to a different clerk and bought a roll of one-inch surgical tape and a pack of six-by-six gauze compresses. These two went into the case.

He found the Hertz booth, presented a phony California driver's license, and rented a sober gray Chevrolet Impala. He was wearing his most conservative clothes: a dark Brooks Brothers worsted wool, white shirt, four-in-hand gray tie, black Florsheim shoes. Dress and the colorless car were well matched. Good for white suburbs. A subdued nigger who knew he was lucky to be making it in a white world and who wouldn't rock the boat. A credit to his race.

Twenty minutes later, driving east on Devon Avenue, he passed a sign which welcomed him to Park Ridge. He slowed and moved into the left lane, flipping his directional signal as he approached South Albine. It was a street of comfortable, tended homes in varying styles, with healthy lawns and shade trees. He drove down the block and pulled to the curb one house short of number 1108. He unfolded the Hertz street map and put on a frustrated and befuddled expression.

His vision went past the map to Perry's house, a two-story structure of fieldstone and redwood. An empty carport on the right. Angling from that, a short walk leading to the front door. No window in the door. Sconces flanking it. To the left of the door, a window bay. Probably the living room. Each of the neighboring houses was roughly seventy-five feet away. No fences; shrubs and bushes demarcated lot lines. Only three lamps on the street itself. If the door sconces were not turned on, the entrance to Perry's house would be in darkness.

He folded the map, started the car, and drove to the cross street, turned left, and then left again at the next one. Halfway down. Park. Open the map. There were no alleys in Park Ridge. Back yards butted directly against each other. Behind the map, Wylie peered past the house on this street into Perry's back yard and at the rear of his home. He saw a glass wall with sliding doors, drapes drawn across it. A screen porch to the side of this. Atop the porch a balustraded sun deck. Kitchen door. A basement entrance. He puzzled over a set of floor-to-ceiling windows on the second floor. A skylight had been cut into the canted roof above them. Drapes blocked them off.

Wylie returned to the airport and left the car on call with Hertz.

He took an elevator up to the terminal's mezzanine level and walked down a gallery to a door marked ADMIRALS CLUB. He rang the bell and was answered by a buzzer, which released the lock. He showed a membership card with a name to match that on the California driver's license to the pretty girl behind the desk in the reception

165

foyer, and went into the large lounge on the left. The room was quiet and restful, and equipped with oversize club chairs and couches, some standing in privacy, others in conversational groupings. A waiter appeared as soon as he sat down. He ordered a double Jim Beam on the rocks and took Joseph Sucher's *Ivory and Ice* from his attaché case. Twelve years ago, when it was first published, he'd thought the book mad and anarchic, but brilliant. Skimming its dialogue last week, it had caught him up anew, and he'd decided to read it again.

He read until six, then moved to the color television at the far end of the room, volume discreetly low, to watch the news. The national and international reports were spirited, the half-hour local roundup akin to dipping into *Babbit*.

After the news he went downstairs and sat in a dim restaurant and ate a filet with mushroom caps. Beef was the best thing about Chicago. The old stockyards were gone now, but Chicago stubbornly maintained the quality of its meat – perhaps because it had little else to offer. Wylie considered ordering another – the first had been that good – but he didn't want to make himself sluggish. Back to the Admirals Club and *Ivory and Ice*, with a snifter of Remy Martin, until it was time to leave. He regretted having to close the book.

Lights were burning in Perry's living room, but the door sconces were not on. Wylie pulled into the driveway and stopped behind the new Oldsmobile in the carport. He wore snug gray silk gloves. The model Smith & Wesson was in his right coat pocket. He walked briskly to the door and pressed the bell stud. He held his attaché case before him in his left hand, took the gun out, and concealed it behind the case.

A man of medium height and weight answered. He was about forty-five, wore black-rimmed glasses, and had a mole on his right cheek. He was dressed in a sportshirt,

166

brown slacks, and suede house slippers. He blinked at the sight of a black man.

'Mr Perry?' Wylie asked politely.

'Yes. What is it?'

Wylie lifted the gun over the attaché case and leveled it at Perry's belly. 'Take three steps to the right or you're gut-shot.'

Perry blanched. He moved as instructed and said, 'Take it easy, mister, you can have anything you want.'

Wylie entered the foyer and closed the door behind him. Perry was standing in an arch that opened to the living room. 'Two steps more,' Wylie said. 'Then lay down on your stomach and lock your hands behind your head.'

Perry got on the floor. Wylie pulled the drapes across the living room windows. At the opposite end of the room was another arch, which gave onto a dining room. The rear wall of that was glass, and was still sealed off with drapes, as Wylie had observed earlier when he'd parked on the next street down. There were no other windows through which they could be seen.

'Look,' Perry said, talking into the carpet. 'I don't have much, but I'll tell you where everything is. My wallet –'

'Shut up.' Wylie listened to the house. 'Anyone else here?'

'No. I'm alone.'

'If you're shittin' me, you get the first bullet.'

'I swear,' Perry said. 'It's just me. My wife and kids are downstate.'

'Hands behind your back,' Wylie ordered. He removed the tape and compresses from his attaché case and knelt beside Perry. 'Be cool,' he said, 'and you'll come out fine. Try to fuck with me and you're dead.'

Perry was sweating. 'I'm listening, mister. Right now you're God.'

Wylie taped Perry's wrists together behind his back. Then he lifted the man's head and told him to open his mouth. He stuffed gauze compresses in and sealed Perry's mouth with tape. 'Just lay there quiet,' he said.

He carried a steepleback chair from the dining room, placed it near the wall, and ordered Perry to sit on it. He taped around Perry's chest and the chair back, then taped Perry's ankles to the fluted legs. He tilted the chair so that its weight balanced between its top, which rested against the wall, and its rear legs.

'If you try to move you'll fall over, and I'll hear it,' Wylie said. 'Best you just relax.'

He searched the house. As he'd expected, he didn't find anything – though he did discover what the skylighted second floor room was: an artist's studio. He spent some minutes going through the canvases. They were Primitives. The country scenes, farms and lead mines, weren't especially striking, but the cityscapes were excellent, with a powerful tension between subject and style. At a gallery, Wylie might have bought one.

The furnishings, clothes, and recreational equipment Wylie saw put Perry in the twenty-to-twenty-five-thousand bracket. There were also indications of the man's medical condition. Sharp and pointed articles were noticeably missing, windows were of safety glass, corners had been rounded with moldings, an electric razor, plastic drinking glasses . . .

Wylie went back to the living room, pulled the tape from Perry's mouth, and dug out the compresses. Perry spat, then swallowed. Wylie tipped the chair so that it rested on all four legs again. He pulled an armchair forward and sat down facing Perry.

'You do nice paintings,' he said.

Perry looked at him in confusion and fear.

'Want a cigarette?' Perry shook his head. Wylie lit one for himself. 'Where have you got the stuff from the Chasteen job?'

'What?' The man looked utterly lost.

'I'll be straight with you,' Wylie said. 'I'm looking for a

gold cigarette case that was part of the take. Solid gold, not an overlay, very thin, plain finish, no jewels or text-uring. A tiny *L* engraved in the lower right-hand corner of the top. There were a couple of scented cigarettes in-side, perfumey tobacco, like sandalwood. I want it back. And that's all I want. As soon as I get it, I go away – and we never saw each other at all. I don't give a damn about anything else.'

'Jesus Christ, mister, I don't know what you're talking about!'

'Aw, come on. I don't want it any messier than you do.'

Perry shook his head in horror. 'You got the wrong man, you got to believe me.'

'I only want the case. I'm not fuzz, I'm not after your action.'

'Call the cops,' Perry said hysterically. 'If you think I took somethin' of yours, for God's sake call the cops!'

Wylie cocked an eyebrow. 'Not bad, baby, not bad at all. Where's the case?'

Wylie drove in questions at him for half an hour. There were tears in Perry's eyes. Wylie felt misgivings. Either Perry was a remarkable man, or Wylie's theory was a loser. Wylie lit another cigarette, smoked in silence, and thought it through again. He had to trust his first judgment.

He went into the kitchen and opened the knife drawer. The drawer had been fitted with clips, and outlines inked, which permitted each knife to be accounted for. The blades were encased in cardboard sheaths. Wylie lifted a carving knife and tested it for balance. He dis-carded it and tried another. That one was all right. He removed a piece of pine shelving from the foyer closet on the way back. He knelt on one knee in front of Perry and began to remove the man's shoes and socks.

'What are you doing?' Perry said apprehensively.

'I want that case.'

169

When Perry's feet were bare, Wylie raised the chair a little and slid the pine under the front legs. Perry's feet rested in the center of the board, about twelve inches apart. Wylie sat down in his own chair and held the carving knife by its tip in his right hand. He waited a moment, then flicked his wrist and sent the knife spinning down. It struck into the shelving midway between Perry's feet and quivered.

Perry jerked his head and cried out. The muscles of his legs flexed. His toes curled under, and his nails scratched against the wood.

'I want the case, Gene.' Wylie retrieved the knife.

'Please,' Perry begged. 'Please, I'd give you anything I have – *I don't know what you're talking about!'*

The knife flashed down and thunked into the wood. Perry gasped.

Wylie pulled the knife free. 'I can keep this up all night. But sooner or later I'm going to miss and hit your foot. And you'll start to bleed. And you'll keep on bleeding until you talk to me. And then maybe it will be too late anyway.'

Perry was chalky. He hung his head. 'You can't do this,' he whispered. 'I don't know anything.'

Wylie threw the knife.

Perry held out longer than Wylie thought that he, Wylie, could have. But when the knife bounced on a bad toss and struck against the man's foot with the flat, Perry threw back his head and shrieked.

'No! No, for the love of God, I can't stand it any more!'

Wylie balanced the knife. 'The case.'

'All right,' Perry gasped. 'All right, you fuckin' nigger, you goddamn black bastard!' He wept convulsively.

Wylie gave him time to take hold of himself.

'You've got to believe me,' Perry said. 'Chasteen's was the first time in my life I ever carried a piece. I do ice once, twice a year, but never a boost – always a prowl, a couple of times a con. But nothin' like the Chasteen thing. I swear on my children's lives. The fuckin' guns were for show – they weren't even supposed to be loaded!'

'*Ego te absolvo*,' Wylie said. 'The case, Gene, the case.'

'I remember seeing one like that, but it wasn't part of my cut.'

'Who got it ?'

'I don't know.'

'All right, take it from the top. How did you get in on the job?'

'Cramer. Chuck Cramer. Usually I work alone, but a couple years back I did a job with him. He called me from New York. I didn't like it, but he said it was a real creampuff, a walk-in, and we'd take at least thirty a man, maybe two or three times that. I still didn't like it. But I was busted, and there was nothing else around. So I said okay, I'd look it over. I went to New York. It was too tricky, and I told Chuck no. But he said everything had been covered and it'd run like a Swiss watch. I worried it up a couple of days, tried some other contacts that didn't work out, then I told him okay, I was in.

'God – I swear the guns were for show. If it turned bad we were going to drop the pieces and take our time. Nobody wanted to go down for the big one. I *know* my piece wasn't loaded. I checked it when they gave it to me. I checked it again just before we went into the place. It was empty, you got to believe that, I never even fired a BB gun in my whole fucking life!'

'Who were the other two guys?'

'I didn't even meet them until three hours before the score. That's the way they wanted it, and it was okay with me. The more people who know you, the harder it gets to stay free. Chuck introduced them as Mickey and Ray, but I don't know if they were using their real names – I wasn't.'

'Where do I find Cramer?'

Perry looked away.

'Come on, man. We've gone this far. Do we have to do the mumbletypeg again?'

'East Eleventh Street, you cocksucker!' He named an address near Avenue B.

Wylie looked at his watch. It was almost one A.M. New York time. He felt bad for Perry. 'I have to spend some time here. If you tell me you won't make any noise, I'll leave the gag off. What about it?'

Perry stared at him with hatred.

'I don't blame you,' Wylie said. 'But you have to nod at least, or I'm going to stuff your mouth.'

Perry's cheek twitched. He flushed, then nodded.

Wylie dialed the operator from the kitchen wall phone. 'I want to make a credit-card call,' he told her. He gave her a false card number, making it impossible for Perry to trace him or ever discover what number had been called from his phone.

'Hello,' Russ answered.

The kitchen door was closed, Wylie's hand was cupped around the mouthpiece, and he spoke quietly. 'Perry's our man. It *was* a hit, but I think they set Perry up. He doesn't have the case. I have nothing but his word, but I believe him. Perry's contact was a dude named Chuck Cramer, who also might have been used. The shooters were named Mickey and Ray, possible aliases.'

'Is Cramer local?'

'Uh huh.' Wylie gave Russ the address. 'Take him. If he doesn't have the case, get us to Mickey and Ray.'

'You better sit there till I can check it out.'

'Right.' Russ took Perry's number, and Wylie said, 'Call me from a pay phone.'

'As soon as I have something. Talk to you.'

Russ hung up. He pulled the back of his hand across his chin.

Beth hadn't been there when he'd come home. The

clothes he'd bought her were gone, and her records. A piece of a brown-paper bag was on the kitchen table. On it she had written 'Bye.'

'Fuck off,' he'd said to it.

And he'd paced back and forth through the apartment, waiting for Wylie's call. Frank had moved at his side, feeling Russ's tension, hackles sometimes rising, and at intervals growling at nothing. Russ hadn't been sure that Perry was the key, and while he waited images of Beth had driven into him like oblique shafts of light through a faulty blind.

Now Beth was wiped from his mind.

Russ patted Frank's head. The dog made an eager sound.

Russ moved the couch away from the living room wall and tapped the blade of a wood chisel between the quarter-round molding and the baseboard. He was careful not to leave marks. He pried the quarter-round off without bending the finishing nails that had anchored it. He pulled back the corner of the carpet and levered up a small section of flooring. He removed two oilcloth parcels. One contained a Mauser .380 Auto Pistol with checkered walnut grips. The other held a shoulder holster and a belt-clip holster, a box of cartridges, and two empty magazines. He broke the pistol down – it was clean and working smoothly. Frank lay at his side, head on paws. The dog whined. Russ counted out fourteen cartridges. He loaded both magazines – seven shells each – slapped one into the pistol's butt, put the remaining one in his pocket, and positioned the holster inside his waistband. He put on his windbreaker and leashed Frank.

They were on East Eleventh Street half an hour later. They walked past Chuck Cramer's building on the opposite side of the street. It was a walkup, dirty, the concrete stairs chipped, an iron handrail twisted into uselessness and rusting. At the end of the block Russ crossed over and started back. He walked by two abandoned cars, both stripped, one paint-blistered and stinking from a recent fire. Beer cans, newspapers, and broken bottles littered the sidewalk. Frank ignored the wild, ghostly cats that bolted in the shadows. Soul, Hispanic, and rock music spilled into the night from open, barred windows. A man was shouting insanely for someone in another apartment to turn down the volume. No one bothered to answer. Television lights flickered bluishly. Three-room apartments could still be rented here for under sixty dollars. And friends, crazy for a fix, murdered friends for half that.

Russ mounted the steps to Cramer's building. The front-door lock had been broken long ago and not repaired; there was no point to it. The overhead lights were out, and the hallway was in blackness save for a small bulb two-thirds of the way down that weakly illuminated a basement door. The door was covered with sheet metal and secured by two big padlocks. There would be nothing worth stealing down there, but at least drifters and junkies wouldn't be using it to sleep. Cramer's apartment was on the ground floor, last door on the right. Russ moved in far enough not to be seen from the street, then stopped to let his eyes adjust to the darkness. Frank sniffed the air and grumbled. Russ dropped to a crouch. His hand went under his sweatshirt and rested lightly on the Mauser.

A tiny patch moved in the darkness beneath the stairs. Russ put a hand over Frank's muzzle, signaling him to be quiet. The dog's muscles were taut.

A minute passed. Two. Three. A youthful voice whispered nervously.

Russ waited to a count of five; then he said, 'Get the fuck out of here.'

Silence tightened. Another whisper – a sudden rush of footsteps. A black and a Puerto Rican boy appeared for an instant beneath the light over the basement door.

174

They fled out to the courtyard in the rear.

Russ waited five more minutes. Then he moved quietly down the hall, keeping close to the wall. He paused at Cramer's door, heard nothing, saw no light around the edges. He went into the courtyard. It was empty except for a bedspring and a cardboard suitcase pulped by rain. Cramer's only two windows, stoutly barred, gave onto the courtyard. They were filthy, and the apartment was dark. Russ couldn't see anything. He returned to Cramer's door and ran his fingers over it in the darkness. There were three locks: a standard cylinder and two deadbolts. A steel flange protected the doorknob side from top to bottom. Russ found a thin crack in the wood of the opposite jamb. He stepped back and lifted his foot, reckoning the position of the bottom hinge. He kicked and felt a little give. He kicked again. He touched the crack – it had widened. He listened: radios, television, an arguing couple. Blindness and deafness were a way of life around here. Two more kicks forced the bottom hinge. Pieces of the split frame clung to the screws. He broke the top hinge free with his shoulder. He squeezed into the apartment. Frank followed him.

He pulled the shades down over the window and struck a match. Roaches went scuttling. The apartment was only two rooms, kitchen and living room/bedroom. He switched on a table lamp in the bedroom, stripped a sheet off the bed, and tossed it over the lamp, sinking the apartment into a dim twilight. He pushed the door back against the broken frame and put Frank in a down-stay beside it and told him to listen.

The apartment hadn't been painted in some time. Plaster had fallen from the ceiling in two places, exposing the lathing. Posters were taped to the wall: Dennis the Menace on a souped-up tricycle giving the viewer the finger, a slim nude with bowed head and the legend BECAUSE YOU ARE AFRAID TO LOVE, I AM ALONE IN THE WORLD. The bed was a sofa-bed that hadn't been closed. A

175

blanket was tangled at the foot, and there were semen stains on the bottom sheet. Bare wood floor in the living room, worn linoleum in the kitchen. The odor of perfume, grease, and marijuana. A bottle of instant coffee on the kitchen table, a plate with a gnawed porkchop bone. More roaches.

Female signs: costume jewelry, blouses and small jeans, two skirts, pantyhose, eye make-up, a half-empty box of Tampax. But in the corner of the closet Russ found a balled-up pair of dirty jockey shorts, in the dust under the bed a pair of man's socks, on the top shelf of the medicine chest a razor clogged with dried shaving cream and tough whiskers. But nothing significant.

Russ turned off the lamp and called Frank to his side. He settled down in a corner of the bedroom and lit a cigarette. He waited through four more cigarettes, fingers moving against the dog's hair. Twice someone entered the building, but each time went up the stairs to other floors. When footsteps approached down the hall, Frank lifted his head and raised the flaps of his ears. Russ laid his hand over Frank's muzzle, commanding silence, then held it before the dog's eyes, ordering him to stay.

Russ slipped the Mauser free and stood. The footsteps stopped outside the door. A key clicked against one of the wrenched locks. A dead moment followed, in which the keyholder realized that something was wrong. The door was pushed, tentatively. It leaned inward.

'Oh shit,' said a girl's voice.

The door opened farther. The overhead kitchen light went on. A plain-faced girl with brown hair put her hands on her hips and surveyed the kitchen. She wore beige jeans and a patched velour coat with a high dandy's collar. 'There was nothing left to steal, you creeps,' she muttered to herself. She turned and saw Russ. Her eyes flickered in alarm; then resignation settled over her face.

Russ directed the Mauser at her stomach. 'Shove the door closed.'

She nodded and pushed it shut. 'I haven't got anything,' she said. Then added scornfully, 'Except what every other chick has got.' She tossed her purse onto the metal sheet that covered the old bathtub in the kitchen. 'Let's make it over with and then you can split and I can get some sleep. I'm wrecked.'

'You live alone?' Russ said.

'Yeah.' She saw Frank. Her eyes moved from the dog to Russ and back again. Fear entered her face.

'Where's Chuck Cramer?'

'In hell with a pitchfork up his ass. For all I know. Or care.'

'Do better.'

She licked her lips in calculation. 'Why?'

'Because you live alone.'

The calculation fled. 'I don't know. I got terrific karma for bastards. You put one within a hundred miles and I'll find him. He was a Scorpio, too. I should of known. He split two weeks ago. One afternoon I come home and his bag and half his stuff is gone. I threw the rest out.'

'Where do you think he might have gone?'

'Paris, Rome, Majorca, Acapulco.' She shrugged. 'Everywhere. He was big on talk. He was comin' into big money, he said. We were going to do the world.'

'When?'

'When what?'

'When was he coming into money?'

'Soon. Maybe he got it, and found a new cunt, too. I don't know. I put him up three months. He took my stash when he left. Maybe you and your mutt want to crash. Nobody's pushed me around in two weeks, and it's starting to feel unnatural.'

'How was he going to get this money?'

'He never said. Hey, you want to put the gun away now? Please?'

Russ holstered the Mauser. 'Give me the names of some of his friends.'

'He didn't have any.'

'You don't spend three months with a guy and not hear a name.'

'I didn't – wait! I got, yeah, I got a phone number. What are you going to do when you find him?'

'Talk about some big money. What's the number?'

'You break down a door and you're waiting for him with a gun. You're not his old Army buddy that wants to guzzle beer with him, right? That's beautiful. When you find him, kick him in the nuts for me. He was going to take me out of this hole if I put him up for a while. Big Scorpio. I should of known.'

'You give me the number and I'll give him one in each nut for you.'

'That'd be nice. Just before you do it, tell him Evie sends her love. Once he had a phone call from some guy – hey! I got a name, too! From some guy named Ray. He had to write down a number, and he didn't have nothin' to write on. He yelled into the kitchen for me to remember it. Look, I mean, I gave you the name and I'm gonna give you the number. But it's going to cost me fifty bucks to get the goddamn door fixed. Could you, you know, since you busted it down, could you kind of help me out?'

Russ took a fifty, two twenties, and a ten from his wallet and gave them to her. 'Fifty for the name and fifty for the number.'

'Hey,' she said. 'Oh wow! That's really beautiful, man.' She gave him the number.

'What's your name?' he asked.

'Evie. Evelyn Weitzman. You wouldn't ... uh ... you wouldn't want to stick around for some coffee or something, would you?'

Russ shook his head 'Thanks, Evie.'

'What the hell. Nice guys aren't my karma. If you run into a bastard, you tell him where to find me, okay?'

It was three A.M. New York time when the phone rang in Perry's kitchen. Wylie listened, then said he'd catch the next flight back.

In the living room he told Perry, 'It checks out, but Cramer's skipped. Where can I find him?'

'I don't know. I didn't see him for five years before he called me. He can be into anything. But he's the kind that gets nervous when the heat's on. He's probably out of the country.'

'Okay,' Wylie said. 'I'm leaving now. Do you know anyone you can trust to be cool and not ask questions about why you're taped to a chair?'

Perry stared at the wall. 'Yeah.' He gave Wylie a number. 'His name is Sal. Just tell him Gene wants him to come over right away.'

'Figure on me calling him in three or four hours.'

Perry's mouth was set hard, but there were tears in his eyes. 'Put my shoes and socks back on, will you? And get rid of that goddamn knife and board.'

Wylie tugged Perry's socks on and laced up his shoes. He returned the knife to the kitchen and the shelving to the closet. He put his hand on the doorknob and said, 'I'll leave this unlocked so your buddy can get in. And if you're wondering, it *is* like I said. All I want's that case. I never even heard of you.'

Perry had not moved his eyes from the wall. 'You would have done it, wouldn't you? You would have cut me and let me bleed to death.'

'Yeah,' Wylie lied, to help the man with his shame. 'I would have.'

He left.

CHAPTER TEN

Russ's scrotum was tight when he stepped from the phone booth. His breathing was shallow, his armpits damp. Close, very close. He wanted Cramer. Or Mickey. Ray. He scratched Frank's ears and looked down the darkened length of Avenue B. Music and dull light washed from the Krishna Fluting. A few freaks and heads were clustered in front of it, a giant Hell's Angel in denims and chains. A couple of blacks with watermelon Afros and shades were intimidating and seducing a pair of teenyboppers.

Dawn was still two hours off. There was time. He could panic Ray and take him. He turned back to the phone and dialed Evadne. She answered sleepily after several rings.

'Vad, it's Russ. Sorry to wake you, but I need help.'

' 'S okay, darlin'. Just a minute.' Cellophane crackle, the scratch of a match, the deep starting-puffs of a cigarette. 'What's happenin'?'

'We're close on this Marecek thing. Do you have a pencil?'

'Yup.'

'Good.' He gave her the number he'd gotten from the girl. 'You're Evie. Evie Weitzman. You have to talk to Ray. If they give you a hard time, tell them it's a goddamn emergency and they can't blame you if the roof falls in. That's what Chuck told you. He called you and said to contact Ray at this number. Chuck has to meet Ray at four thirty at Pier Fifty-eight – if he doesn't, everyone's in bad trouble. If they grill you, tell them to piss off, you don't even know why you're doing this for Chuck after the way he ran out on you. Talk white, twenty, twenty-one years old, downbeat, a little slangy, you get used a lot. Do you have that?'

'I think so.'

'Give it back to me.' He listened. 'Good.' He read off the number of the phone he was speaking from. 'Call me back as soon as you're done.'

Russ waited ten minutes. A patrol car drifted toward the curb and slowed as it neared him. The two cops looked him over. He gave them a small wave. The one in the rider's seat nodded curtly. The car picked up speed and went by, slowing again for the people in front of Krishna Fluting. The phone rang.

'Some chick answered and got stiff with me,' Evadne said. 'I told her Ray would kick her ass if she didn't wake him up. I'll tell you, that Ray has the vocabulary and the sweetness of a Mississippi deputy sheriff.'

'Is he coming?'

'I can't say. I gave him the message. Is it dangerous?'

'No.'

'Be careful anyway. A big kiss.'

'I will. Thanks, Vad. Talk to you.'

He had to walk up to Fourteenth Street and a few blocks west to find a cab. They shunned the East Village. But because of the hour, Frank was more asset than liability: A man with a dog was less likely to mug you than were the other fares.

He took the cab to the end of Fourteenth Street, walked up to Sixteenth, and crossed beneath the elevated West Side Highway. Pier 58 was abandoned, sealed off by an eight-foot cyclone fence. The City could not prevent people from entering vacated property, but it was obligated to observe the forms nonetheless. It erected fences, it boarded over windows, it bricked up doors, and then, hands washed, it turned away, hoping that whoever breached these defenses would not be a major nuisance or embarrassment – like a group of Welfare families barricaded in a condemned brownstone.

Cars on the highway were infrequent; there was no one in eyesight. Russ unleashed Frank and walked the fence until he came to a tear in the links at the base of a post. He and Frank went through; then he bent it back into position.

Pier 58 had been rotting for years. Russ had used it once before, when he'd needed a private, isolated place where odd sounds would not be noted. Its shed was two stories tall, each story soaring fifty feet to the ceiling. Toward the rear of the first floor were two old house trailers that had once been used as command centers at construction sites. One was a burned-out shell; the other had been smashed by vandals. Russ looked at his watch: 3:25.

He entered the shed with Frank. 'Search,' he ordered.

Frank moved ahead and disappeared into the darkness. Russ wanted to find and clear out any vagrants or junkies who might be sleeping here. He followed the dog.

The boards beneath his feet were spongy, and he had to step over and around the detritus of age and droppings of the nameless. Stygian blackness. The clinking of cans and the crackle of glass he stepped on were magnified. Pieces of the ceiling above him were missing, and, far higher, a roof panel had fallen in. Through the gap he could barely make out a single star glimmering weakly through the fouled air. Water slapped rhythmically against the pilings. A light breeze was blowing in from the Jersey shore. The river smelled like the breath of an old and sick man.

Frank came up to him and butted his hand for petting. The shed was empty. In ten minutes a dog could search an area that would require an hour's effort by a team of eight men – and do it better. Russ didn't bother with the second floor. It was too treacherous even for the drunkest man to chance.

A water rat squealed angrily and went scrabbling away. Frank barked and lunged after it. '*Aus!*' Russ snapped, 'Heel.' The dog checked himself and returned to Russ's side, quiet.

A third of the way into the long shed, Russ stopped and looked back. The entrance was a large rectangular block of empty space that stretched from wall to wall and from the ground to the ceiling. It shone a paler shade of black than the interior of the shed. Russ doubted that Ray would arrive within the next half-hour. After that, the first gray seepage of false dawn would progressively lighten the mouth of the shed, and a man entering could easily be seen in silhouette, while a man within would still be hidden.

Whether he'd believed Evadne or not, Ray would have to know who could tie him to Chuck Cramer, and how much information that person had. It would be easier if he'd fallen for it and come alone, but either way he'd be jittery and not thinking well, and the help he'd bring, assuming he could muster any that was trustworthy on such short notice, couldn't be more than a man or two.

Russ moved to the north wall. He dropped his windbreaker and began working toward the entrance, moving rubbish. He counted his steps, and at fifty he piled up an obstacle of junk, another at one hundred, and a third fifty paces later. Fifty, one hundred, fifty; he could creep along the path soundlessly, but the barriers would trip up a man trying to come at him from the other end.

He returned to his windbreaker and settled down with Frank to wait. He listened to the river. It splashed; it sucked and moaned. Through a rent in the wall he watched the shrouded, spectral lights of a tugboat pass. Frank did not relax. His muscles ticked with each rustle and scratch of a rat. Once, several of the beasts engaged in a bumping, squealing fight. Frank trembled, but he remained silent and held his stay.

A scout dog's alert was a subtle thing. To the inexperienced, the dog reacted no differently to the scent or sound of a man, an animal, or a branch snapping in the wind, but a good handler who knew his animal could tell you precisely what it had focused on. An expert could even distinguish between the dog's scenting of a native and a foreign citizen.

So Russ ignored Frank's quick tensings and waited until the dog lifted his head to the fullest extension of his neck, hardened his muscles, and stared at the mouth of the shed. Then he patted the dog atop his broad skull and gave him the hand signals to stay and remain quiet. Russ crouched on the balls of his feet, arms resting lightly across his knees. He squinted and cocked his ear, but discerned nothing.

Frank moved his head, as if on a gear with infinitesimally tiny notches. Russ calculated the dog's line of attention. Someone was in the shed already, about twenty feet in, close to the south wall. Frank looked to the entrance again, studied it a moment, then returned to the man along the south wall. The man was progressing slowly. Russ admired his skill. Frank followed the painstaking advance. At roughly a hundred fifty feet the man stopped and held. Frank alternated his attention between that area and the entrance. Russ awaited the appearance of the second man, whom Frank had told him was lurking out there.

Several minutes later a figure emerged from the waning murkiness and walked openly toward the entrance. It paused and peered into the shed.

'Chuck?' The voice rolled over Russ.

Russ didn't answer.

The man entered. 'Chuck. It's me. Ray. Where are you?'

Russ looked to Frank: The first man was staying fast. Russ cupped his hands to his mouth, turned, distorted his voice, and tried to throw it behind and to the side. 'Yeah, Ray. Meet you halfway.'

'Sure. What's the problem? I thought you went to ground in New Mexico.'

Russ moved carefully down the lane he'd prepared, keeping low.

'Hey, man,' Ray called. 'You in trouble? Where are you?'

Russ skirted the first obstacle.

'What the hell?' Ray said with a touch of anger. 'What is this? ... Chuck? ... Listen, mother, you don't drag me down to this graveyard in the middle of the night to play games. Now where the hell are you?'

Russ reckoned he was abreast of the man along the south wall. Ray was still some ten yards farther toward the entrance. They had planned to box Russ.

'If you got somethin' to say, start talkin', or I'm walking' out,' Ray called.

Russ was on his hands and knees now, probing the floor before him and moving with excruciating care.

'Come on, you gutless bastard,' Ray said.

Russ lunged and seized both Ray's ankles, jerked hard. Ray shouted and crashed to the floor. A gun in his hand went off, stabbing a bright tongue of fire.

'Mickey!'

Ray's cry merged with a ragged snarl.

Russ had Ray's gun hand trapped by the wrist. He chopped against the underside of Ray's forearm with the hard edge of his other hand. Ray gasped and dropped the gun.

Headlights flared suddenly behind the fence at the end of the pier, ballooning bright light into the shed. The motor raced, and the car plunged forward and struck the gate in the center, bursting the Yale lock and throwing back the two sections, plunging through.

Ray got a knee into Russ's stomach and levered him off and back. Falling, Russ saw Mickey illuminated in the headlights. Mickey was leveling a .45 automatic. The gun discharged at the same moment that Frank, hurtling through the air, sank his teeth into Mickey's arm. They went down with a shout and growl.

Russ gained a knee. Ray was already on his feet, face raging. A switchblade knife sprang open even as he began a looping swing with it. Russ parried reflexively, slashing the stiffened edges of both hands into Ray's arm. In an instant: the knife clattered to the floor, Russ's right hand locked Ray's wrist, his legs pistoned up his weight, and – as he tried to check himself, too late – the heel of his left hand struck powerfully against the bottom of Ray's nose, driving up. Ray collapsed as if his spine had been severed.

The car was at the base of the pier, its motor racing. Gunfire spat from the driver's window and boomed within the confines of the shed. Frank was roaring and savaging Mickey, whose legs flailed ineffectually. He was screaming. A slug kicked up a can close to them and spun it away.

'Frank, *aus!*' Russ shouted. 'Come!' He wasn't going to risk the dog's being hit.

The animal disengaged and came running. Mickey got to his feet and went stumbling toward the car, clutching at his right arm, which dangled, torn and useless, at his side.

A bullet chunked into the floor between Russ and the dog. Russ grabbed the .38 Ray had dropped and dove for the nearest wall, where the angle would remove Frank from the shooter's field. Frank bounded up and smeared his tongue over Russ's face, tail stub beating.

Russ thumped the dog's shoulder. 'Good boy! Down! Stay!'

The dog dropped, and Russ ran into the open and brought the .38 to aim, its longer barrel more accurate than his own weapon. The car was already moving when Mickey hurled himself into the back seat through the door the driver had opened. It made a skidding and screeching U-turn. Russ's first shot had missed. His second starred the rear window. He squeezed off a third as the car roared through the sprung gates. It swerved crazily, but straightened out, managed the turn, and went speeding down Fourteenth Street.

Breathing heavily, Russ stood and listened. A car passed above on the highway. That was all. He walked down the shed and out to the pier. There was no one about. He closed the gates, found the ruptured lock, and positioned it. It would pass if it weren't examined closely.

He returned and released Frank from his stay. The dog sniffed once at Ray, then turned aside. Frank had no interest in corpses. Ray's crushed nose was filled with blood. Blood also darkened the inside corners of his eyes. Russ went through the dead man's pockets and found a wallet. He struck a match and read the driver's license: Raymond Fowler, Secaucus, New Jersey. Russ put the wallet in his pocket.

He dragged Fowler deeper into the shed, to the side of a rubbish pile. He wiped Fowler's pistol free of prints with a rag, then pressed the fingers of both Fowler's hands at different places on the gun. The single shot Fowler had discharged would cause a paraffin test to read positive – if anyone bothered to make one. He covered the body and gun with junk, searched for and found Mickey's .45. He cleared it of prints and dropped it through a hole in the floor into the river below. He called Frank and left the shed.

It was nearly light. He waited in the shadows for a pair of cars to pass, then went through the fence the way he'd entered. He walked east on Fourteenth Street, feeling vibrancy and fullness and something that was close to joy. He turned south on Greenwich Avenue and went to Herbie's, an all-night diner where he was known and where they didn't mind Frank's settling into a corner. He told the counterman, Julio, to put up sausages and scrambled eggs for him; then he sat in the phone booth and closed the door.

He obtained Fowler's phone number from New Jersey Information and called it. No one answered. He ate

187

breakfast and walked to the Kinney office on Sixth Avenue. He rented a car, using Fowler's license, and drove to an all-night drugstore, where he bought a pair of Playtex gloves. Then downtown to the Holland Tunnel.

Fowler had lived in a cramped, artificial, polluted valley. It was bordered on the east by a dead river, on the south by a line of massive oil-storage tanks, on the north by a breastworks of power dynamos, and on the west by tall factory stacks that billowed reddish-black smoke into the sky.

The house was a peeling one-story clapboard structure with rusted automobile parts in the overgrown yard. Russ drove by it and continued another block to the street's end – the river, oily and cluttered with debris. A houseboat was moored to the pilings of a rotted pier, wash hanging from a line. Two more had been forsaken and were only partially afloat. Green moss had climbed up from the waterline over their weathered boards. Russ turned around and went back. He parked three blocks away on another street, across from a fenced new-car depot.

He walked to Fowler's house. Frank heeled at his side. Two bearded youths from what looked to be a commune watched him pass. From the porch of a house with half a dozen Harleys in the drive, a man in a sleeveless denim jacket with a death's head on the back and an iron cross over the heart gave him a bellicose look. But no one else paid him any attention. The morning was overcast. People were rising for work, lights were on in some of the small houses, querulous voices sounded, radios, cooking smells.

Fowler's house was dark and quiet. Russ didn't think Mickey or the man who had driven the car would have chanced coming here. There were too many unknowns. But he put the Mauser in his jacket pocket and thumbed off the safety. The porch boards creaked. Springs stuck though an old sofa in the corner. No one answered his knock. He went to the back door and knocked. Nothing. He put on the Playtex gloves, broke a pane of glass, reached through, and opened the lock. Pistol in hand, he signaled Frank to stay; then he banged open the door and rushed into the kitchen, hard to the left. Most men are right-handed, and a right-handed gunman has more trouble following a target moving to his right than one moving to his left.

The kitchen was empty. Russ called Frank in and said, 'Search.'

The dog prowled through the house with his head high, snuffling the air. There was no one.

Russ tried Wylie from the phone in the living room. He got no answer. He called the doorman of Wylie's building, gave his name and Fowler's number, and asked that Wylie call him as soon as he could.

The house was six rooms and an unfinished basement. Russ set about searching it. He was thorough and destructive. Wylie called while he was working on the third room.

'The girl gave me a New York City number for Fowler,' Russ said. 'I don't know if he has a pad there or a chick he shacks up with or what. This place looks like he lived here on and off. I haven't turned up anything so far.'

'I'll be right out with Ahab. Just let me change shirts and shave.'

'Don't bring the Mercedes. It'd stick out around here.'

'I'll take the new van, the one that doesn't have the logo painted on it yet.'

'Pull right into the drive. It curves to a garage behind the house. You're covered by fences on both sides, and I don't think anybody much cares what's going on.'

'See you soon.'

Frank barked. Russ went to a window. The blue van

189

was pulling up. Frank stood on his hind legs and put his paws on the sill. He saw Ahab get out with Wylie, and he growled.

Russ took the dog into the kitchen, downed him and told him to stay, and opened the door for Wylie. 'The living room's through there,' he said. 'Take Hab in and I'll bring Frank out to the van.'

The dogs glared at each other with raised hackles.

Russ opened both the van's windows a little for ventilation and left Frank there.

He told Wylie, 'I found two pistols in a compartment behind the bathroom medicine chest. And a bottle of speed caps and about three hundred cash in a dresser drawer. But nothing else.'

Wylie nodded, pulling on his silk gloves. 'Was there any coffee?'

'A jar of instant.' Russ got it.

Wylie ran water in a pan. 'You want any?'

'No.'

Wylie shut the tap and put the pan on the stove. He leaned his buttocks against the edge of a counter. 'Russ, did you have to kill Fowler?'

'He was trying to gut me.'

'Okay.' Wylie was quiet for several moments. 'I hope we find it here,' he said. 'It's getting grubby.' He blinked to clear the image of Perry's tormented face from his mind.

'If we don't, we can move on that guy Mickey. I made him. Mickey the Hammer – Michelangelo Guida. He's a street soldier and muscle for a small-time juice racket. I've seen him around the bars.'

'Did he make you?' Wylie asked with alarm.

'No way. He doesn't know I'm alive.'

Wylie poured boiling water into his cup and stirred the coffee. He sat down at the table. He yawned. 'This all-day-and-all-night stuff is rugged. How are you holding up?'

Russ was charged with frustrated energy. 'Okay,' he said. Ahab was leaning against him. He petted the dog. 'Do you have something Hab can take a scent from?'

Wylie tore open the top of a lavender pack of cigarettes and tossed the pack to Russ. 'She had some of these in the case.'

Russ sniffed. 'I could almost smell 'em out myself.'

Wylie finished his coffee, took the cigarettes back, and leashed Ahab. The dog tensed in anticipation of a command. Wylie held the pack before Ahab's nose. Ahab sniffed deeply. 'Find it!' Wylie said. The dog sniffed rapidly, graving the scent into his mind. His tail swished excitedly. Wylie flipped the cigarettes to Russ, who opened a window and dropped them outside where they wouldn't distract the animal. Wylie turned Ahab toward a cabinet. The dog sniffed its interior, browsed his nose over the canned goods Russ had spilled out, then went to the next cabinet.

Much was being asked of Ahab. Most search dogs were specialists – trained for nothing but scent work and to seek only one type of article, such as marijuana, or guns, or explosives. A general scent dog, one that could immediately internalize a new scent and relate it to previous experience as the object of the moment's quest, was rare, and required an animal capable of abstraction to a degree not frequently found in creatures whose comprehension was mostly literal and specific. The success ratio of such generalists was not high, but Ahab was intelligent, flexible, possessed excellent olfactory capacity, and had a mania for accomplishment.

Wylie handled him softly. A taut leash could make an animal feel restricted, even censured, which could dampen its ardor, or, if used to direct the dog too heavy-handedly, could distract or blur its focus.

Russ watched Ahab with pleasure. He loved the dog almost as much as he loved his own.

Ahab finished the kitchen in ten minutes, and Wylie

brought him into the living room.

'I think,' Russ said, careful not to offend – (Ahab was not *his* dog), – 'that he's a bit too geared. Maybe he should be slowed, not cramped, but backed off a bit.'

When a dog was eager, a scent search plunged it into a holocaust of concentration. The animal could burn itself out in a matter of minutes if given its head.

Wylie studied Ahab. 'You're right,' he said. Gently, he tempered the dog.

The dog was working hard. Russ hoped – for Ahab's sake, and nothing more – that he would discover the case. Too many runs over barren territory could depress a dog. The sense of failure was strong. Russ decided that if the case were not here, he'd hide the cigarettes Wylie had brought and allow Ahab to find them so that the dog could have the pleasure of success.

He said, 'There's a bunch of sealed cartons down in the basement. About thirty. Hab can do them a lot faster than I could've, so I left them alone. While you finish the house, I'm going to do the garage.'

Wylie nodded, watching Ahab go over a stereo speaker.

Russ stopped at the van for a few moments with Frank. The dog wasn't happy, and Russ roughhoused him into better spirits. 'You worked your ass off, old buddy, and I'm proud of you and I love you for it. But we've got to let that other dog do something too,' he said. 'Just to keep him happy. I know he's a pain in the neck, but we all have to make a little sacrifice now and then.' He hugged Frank. Frank washed his face. 'Good boy, good ol' dog.'

Frank didn't want Russ to leave, but accepted it gracefully.

Russ was prying a tire from a rim when Wylie brought Ahab to the garage.

'We blanked,' Wylie said.

Russ set aside the tire iron and looked into the tubeless tire. 'Out here so far too. We'll have to go after Guida.'

Wylie unsnapped Ahab's leash. 'Okay, Hab. Break time.'

But the dog didn't want to stop. He went to a bench and began sniffing.

Russ clapped his hands. 'Come on, boy. Lay off and goof with me.'

Ahab froze. He swiveled his head toward the Pontiac station wagon on the far side of the cluttered garage. His nose went high. Sniffing, he moved forward.

Wylie and Russ glanced at each other.

Russ had searched the car. Its hood, doors, and tailgate stood open; the carpet had been ripped up from the floor, the upholstery cut and the stuffing probed, the spare tire popped from its rim.

Ahab pressed his nose to the front fender and worked his way down the car, emitting machinegun-quick snorts and leaving a thin trail of moisture on the metal. He barked suddenly, and leaped into the cargo section and began clawing at the floor. Russ and Wylie hurried to him. The dog jumped down and squirmed under the bumper. He barked again, then growled. There were scraping sounds. Russ and Wylie went to their knees Ahab was growling and whining and biting at the gas tank.

'We're home, baby,' Wylie said.

He called Ahab out. The dog came reluctantly. Wylie put him in a down-stay and petted him and talked to him softly to ease his tension.

Russ took a flashlight from a rack above the workbench and crawled under the car. 'I checked the undercarriage before, and I still don't see anything,' he called. 'It must be in the gas tank.'

He slid out, hotwired the car, and checked the dashboard. 'Shit, the tank's full. That's better than twenty gallons, too heavy to drop.'

'We'll have to drain her.' Under Wylie's hand, Ahab was calming, but he didn't look away from the car.

Russ removed the hotwire. He rummaged up two old galvanized buckets, a chisel, and a hand sledge. He set the Pontiac's parking brake, chocked the front wheels, jacked up the back, and braced it with blocks of two-by-four scrap. 'It'll come fast,' he said, going back under the car. 'Get ready.' With the sledge, he punched the chisel through the gas tank. Pinkish gas sprayed around the edges of the chisel and stained his shirt. He swore and yanked the chisel free. The gas poured down into a bucket.

Wylie squatted at the bumper. As the bucket filled, Russ slid it aside and moved the second one into place. Wylie took the full bucket out the side door, and spilled the gas onto the brown grass. He returned, gave the bucket back to Russ, and received the second one almost immediately. He dumped that and came back.

'Son of a gun,' Russ said curiously from beneath the car.

'What?'

'We've got about half this bucket and the tank's drying up. It's down to a trickle ... drops now ... that's it. But we can't have emptied more than five gallons.' He rapped his knuckles against the tank. 'It's empty all right. Maybe the gauge is busted.'

He came out and foraged for the tools he needed to remove the tank. 'Don't light any cigarettes. It's lousy with fumes.'

Wylie took Ahab out of the garage to relieve himself and to relax. But Frank pressed his snout to the van's window and rumbled menacingly, and Ahab walked about the vehicle with stiff legs and bristling hair, so Wylie took him back inside.

Loud hammering sounded under the car. Russ grunted. There was a wrench of metal. The gas tank clanged against the concrete. Russ dragged it into the open. He forced the midseam and pried the two halves apart.

'So that's how he did it.' He showed Wylie a large soldered compartment mounted within the tank. 'Watertight. It takes up most of the space. The gas fills the area between the outside of this and the inside wall of the tank. The gauge reads full, even though you have only five or six gallons. Great for smuggling.'

Russ broke the solder seal and exposed the interior of the compartment. Five canvas pouches lay within, closed with knotted drawstrings.

'Let Hab finish it,' he said.

Wylie brought the dog from his stay. He strained at his collar. Wylie said, 'Find it!' and released the animal.

Ahab lunged, grabbed a pouch and pulled it aside, and seized the one beneath it. He shook it and barked around it and whipped the air with his tail.

'Good boy!' Wylie said. 'Good boy!' He rubbed the dog, then held out his hand and said, 'Give.' Ahab released the pouch.

Russ petted Ahab, smiling.

Wylie opened the pouch and dumped its contents on to the floor: bracelets, watches, necklaces, pendants, earrings, cuff links, lighters, jeweled pillboxes, and other exquisite trifles – and Lesley Marecek's gold cigarette case. Wylie flicked the catch, flipped out the cigarettes, worked a fingernail beneath the bottom plate, and lifted it against the light spring pressure. Two strips of 35-mm. negatives lay there, ten frames each. Wylie held one up to the light.

'That's the job,' he said.

CHAPTER ELEVEN

They opened the other pouches. One was stuffed with paper money and a packet of negotiable securities. The cash went over six thousand dollars, some thirty-four hundred of it in older, circulated bills. They took that and left the new bills and the securities.

There were also three glossy photos of businessmen at different banquets, one a political affair with the governor as featured guest. Julius Hollander appeared in each, his ascetic face smiling politely and circled in red grease pencil.

'It was Hollander they wanted,' Wylie said.

Russ was stroking Ahab. He looked at the photos without much interest.

Wylie turned them over. On the back of one, written with the same grease pencil and in a bold vertical hand, were Malcolm Chasteen's name, address, the date of the party, and the time at which guests would begin arriving. Beneath that another hand had scrawled in pencil: 'Ray. Memorize the hit and burn this shit. M.'

'M – Mickey,' Wylie said. 'Ray should have burned these. Dumb.'

'Maybe he planned to squeeze the guy who set this up.'

'It'd be nice to know who that is.'

Russ shrugged.

Wylie handled some of the jewelry. 'Some of this is really fine. You could turn a nice dollar even taking the bottom from a fence.'

'Don't even think it, man. You've never seen anything hotter.'

Wylie sighed. 'I guess.' He began bagging the jewelry. 'But, oh sweet mama, it does hurt a boy!'

'Just leave it.'

'That would bother my sleep, thinking it was laying for any rummy to trip over.' Wylie reflected. 'Fowler's house is oil-heated. I'm going to stick it on the upper ledge of the firebox and disconnect the thermostat. If anyone finds it, at least I'll know he had to do some figuring.'

Still, it hurt him to leave the jewelry.

He dropped Russ and Frank at Russ's rented car. He looked at his watch, and realized he'd forgotten to phone the school. 'Did you call Pat and tell her we wouldn't be in today?'

Russ shook his head. 'I'm heading there now.'

'You're a stronger man than me. The only place I'm heading is to bed – well, I might show in the afternoon.'

'Take the day. I'll handle everything.'

'I'll see how it goes.' Wylie put the van in gear but kept the clutch depressed. He looked across the seat through the opposite window at Russ, who was behind the wheel of the car, lighting a cigarette. 'You did a nice job, Russ.'

Russ nodded. 'You too. It went okay.'

Wylie pulled away. Russ sat and petted Frank, looking out the windshield at a broken wooden fence. Scaling paint, long rust stains tailing down from nailheads. He started the car.

He drove back to Manhattan at a moderate speed, not thinking, his dog asleep with his head in Russ's lap. He felt dead in a small way. It was always so at times of ending. He was weary. But he did not want to return to the emptiness of his apartment, to its entombment.

He steered with one hand. The other rested on Frank's head.

That Russ had gone to work shamed Wylie out of sleeping all day. He was annoyed at his vanity for not permitting him the collapse he wanted. But he felt good after the alarm woke him, and he showered and dressed.

He'd have slept through the early evening otherwise, and thrown his schedule off for days. He called Evadne, endured her abuse for having ignored her these last few weeks, and cajoled her into breaking a date and fixing dinner for him that night.

He arrived at Cerberus at four, buoyant and filled with bonhomie. He wore a severe black leather vest over a brown-and-gold paisley shirt, belled tweeds with a chain belt through the loops, and ankle-high shoes of low-gloss brown.

The staff was gathered around a desk singing 'For He's a Jolly Good Fellow.' Wylie offered them a modest bow, but was aggrieved upon straightening to discover that no one had even noticed his entrance. Kenroy and Cheryl had their arms around each other's shoulders. George and Russ were shaking hands. Abbie kissed Harold, who turned scarlet. Everyone was drinking from paper cups. An empty magnum of champagne stood next to Pat's phone console.

The song ended, and Kenroy led a 'Hip-hip-hurrah!'

Wylie approached and said, 'What obtains?'

Pat turned and said, 'What whats?'

'It was a pompous joke,' Wylie apologized.

'Oh. Tickle me and I'll giggle.' She raised her paper cup to him.

'My God, I'm employing a gang of drunks.'

Pat stepped aside 'I give you Kong – graduate of Cerberus School for Dogs.'

The Welsh corgi was atop the desk. His tail was metronoming allegro as he finished what remained of a thick marbled filet which rested on butcher's paper.

'You mean...?'

Cheryl nodded 'In the last thirty-six hours he has urinated nine times and defecated three on the street and hasn't had a single accident inside. I declare this dog housebroken.'

There was applause.

Kong gobbled down the last piece, raised his head, and went, 'Rowff!'

Wylie congratulated the dog. Then he asked, 'Who's funding this party?'

'Uh ... petty cash,' Pat said.

'Cerberus is generous,' Wylie said.

Cheryl snuggled up against him. 'That's why you manage to keep us while the other schools lose all their good trainers.'

'Sometimes,' Wylie said, 'I am moved to clap my hands in happiness.'

'We'd give you some champagne, but there isn't any left,' Abbie said.

'Call the store and have them deliver another bottle.'

'Terrific.' Abbie hesitated. 'Uh ... who's paying for it?'

'Petty cash,' Wylie said 'It's one of the ways I manage to keeep all my good trainers.'

Cheryl said, 'We really shouldn't. We have a group class scheduled in fifteen minutes. It wouldn't look right.'

'I think what I need is some mediocre and irresponsible trainers.'

Cheryl looked offended.

The school was back to normal in half an hour. The group class was under way, a client's puli was being sharpened for the last leg of its Utility Dog degree, and the first of the area guards was loaded into a van.

Wylie went over the log. Russ had dealt with everything immediate. There were a few calls to return, but they could wait until tomorrow. Joseph Sucher's name was on the list. He wondered what Sucher wanted, and decided to phone him now. He was putting off the call to Lesley Marecek, extending the sweetness of accomplishment.

He gave his name to Sucher's secretary, and she asked him to hold. Sucher picked up a moment later.

'Lincoln, good of you to get back. How's it hanging?'

'A little at an angle.'

'Right – proportionate to the mass of the ass. There's a science in there somewhere.'

'How are you feeling?'

'Like a bull who survived the ring. Bit a nurse on an unmentionable last week, and they threw me out. Goddamn charnel house. Now I can breathe again.'

'I'm glad to hear it. Incidentally, I've been rereading *Ivory and Ice*. It's superb. The sequence –'

'That piece of shit! I'd like to buy up every copy and burn 'em. Living with that book is like living with a big *zits* in the middle of your forehead.'

When you complimented a man's work and he answered by condemning it as inept, he was denigrating your taste and intelligence. It was a particularly nasty form of entrapment and put-down.

'Oh, I don't know,' Wylie said. 'There were some good things in it. The grammar and the spelling, for example.'

Sucher paused. Then he laughed. 'A hundred and twenty years ago, I'd have had to put you on the block and sell you. You'd have been too much trouble to keep around.'

'A hundred and twenty years ago you'd have been pissing your pants and running from Cossacks.'

'Sucher one, Lincoln one. *Fin*. Listen, I'm working on a film and I need your help.'

'I thought you were doing the Chasteen book for Harper's.'

'Oh, yeah, yeah. That's moving. I've profiled the first of the killers already – a graduate student at Chicago U., probably European Literature. The second one's coming. He's a telephone lineman or a backhoe operator from New England somewhere. I haven't been able to reason out the others yet, but they'll shape soon. Right now I'm doing this film – did you see my last one, *Stone Phallus*? – well, I'm elaborating and refining the same premise in this one. *J.S.*, it's called. Anyway, I need a big, tough, ugly son of a bitch of a dog. You have any real savages on hand?'

'A couple. What do you want it to do?'

'I want it turned loose against me from about fifty feet. I'll stop it before it reaches me.'

'How?'

'By bringing energy to bear. Focusing the power of the universe through my mind. You know, the ascendancy of man.'

'Well, we can order the dog to drop before it hits. But we should work from eighty or ninety feet to be sure we have enough time. It's a matter of split seconds.'

'No, no. You just send it at me. I'll do the stopping. This is a *truthful* film.'

'Mr Sucher,' Wylie said. 'It won't work.'

'You don't think man can tap the power of the cosmos?'

'It's what the dog thinks that counts. You'd be mutilated.'

'Impossible.'

'Last year a karate master bet two thousand dollars that he could stop any dog in the world. A trainer took him up. The karate man pistoned a kick that would have smashed bricks. The dog caught his foot, broke it with one bite, then cut the guy's calf muscle before the trainer could get it off.'

'I'm not impressed by karate.'

'Neither is a dog.'

'Okay. You leave the universe to me, and I'll leave dogs to you. We'll fake it.'

'But what happens to your reality then?' Wylie asked pleasantly.

'Don't be specious. Reality is an illusion. Sometimes you have to go beyond it to find truth.'

They fixed a rehearsal date.

It was after five. Harold was winding up the group

201

class, the last of the area guards had been loaded, and Pat was closing down her desk. Wylie wasn't due at Evadne's for two and a half hours, which gave him enough time to meet Lesley. He went to the rear office and dialed her number.

She answered before the first ring finished. 'My God, I was just picking up the phone to call you. Victor's on to one of those people – some cheap Syndicate thug. He's expecting the name any minute.' Her voice cracked. 'What am I going to do! He'll get those goddamn negatives and he'll kill me!'

'No one's getting the negatives but you, Lesley. I have them right in my pocket.'

She gave a little cry. 'You do?'

'Yes. Just tell me where to meet you, and you can have them as soon as I get out of the cab.'

'Oh Christ. Oh Jesus. Oh thank you! Oh God, *thank you!*'

'You're welcome.'

'I'll do anything for you. Tell me and I'll do it.'

'Just bring the money.'

'The money,' she said. 'Yes, I forgot that. Very well. What does it come to?'

'You gave me twenty-five hundred against five thousand. Call the expenses seven fifty. So there's a balance due of thirty-two fifty.'

'You want cash, I suppose.'

'Of course.'

She named an uptown bar on Third Avenue and said she'd meet him in an hour.

Wylie called Lamorena's office.

'Hey,' Lamorena said, 'I gotta thank you for Raphaela Bracey's boy – that Christian Wright kid. He's not human, he's something IBM made up. It's costing me a fortune, but the government's going to get a big zero. We'll fly that tax suit like a kite.'

'Congratulations.'

Lamorena's voice became guarded. 'What's up?'

'I made a little progress.'

'Yeah?'

'I have a name you might like. It belongs to man with a shotgun.'

'You don't say.'

'I do.'

'And you want to give it to me because I'm a nice guy.'

'Are you?'

'Oh yeah. I'm so nice, it doesn't even rain on me.'

'Well, I figured you'd probably be nice enough to give me a name in return.'

'Whose?'

'The man behind the man with shotgun.'

'I don't know any names like that.'

'Maybe you'll stumble across it.'

'That'd be a funny thing to stumble across.'

'Hilarious. But these things happen sometimes.'

'Sometimes. What's the name you got?'

'Michelangelo Guida. They call him Mickey the Hammer.'

'That's a cute name.'

'I thought you'd like it.'

'Sure. Good to hear from you, Lincoln. Stay in touch.'

Wylie said good-bye.

It was a long shot. Guida was probably already trussed up in the warehouse below Lamorena's office. The man would be a cancellation by morning, and would have been whether Wylie had called or not. But this way Lamorena might, possibly, pass on to Wylie anything he happened to learn from Guida. Wylie had done what he'd been hired to do, but he was still pricked by the missing parts. It bothered him more or less the same way the *Unfinished Symphony* did.

The Jubjub Bird was a singles bar, token sawdust on the floor, open barrels of peanuts, color organs and deaf-

ening music, a small platform at the back for poetry read-
ings and tight theatrics. The platform was empty now.
Wylie got to the bar as it was beginning to fill, and he
managed to beat a young man with a sculpted beard and
a corduroy jacket to the only remaining table, jammed
into a rear corner.

It was a good place to meet – no one in this social
stratum would recognize either of them. A green-eyed girl
with streaked hair, in a leotard and black tights, her
crotch covered by a tiny white frilly apron, took his order
without interest. She returned with a big mug and a
pitcher of Lowenbrau Dark.

Wylie had finished half the pitcher before Lesley arrived. She wore a simple cotton dress, bright, countryish
and full-skirted, and a red collar around her neck. She'd
applied minimal make-up. Her hair fell carelessly over
her nearly bare shoulders. The effect was calculated to
give her an air of innocence that might be toppled by the
right man. If he was gentle, of course. And sincere. Walking past the stag line at the bar, she twanged chords of
lust. A man with bushy mutton-chops looped an arm
around her waist and drew her in. She jerked her head
up with a look of confusion, fear, and betrayal. He apologized and released her. She thanked him with a sweet
and timid smile and made her way to Wylie. Here and
there a face soured as she sat down with this very black
nigger.

'You can't possibly conceive of how grateful I am,' she
said earnestly.

'I'm glad it worked out for you.'

'*You* made it work out, I'll never forget that.'

Wylie demurred.

The waitress appeared. Lesley ordered a sweet dai-
quiri, which Wylie thought was overdoing it.

'Was it terribly troublesome for you?' she asked.

'Not too. Mostly a series of lucky breaks.'

'I was very worried. I couldn't have lived with myself if

204

I'd been responsible for your getting ... hurt, or anything.'

'You shouldn't have concerned yourself,' Wylie said reassuringly. 'This kind of thing is mostly paperwork and contacts.'

The waitress brought Lesley's drink.

'Did you ... uh ... did you...' She averted her eyes. 'Look at the negatives?'

'Well, I did have to make sure a switch hadn't been pulled,' Wylie admitted.

Her cheeks and ears reddened.

Wylie's estimation of her soared – that was no simple ability. 'I'm sorry,' he said. 'It was necessary.'

She nodded. Then she sucked in breath, appeared to pull herself together, and looked up. 'Well. It's over now. I can put it behind me.'

'That's best.'

'Do you have the negatives with you?'

'Yes, I do.'

She smiled shyly and held out her hand.

'Do you have the money with you?' Wylie asked humbly.

'I'm afraid I couldn't raise it in cash so quickly.' Lesley pressed her lips together and shook her head in apology, her hair swirling prettily. 'But I'll have it for you by Monday. I promise.' Her voice was girlishly determined.

'Monday will be fine,' Wylie said. 'And don't you worry about the negatives. They'll be safe with me.'

'Oh, I'm sure they would. But I'd feel so much better if I could have them now. It's been such torture.' She laid her hand atop Wylie's.

'I would too. And I'd feel even so much better than you if I had the money.'

She looked softly into his eyes a moment. Then she leaned back abruptly and said, 'Oh, fuck it!'

Wylie grinned.

The waitress walked by, carrying four drinks on a tray.

Lesley shot her hand out and snatched a double Scotch from it. The waitress stopped short, turned angrily, and said, 'You can goddamn well wait your turn, baby. Now gimme that back.'

Lesley fished in her purse and put a five-dollar bill on the tray. 'Be a love, and buy one for yourself, too.'

The girl crumpled the bill into the pocket of her apron, shrugged, and turned back toward the bar.

Lesley took a good belt of Scotch, rested her forearms on the table, and hunched forward. 'Lincoln, you're twenty-five hundred to the good already. The negatives are out of those clowns' hands – my sweat is over. I think you got enough for the job. So you can shove the negatives. Stick 'em under your pillow if you want, and give yourself sweet dreams.' She smiled dazzlingly, raised her glass to him, and drank again.

'It's a sad life,' Wylie said unhappily.

'That's not the half of it, sweetheart.'

Wylie produced a folded envelope. He flattened it on the table, took a pen from his shirt pocket, and wrote a name and address on the front. He removed a stamp from his wallet, licked it, and pressed it onto the upper right corner.

Lesley watched incredulously.

He put her cigarette case on the table, slipped the negatives out before her staring eyes, placed them in the envelope, and sealed it.

'What the hell are you doing!' Lesley had read Victor Lamorena's name and office address upside down.

'Going to mail a letter. There's a box right on the corner. He might even have these by tomorrow morning.'

'You wouldn't do it. You wouldn't!'

'We had an agreement. I fulfilled my end of it.'

Lesley slammed her purse on the table, snatched a manila envelope out, and threw it against Wylie's chest. It bounced off and fell into his lap. 'It's all there,' she spat. 'You can count it if you'd like.'

'I will,' Wylie said. He opened the flap and went through the corners of the bills with his thumb and forefinger. 'You're right, it's all there.'

She glared in dumb rage.

He pushed the envelope containing the negatives over to her. 'As Evadne told you – I'm a real prick.'

Evadne opened the door to him in a silken blue lounging gown cinched at the waist with a tasseled white cord. The neckline opened casually to the first mounding of her belly. Her large nipples and the delta between her thighs were faint shadows. It was not a garment in which to receive callers – unless you received callers for a living.

Wylie moved to embrace and kiss her. She slipped away from his hands and turned her cheek to his lips.

'I want to kiss you,' he said.

'Why? Has Scandinavia declared you *persona non grata*? Is everyone else on vacation?'

'Aw, come on, honey. I thought we did that on the phone. I've been *working*.'

'We might as well get married again, for all the attention you pay me.'

Wylie feigned reflection. 'You ... might be right.'

She jumped away. 'Not on your ass, brother!'

Wylie laughed and grabbed her wrists. 'Then treat me right or I'll propose, you bitch. You didn't dress that way for the doorman.'

'A girl has to get it where she can.'

He pressed his mouth to hers and ran his hands down her back to the high roundness of her buttocks. She returned his kiss, put her long fingers into his hair, and did his scalp with her nails. He lifted her bottom up and forward, which brought her groin strongly against his. She moved on him, crooked a knee, and stroked the inner part of his leg with her bare foot.

They separated and looked into each other's faces with the pleased expressions of two neighboring, wary, but generally amicable warlords.

'Well, it *is* about time you gave me a thought,' she said.

'Way, way past time, chile.'

She led him into the living room. 'Sit down, remove shoes, liquefy yourself.'

He dropped onto the couch. She went to the bar and fixed him a large bourbon. He accepted it gratefully. She walked behind him, leaned over the back of the couch, and began to massage the muscles of his shoulders. He sipped his drink and sighed.

'You have to amuse yourself for about fifteen,' she said. 'While I finish in the kitchen. Dinner in an hour?'

'Great. It smells terrific.'

'It is.'

She kissed the crown of his head and went into the kitchen. 'I assume,' she called from there, 'that your obvious smugness means you've finished the job for Lesley.'

'Yup. Want to hear all the exciting and brilliant details?'

'Not tonight especially. Tomorrow morning.'

'A woman should take more interest in her man's work.'

'Oh, I intend to take a strong interest in your work tonight.'

'Work? That's how you see it?'

'I'm feeling very narcissistic. I'm going to make you work.'

'Hey, speaking of that, did you tell Lesley that I was a real prick?'

'Sure. You are.'

'Yeah, but I don't think you should be mentioning that to strangers.'

'Oh, Lesley's not a stranger. We've been friendly for a while.'

'She does seem the type you'd get along with.'

Evadne came to the kitchen door. 'What does that mean?'

'*I* never talk about people to other people.'

Evadne eyed him suspiciously, then turned back into the kitchen.

'Who's sending flowers?' Wylie asked. On a table at the far side of the room was a large arrangement of deep-hued red and purplish flowers. Exotic, meaty petals, strangely voluptuous.

'Neal Cummings.'

'That Wall Street number who wants your ass?'

'To be crude, yes. And he's getting more difficult. I went out with him last night. He has one arm in a sling – pulled some muscle in a polo accident – but he still gave me more trouble than a rutty gorilla with two good ones. He had me down to my panties before I could shove him out the door. These came today, I think they're an apology. Men in his class aren't supposed to get so pushy about things.'

Wylie walked across the room. 'They look expensive.'

'They are. The deliveryman was very impressed. They have a twenty-six-letter name, and he told me they're flown in from the Amazon River or some place. That's about a hundred and fifty dollars worth of transient beauty. At least *he* appreciates me.'

Wylie fingered the envelope attached to the stalks with green florist's wire. It was sealed. 'Don't you even bother to read the card?'

Evadne came into the living room with a drink in her hand. 'There. All done. No. Tell you the truth, he has nothing to say that I really want to hear.'

'Poor boy.' Wylie opened the envelope. He read the card and set it down carefully. 'Vad,' he said, 'I'm sorry, baby, but I've got to. I'll –'

'You *what*?!' she said unbelievingly.

Moving to the door, Wylie said. 'It's too complicated. But it's important. I have to run.'

'Oh no. You are not walking out of here.' His hand was on the doorknob. 'You are not leaving me tonight. You are not. Do you understand?' Her voice shrilled as he turned the knob: *'You are not!'*

He opened the door. 'Please, baby. I'll call you later. But I —'

She screamed and hurled her glass at him. It trailed Scotch as it came. He slammed the door behind him, just in time to intercept the glass, which shattered.

He hurried down the hall, hearing Evadne's muffled voice: 'You prick!' she shouted. 'You prick! Prick! Prick!'

CHAPTER TWELVE

Wylie rapped on the door. Behind it, Frank barked. Russ's voice said, '*Aus*,' and the dog went silent.

'It's me,' Wylie called.

Russ was slack-faced; there were pouches under his eyes. 'What's on?'

Wylie entered and turned in to the kitchen. On the table were a water glass with red wine and a partly eaten TV dinner in its aluminium tray.

'I think I know who paid to have Hollander hit.'

Russ sat down and picked up his fork. 'That's cool,' he said. He cut a piece of Salisbury steak and put it in his mouth.

Wylie took ice from the refrigerator and helped himself to a bourbon. 'You want to know?'

'It doesn't mean a thing to me.'

'What are we going to do?'

'Nothing. We already did what we were hired to do.'

Frank curled up on the floor beside Russ.

'Hey, baby. We're talking about a goddamn killer.'

Russ chewed a mouthful of peas and carrots. He lifted his wine and drank.

'We can't just let it go,' Wylie said. He was pacing the room.

Frank followed Wylie with his eyes.

'Why?' Russ reached down and patted the dog.

'Because he had a man *murdered*.'

Russ's face was empty. Wylie looked away from it.

'The son of a bitch shouldn't get away with that,' Wylie said.

'Did you ever kill anyone?' Russ asked.

'Come on.'

'Tell me.'

'Yes,' Wylie said.

'Uh huh,' Russ said. 'One when you were a cop and three when you weren't. I tell you, Wylie – you kill somebody, he dies. That's what killing means. It doesn't change shit whether the killer was a nice guy or not or whether the corpse was a nice guy or not. Why the fuck should you get away with it?'

Wylie took his bourbon in a big swallow and poured another. He sat down across from Russ. 'There are differences.'

'Sometimes. But they don't mean anything.'

'Killing and murder are two separate things.'

Russ continued to eat.

'For Christ's sake, you never *murdered* anyone. Right?'

Russ stopped chewing. 'You don't want to ask me that, Wylie. Not really, you don't.'

Wylie's stomach turned over.

Russ swallowed, and lifted another forkful of food.

Wylie looked into his glass. 'I don't like just walking away from it, man.'

Russ pushed the TV dinner aside and laid his palms on the table. There was strain in his voice. 'We have three choices. One – we forget about the mother, he doesn't exist. Two – you can kill him. You, not me. Because I'm not God's Soldier. If it's going to make you sleep better, then take him off. But don't try and lay it on me. Three – we can turn him in to the cops, and that would just be smart as hell, because they'd start digging, and they'd find that we've done a lot of interesting things, including making a body of our own last night.' He got up and refilled his glass. 'So what I'm going to do about it is, I'm going to finish this bottle of wine and then take a warm bath and then go to sleep.' He lit a cigarette and began to scratch Frank's chest.

Wylie sipped his bourbon is silence.

After a few minutes Russ said, 'I'm sorry.'

'It's okay.'

The telephone rang, and Russ answered. 'Yeah, he's here,' he said. 'Uh huh.' He caught the receiver between his shoulder and neck and dug a pen and a scrap of paper from his pocket. 'Go ahead.' He wrote down a number. 'Thanks, Kenroy. See you tomorrow.'

Wylie arched his eyebrows.

'Victor Lamorena's been trying to get in touch with you,' Russ said. 'He says it's urgent.'

Wylie called the number Kenroy had given Russ. Lamorena answered.

'This guy Mickey,' Lamorena said. 'I thought maybe you'd like to know that he's gone on a very long trip. He left the names of some friends before he took off.'

'Any I might be interested in?'

'One, maybe.' He told Wylie what Wylie already knew. 'What do you have in mind for him?'

'Nothing. All I wanted were the two who made the loud noises. A funny thing. Mickey said someone else arranged a long trip for the other noisemaker. You wouldn't be in the travel business yourself, would you?'

'I rarely even get out of Manhattan.'

'You work too hard. You should take a vacation once in a while.'

'Listen, I've come across another name, too.'

'Yeah?'

'A guy who lives in a Chicago suburb. A really nice guy. I want to vouch for him personally. Mickey made a fool of him a couple of weeks ago. He didn't have any idea what he was getting into, and he wasn't noisy at all. I wouldn't like to see him hassled.'

'It's okay by me.'

'That's nice. I appreciate it.' Wylie paused, thinking. 'Is there any chance Mickey might come home again?'

'Not in hell. He was very obvious about it when he left.'

213

'There was one more man. You know anything about him?'

'Oh yeah. I know all sorts of stuff. Mickey found out that one of the things he was best at was talking. The last guy, he's taking a rest cure in a private clinic in New Mexico. It's going to change his entire appearance. He plans on retiring in South America. He's no special interest, in case you got a soft spot for him too.'

'Doesn't matter to me. Is this clinic really good?'

'The best. They'll fix him up so nobody, and I mean nobody, would ever make the connection.'

After he hung up, Wylie toyed with the salt shaker several moments. 'There's a way to get this guy,' he said. 'As long as we're kept out of it, do you have any objections?'

Russ removed the empty dinner tray and dropped it into a paper bag near the sink. 'No. Do what you want. Be sure, though. I owe you, but it's my life at stake. Nobody's going to put me in a cage again.'

'Baby,' Wylie said softly, 'there's nothing I hold more precious than my own sweet ass. And I will never, never set it up for a fall.'

Russ shrugged.

Wylie picked up the phone and called Evadne.

'You prick!' she said. 'You prick! Pr—'

'Stop! I left on that very same line, and redundancy hallmarks a sluggish imagination.'

'You cocksucker, you baby-raper, you shiteater, you—'

'Much better.'

'You liverfucker.'

'I'm sorry, honey.'

'Pig-rimmer.'

'I apologize. I mean it.'

'Armpit sucker.'

'Are you done now?'

'No, but getting there. The doorman's in my box, the elevator boy's in my ass, and the super's about to stick himself in my mouth. I'll be done soon, I imagine.'

'You are harsh, woman.'

'Excuse me if I moan, but these guys are hung like horses. Keep talking, lover man.'

'Evadne. I – am – sorry. I'll explain.And I'll make it all up to you. Tomorrow night. I swear.'

'Tomorrow night.'

'Yes.'

'Or I hang your balls over the fireplace.'

'I'm *sorry*.'

'Mmmm.' Thomas, when told the Lord had risen.

'Honey,' Wylie said lovingly. 'I want you to call Neal Cummings and make a date with him for tomorrow night.'

'MOTHERFUCKER!'

She slammed down the phone.

Wylie dialed her again. She didn't answer for a long time.

'Don't hang up,' he said quickly. 'Just trust me, baby. Please. Trust, it's not much to ask.'

'You're up to something.'

'Sure.'

'You're no good,' she said wearily. 'Just no good. You'd sell my pussy if you thought it would help you out.'

'That is a lie. Rent it, possibly, but not sell it.'

'Nigger, put it to your dogs. It ain't welcome here no more.'

'I promise you, babygirl, the pale gray ain't even goan raise its sickly head. Goan be nothin' but Daddy's big black beauty for you.'

'I'm sick,' Evadne said. 'I'm sick out of my head, and I should be put away for my own good. Because, okay, I'll take you on faith this one more time. But this is the last, Wylie. The absolute and final time. If you mess me up again, I'm going to declare you dead, and I'll shovel manure onto your grave and scratch the eyes out of anyone who so much as mentions your name for the rest of my life.'

'Thank you, sweet thing. Really. You give me more than I deserve, and –'

'You've never said anything truer.'

'– and I *will* make it up to you.'

'Uh huh. What do you want me to do with Cummings?'

'A dinner date. Some place midtown or a little up. Getting to your coffee about ten o'clock.'

She thought a moment. 'How about La Rencontre? Reservation for about nine?'

'Good.'

'Got to run now,' she said. 'The super's getting impatient.'

Wylie whistled through most of the next day, growing progressively more cheerful as the hours passed. When Kenroy took him aside to speak about a raise, he hardly reflected before adding a thousand dollars to Kenroy's annual salary. Kenroy shook his hand energetically and went rushing upstairs to tell his wife. Wylie felt terrific. He stopped at Pat's desk. Pat had been moping about all morning – trouble with a boyfriend or roommate or something. Wylie wasn't sure. He told her she'd been doing a great job, and he upped her by ten dollars a week. The girl brightened substantially. Wylie was swept up in happy magnaminity, and he considered granting across-the-board raises to everyone at the school. But practical economics, like a weight tied to the end of a child's helium balloon, held stolidly against the tugs and bobbles of his fancy, until he took hold of himself again; he compromised by deciding to agree to any raise requests presented to him the coming business week.

At nine thirty he was with Russ on Lexington Avenue, outside the heavy bolt-studded door of La Rencontre. The door was bracketed by gaslights.

Russ was not interested much in this. He didn't like Cummings, or the abstraction the man represented, but he was indifferent to the man's fate. He had perceived, though, that not to be present would give him a sense of incompletion, would be a kind of default.

They went in. The cloak room was to their left, a small bar to their right. The maître d' stood at a podium at the base of four stairs rising to the softly lighted dining area. He smiled and laid his hand upon the open pages of his reservation book, as if he were touching the written law to assure them all that the universe was indeed known and orderly. Wylie smiled back, then sat at the bar with Russ. The maître d' looked at them with stern disapproval.

Proper appreciation of the subleties of French cuisine requires a pure tongue; the stunning and laceration of that organ with the bludgeon of hard alcohol is judged a gaucherie of the lowest order. La Recontre's bar was essentially an ornament, a grudging acquiescence to New York philistinism. There were only four stools: one observes the necessities, but need not give the heart to them. The bartender served them with polite expertise, then retired to the opposite end and ignored them, to demonstrate his disdain. Wylie was tempted to summon him back to mix a sloe gin fizz or something equivalently awful.

They faced the street, backs to the diners. A panel mirror was mounted above the window, and in it Wylie found Cummings and Evadne. Evadne was wearing her butchy black pants suit, short tight jacket, slash pockets, white western-style stitching, many large metal zippers. Cummings was speaking to her with a looseness and ease that belied his conservative London suit. He emphasized some comment with a small, graceful gesture of his right hand. His left arm was in a sling.

Wylie got off the stool, asked the cloakroom girl where the telephone was, and went downstairs to the booth,

217

which stood in a small chamber between the rest rooms. He dropped a dime in the slot and dialed the 19th Precinct. A Sergeant Cipriano answered.

'Pick up your pencil and listen,' Wylie said. 'I ain't gonna say this twice.'

'May I have your name please, sir?'

'Just listen: The guys who did the Chasteen job were Mickey Guida, Ray Fowler, Jerry Brady, and Tommy Abel.' Brady and Abel were random names. The confusion over them wouldn't matter. 'Tommy was my old buddy. He was scared for his life and trying to split the country. He said if I didn't hear from him by noon today, then he was dead and I should spill this to you guys.'

'*Who is this?*' Sergeant Cipriano said.

'Shut up, I don't like playin' pigeon, but I promised Tommy.'

'Hang on a minute, please. I –'

'You get it now, or you never get it. Dig this – it wasn't no robbery at all. It was a hit. A fat cat named Neal Cummings wanted some old dude named Hollander taken out, and he bought Mickey Guida to do it. Guida put the team together. Then Cummings got cute and figured he wouldn't leave no fingers to point at him. He chopped Guida and Fowler and Brady, but missed Tommy the first time. Fowler's under a pile of junk in an old pier by Sixteenth Street. You find Tommy, you bury him nice – he's makin' you over from assholes into heroes. Right now, Cummings is havin' dinner with a nigger broad at La Recontre. If you put it in gear, you can get him there.'

'How do you know where he is? What proof do –'

Wylie hung up and returned to the bar. The ice in his bourbon had melted at a good pace, and the drink was very much to his palate at the moment. He sipped it. He lit a cigarette, glanced at his watch, and looked past the bartender into the street.

He checked his watch when the patrol car braked to a

halt in front of the restaurant. Six minutes. Good time, considering that before they moved they'd have sent a car racing to check the pier for Fowler's body and would have had to consult some fairly high authority for instructions. A gray Ford swung in behind the patrol car, and a blue Chevy pulled up behind that. Two men left each car, moving toward the restaurant even as they slammed the doors behind them. A pair of detectives disappeared, presumably to cover other exits. The uniformed officers flanked La Recontre's entrance. One of the remaining two detectives unzipped his windbreaker and tilted the butt of a holstered revolver forward. Then he and his partner were inside.

They paused, eyes flicking about as they weighed and categorized and sought possible trouble. Their gaze lingered momentarily on Wylie and Russ, but passed on. The one who'd adjusted his gun remained near the door. He was young and thin, and had tiny black eyes. His nostrils flared. He looked eager and belligerent – the kind who'd shot his way to promotion.

The other man was many years older. His suit was pressed but worn. His hair was thin. His mustache was mostly gray. He moved with slow assurance, a man whose experience had made him efficient and sad. Wylie had seen him note Evadne and Cummings a moment after he'd entered, and carefully avoid looking at them again. The maître d', perplexed by the inappropriateness of the detectives' dress, stepped forward to meet the older detective. The detective bent his head to murmur something, and unobtrusively opened his wallet and allowed the maître d' a moment's look. The maître d' pinched his mouth and shot an anxious glance over his shoulder to Cummings and Evadne.

The detective laid a friendly hand on the man's shoulder, and gently but firmly moved him aside. He signaled his partner, who nearly leaped forward, and together they mounted the stairs and walked to Cum-

mings's table. Hostility and suspicion were obvious on
the young detective's face. But the older one was smiling
and amicable. He excused himself to Cummings and
offered his identification for inspection.

Cummings looked from one to the other in surprise.
He accepted the wallet and read the credentials with
lifted eyebrows and a baffled mouth. He grinned and
returned the wallet. His expression and movement as he
spoke to the older detective suggested that obviously a
mistake had been made, but that, with the largesse of the
wealthy, he understood that these things happened, and
he certainly didn't hold it against them. The detective
shook his head. Annoyance spread over Cummings's face,
and he gestured at the dessert and espresso the waiter had
brought only moments before. Again the detective shook
his head. Cummings switched to anger. The younger detective stepped suddenly behind Cummings's chair, right
hand hovering near his hip.

Cummings's face went neutral. Then he lifted his cup
of espresso, took three deliberate sips, placed it back on
its saucer, raised his napkin, and delicately patted his
lips. He smiled beautifully at Evadne, leaned and kissed
her on the cheek. Then he stood. He buttoned his jacket
and with a sweep of his hand courteously invited the detectives to precede him.

They declined.

Cummings led the older detective down the stairs. The
younger one sat in a chair opposite Evadne and took a
notebook and pen from his pocket.

The maître d' had called the manager from his office,
and was watching with wringing hands. The manager,
short and manicured, wearing steel rimmed glasses,
looked on with minor interest. Cummings went directly
to the manager and conferred with him. The manager
snapped his fingers. A waiter hurried up with Cummings's bill. The manager accepted Cummings's credit
card and ran it through the franking machine himself.

He obtained Cummings's signature, then returned the card with a small bow.

Cummings and his escort left.

The manager said something curt in French to the maître d'. The maître d' returned to his station and worked hard to recompose himself.

Wylie finished his bourbon. Russ downed his drink.

The detective with Evadne closed his notebook and took his leave.

Wylie set money on the bar. Evadne was watching the detective's retreating back. Wylie stood as the detective passed. Evadne registered him with widening eyes. Wylie and Russ followed the detective out to the street, turned left, and ambled leisurely downtown.

Evadne overtook them at the second traffic light. 'Hi, Russ.' She squeezed Russ's hand. Then she said to Wylie, 'I trust – no, I hope, very much – that you have an explanation for all this.'

Wylie took her arm. 'Sure. Not only does your date tear clothes off my ex-wife, but he hires people to kill Julius Hollander, too.'

'You've lost your mind,' Evadne said. 'You've really gone stark mad this time.'

'It pleases me to recall that people felt the same way about Billy Mitchell and Cassandra. And look what that got 'em. Be warned, my love.'

'What makes me reserve final judgment,' she said, 'is that you're always insufferable when you're right. As you are insufferable now. On the other hand, you're frequently that way when you're wrong, too.'

'You know, you're just not going to go very far so long as you continue to mistake charm for obnoxiousness.'

'Tell me,' she sighed.

'Say "please." '

'Don't push, Wylie!'

He cleared his throat. 'Actually, you told me. The night of Chasteen's party. You said Cummings had been crushed in a proxy fight back some years ago, remember? Well, the man who did the crushing was Hollander. Old dogs may be tough, but young ones are vicious. It was a long climb back from the financial gutter for Cummings, but he did it. What he didn't do was forget his humiliation. He wanted revenge. You ought to be more selective with your boyfriends. That was a very sick man. Not only did he want Hollander hit – but he wanted to *be* there, too, to *see* it. Nicely planned, though; it looked like Hollander just happened to be in the way of a shotgun blast during a robbery.'

It was going to be a tidy package. Cummings, according to what Guida had told Lamorena, had relied on Guida to pick the other men, didn't know any of them, and had met none but Fowler, and him only on the night Fowler had died. Eugene Perry would never be tied into the job. Searching for four bodies, the police would find just one, but that would suffice. Cummings had driven the car when Guida and Fowler had gone to meet Russ at the pier. Wylie suspected that Cummings's bad arm would be found the result of a gunshot, not a polo accident – Russ didn't miss often – and they might even locate the doctor who had treated it, possibly the slug itself. That would be great luck, since it had been fired from Fowler's gun, but not really necessary to the prosecution. They'd have Fowler's identity within hours after taking the corpse's prints, and his Secaucus address not much later. If by some miracle of incompetence they missed the gems and photographs Wylie had hidden, he'd make another anonymous phone call.

Wylie said, 'Looking at those fence-post verticals on the card that came with your flowers was like looking at the writing on the photographs of Hollander again.'

'It's true,' Evadne said. 'You've gone utterly out of your mind.'

'It won't be enough,' Russ said. 'Not with the kind of lawyers a guy like that can buy. He'll walk away from it.'

'Maybe, but I'd give three to one against that.'

'So why did I have to go to dinner with him?' Evadne asked.

'He was giving you a hard time. I saw it as a little present for you. I thought it might help make up.'

'You have a hell of a lot more making up to do before you're home again.'

'Oh, I know that,' Wylie said. 'And I intend to begin tonight and continue through tomorrow, and far into tomorrow night, too.'

'My, but we have an exalted opinion of ourselves.'

'Simple recognition of reality.'

They strolled, bantering, down Lexington, heating themselves.

Russ began looking for a cab. He saw one a block down and drifted toward the curb to hail it.

'No,' he heard Evadne tell Wylie. '*My* place tonight. You're going to be my slave until dawn.'

Russ didn't hear Wylie's reply. But Evadne responded with a velvety laugh.

Russ flagged the cab.

'Russ?' Evadne said. 'Do you want to stop for a drink with us?' And she and Wylie both waited in embarrassment, because it was obvious that neither really wanted him to.

Russ opened the door. 'Thanks, but next time. I got a couple of things to do.'

'Okay.' Evadne put her hands on his shoulders and kissed him good-bye. The tips of her breasts grazed his chest. Her lips were warm. It was a tender kiss.

Deep inside Russ, something shuddered.

He said good night and gave the driver his address.

He sat on the living room floor, playing a slow, affectionate game with Frank. He swatted Frank's muzzle lightly and let the dog bat him with his paws in return and catch Russ's hand in his mouth. The television was on, but the volume was off. Strange, unreal people came and went across the screen. No sense could be made of their activities, though clearly they were swept up in them.

The Monopoly set he'd bought for Beth was on a shelf behind him, already thinly filmed with dust. He couldn't see it, but neither could he suppress his awareness of it: a growing pressure at the back of his neck, an intimation of pain behind his eyes. He got up and put the set in the closet, beneath a duffel bag.

He poured a drink. But he didn't want it, so he spilled it out into the sink.

He went to the phone and dialed Judy Rukeyser's number. Frank sat at his side, happy under Russ's moving hand.

'Judy? This is Russ Turner. I want to ap –'

'Swine!' The line went dead.

He massaged Frank's ears.

He called the girl who had lived with Chuck Cramer, Evelyn Weitzman. He hung up on the twenty-third ring.

Frank licked his hand. Unaware that he was speaking, Russ said, 'Good boy, that's a good boy.'

He called Donna. She had company over. She was sorry.

He scratched Frank's chest awhile.

He picked up his jacket from a chair and went to the door. 'Want to go out?'

Frank barked and wriggled the stump of his tail.

Russ walked the dog to Hudson Street. There was little traffic, no one on the sidewalk.

He unleashed Frank and said, 'Okay.'

The dog bounded forward. Russ caught up to him. Frank yipped and leaped joyfully into the air, increased his speed. Russ pounded alongside him, running into the night.